STARTING OVER IN STARSHINE COVE

DEBBIE JOHNSON

Storm

This is a work of fiction. Names, characters, businesses, places, events and incidents are either the products of the author's imagination or used in a fictitious manner. Any resemblance to actual persons, living or dead, or actual events is purely coincidental.

Copyright © Debbie Johnson, 2025

The moral right of the author has been asserted.

All rights reserved. No part of this book may be reproduced or used in any manner without the prior written permission of the copyright owner. This prohibition includes, but is not limited to, any reproduction or use for the purpose of training artificial intelligence technologies or systems.

To request permissions, contact the publisher at rights@stormpublishing.co

Ebook ISBN: 978-1-80508-782-3
Paperback ISBN: 978-1-80508-784-7

Cover design: Rose Cooper
Cover images: Shutterstock

Published by Storm Publishing.
For further information, visit:
www.stormpublishing.co

ALSO BY DEBBIE JOHNSON

Starshine Cove Series

Escape to Starshine Cove
Secrets of Starshine Cove
Finding Hope in Starshine Cove

A Very Irish Christmas

The Comfort Food Café Series

Summer at the Comfort Food Café
Christmas at the Comfort Food Café
Coming Home to the Comfort Food Café
Sunshine at the Comfort Food Café
A Gift from the Comfort Food Café
A Wedding at the Comfort Food Café

Maybe One Day
The Moment I Met You
Forever Yours
Falling for You

To the fabulous team at Longmoor House in Liverpool – thanks for making the unbearable bearable, for making me laugh when I felt like crying, and for one of the most memorable birthdays I've ever had. Keep up the good work – you're the best of the NHS!

ONE

Summer, twenty-five years ago

I'm driving too fast. I know I am, but I don't seem able to slow down. My foot feels like it's stuck on the gas pedal, the engine is roaring, and the brake seems like a distant land.

I need to slow down.

I push the pedal a bit harder, and I go even faster. This, I think, laughing as I zoom past a Porsche Carrera, is the story of my life – knowing I should be doing one thing, and actually doing the opposite.

I'm so tired. I haven't slept properly for days, and I haven't eaten solid food for almost as long. I was working in the restaurant until the early hours, then went clubbing with people I barely know – because it seemed like a good idea at the time.

The club was awful, all neon lights and coked-up monsters, the music a tuneless attack on my eardrums. I should have gone home, but I danced my way through it.

I went straight from there to a business meeting with my agent, and the TV producer who is offering me a slot on his new reality show. Celebrity head judge, at your service. I don't think they were put off by my appearance – a skin-tight pink mini-dress and last night's make-up. In fact, I saw the producer's eyes light up as I wandered in clutching an iced coffee, sucking desperately on the straw. I looked like a train wreck – I am a train wreck – and maybe he thinks that will make good television. Me with a hangover, telling wannabe chefs where they went wrong with their bouillabaisse.

He's a good-looking guy, Zack the producer – long hair, broad shoulders, glasses that give him a touch of intellect. We've always flirted whenever we've met; there's a spark there for sure. Even in my fatigued post-clubbing state, I winked at him as I blustered my way into the room. He gave me the kind of lop-sided grin that would normally make my heart beat faster. But that day it just confirmed what I already suspected – my heart is pretty much dead these days.

My agent, Sal, just shook her head. She's used to me by now. Used to the crazy nights and panda eyes and the fact that I'm late for everything. I think she'd like to kick my arse, but there's too much money at stake – the TV show, the recipe book, the tour. I'd like to kick my own arse, but that's too much trouble.

I left the meeting with an even bigger deal than I walked in with – so much money it makes my eyes swivel. I should've been happy. I should've been thrilled – I have everything I've ever wanted. Everything I've ever worked for.

None of it helped. None of it made me feel less empty inside. Not the Michelin star, or the big-name endorsements, or the possibility of seeing my own stupid face plastered over billboards and TV screens. Not the men, or the cash, or the fact that I was winning at life. Technically, at least.

I swaggered out of the TV offices and went shopping in Mayfair. Spent a small fortune on a new handbag and some killer heels to add to the dozens I already have. Realised that I had nobody to tell about my TV deal, that nobody in my life would care unless there was something in it for them.

I went home to my swanky flat in Kensington and tried to sleep. Still in last night's clothes, still in the make-up. My hair is naturally blonde and curly, but I'd had it straightened the day before. When I woke up from a restless half-hour nap, it was rebelling, and my head was the size of a planet stuck on top of my skinny body. For someone who cooks for a living, I'm not very good at eating.

I stared at the mirror, hating what I saw so much that I went into the kitchen, got one of my fancy Le Creuset pans, and threw it at the glass. I didn't look any worse when it shattered – in fact the crooked fun-house version of me was closer to how I was feeling inside.

After that, I got in the car. It's a nice car, German, a sleek machine built for eating up the miles on an autobahn. It's the kind of car that a person like me most definitely shouldn't have. Right now, I'm proving that by heading into my third hour of relentless driving. I have no idea where I am, no idea how I got here, no idea what time or day it is. I'm going so fast I feel like Sandra Bullock in *Speed*, but at twice the MPH.

I'm driving too fast, and I need to slow down.

I'm on a busy A-road, surrounded by people who are far more sensible than me. I spot a big seven-seater packed with kids – mum and dad up front, children between the ages of maybe three and ten in the back. The dad gives me a worried look, and one of the boys sticks his tongue out at me through the window.

I return the gesture, and wonder what that would be like. To not be driving too fast. To be driving sensibly, with a bald husband who looks like the kind of man who could build flat-pack furniture, raising a gaggle of offspring. It would be nice, I think, blinking my sore eyes rapidly to try and clear them of the tiredness. Nice, but not for me.

I zig-zag across into their lane, tucking myself behind them. I see their hazard lights flash on, realise that I'm too close. That I am almost touching their bumper.

I need to slow down – not just for my sake. I can't hurt anyone – the only person I hurt is myself. I don't want to crash into that family, ruin their holiday or maybe their entire life. I need to remove my disaster zone from this busy place, from these busy people, before I infect them.

I see a turning coming up on the left. There is no sign, and I have no idea where I am going – as usual these days. I have been ambitious and determined my whole life, taking every challenge that the universe threw at me and turning it into a strength. Surviving my childhood, for one. Managing my first restaurant by the time I was twenty-one. The first Michelin star at twenty-six. Now, at thirty, I have even more – and none of it makes me happy. I am driving too fast because I need to escape my own life.

I twist the steering wheel, taking the mystery turn while I'm still in third gear. The engine shrieks, the tyres skid, and I barely keep control as I rocket down the road. It's quiet, no other traffic. No other potential victims. I stare ahead through the sunlight, seeing a glittering patch of turquoise blue sea at the bottom of the steep hill. I wonder how far away it is, and whether I'll be able to brake in time to avoid it. My next challenge.

Foot on the pedal, I wind the windows down and feel the breeze on my face. The speed should be exhilarating, but I barely notice the blur of my surroundings. I am in my metal cocoon, and the rest doesn't matter.

Faster and faster I go, only realising quite how fast when I see a cat run into the road. Right in front of me. A black one, which is either good or bad luck depending on your superstition.

"Shit!" I yell, swerving to avoid it. I can't kill a cat. I've already broken a mirror, and what if this cat has already used up eight of its lives? I am many things, most of them bad, but I am not a cat murderer.

The next few minutes are a riot of noise, panic, and a brief feeling of weightlessness as the car seems to fly, and my body is lifted up beneath the seatbelt. I am scared, but I am still laughing – right up until the point where I black out.

I don't know how long I am out for, but when I regain consciousness, I am being smothered by a now-deflating airbag. When I bought the car it came as a fancy option and cost more money, so of course I said yes to it. Now, I think, batting it aside with weak hands, it has possibly saved my life. I have no idea how I feel about that. If I could go back in time, to that day in the car showroom, would I still choose it? Have things really got that bad?

My seatbelt won't come loose no matter how many times I click it, and all I can see through the windscreen is dirt. It appears that I am stuck in a ditch. This definitely never happened to Sandra Bullock.

I feel a bit battered, and pretty bruised, but mainly I feel frustrated – because now I am not going too fast. I am going nowhere. I shake my head to try and clear the mist, and realise that I am bleeding from my scalp. I'm a chef, I'm used to cuts, and blood doesn't bother me – not a night goes by that we don't crack open the first-aid case. I rub my hair clear of my eyes, and my fingers come away red. Huh.

The windows were open, and I am surrounded by green stuff. Broken branches, sheared tree roots, a few pink flowers hanging desolately from crushed stems. I start to swear, because the situation seems to call for it. I've just let out an especially ripe string of curses when I hear a voice.

"Hey! Are you all right?"

It's a man, and obviously a stupid one.

"No, I'm not all right!" I yell back. "I'm stuck in this damn car!"

I follow up with another set of f-bombs, and if the air could actually change colour, it would definitely be blue.

I hear laughter from outside. Annoying.

"Yeah. Right. I'm guessing that you're doing fine, or you wouldn't have the energy to swear like that. I've called for help, won't be too long. What's your name?"

"None of your effing business!"

"Oh. It's like that, is it? Do you have a head injury or are you always this rude?"

"Both! And... well, it's Connie. My name is Connie."

"Is it really Constance?"

"Only when I'm naughty."

"That's probably a lot of the time, I suspect. Look, Connie, I'm going to try and prise open the door with a crowbar, okay?"

"Why do you have a crowbar?" I ask, suddenly a bit concerned. I am in the middle of nowhere, and not a soul knows where I am. "Do you have duct tape and rope as well?"

"I do, as it happens, but don't worry, Constance – I'm trying to help you, not abduct you. I'm a man who likes peace and quiet, and I don't think I'd get much of that with you around."

I can't help but smile at that, despite the circumstances. He's dead right.

I hear him clamber down into the ditch, but all I can see of him from this angle is his hands and arms. He goes to work on the door, but nothing happens apart from some horrible grinding sounds.

"Constance, I can't get it open – do you want to wait until someone comes with a truck that can hoist the car out, or do you want me to smash the window?"

"What do you think?"

"I think you're a smash-the-window kind of girl."

I smile once more. He's dead right again. I tell him to go for it, and he instructs me to cover my eyes and look away.

Within seconds he's broken the glass, and used the crowbar to clear the frame of any jagged shards. He leans down to peer inside the window, and when our eyes meet I literally lose my breath.

He is gorgeous. Blonde hair, diamond-blue eyes, tanned skin. Crinkly laughter lines that finish me off. He's not my normal type. He doesn't look like a bad boy. He looks decent, and kind, and strong. Like he spends a lot of time outdoors, and lives healthily. He's wearing a plaid shirt with the sleeves rolled up, and his arms are lean and muscular. Maybe he's a farmer, or a surfer, or an angel. Yeah. That's it – maybe I'm actually dead, and this is heaven.

He grins at me, making those laughter lines crease, and I feel dizzy – in a good way.

"I'm Simon," he says, reaching in and offering his hand. "Do you want me to get you out of there? The sides of the ditch are pretty steep, and I'm not sure you're dressed right for a climb."

I glance down at the pink mini-dress, and the stupidly tall wedge heel sandals. No. I'm dressed for nothing good at all.

"Yes please," I murmur, leaving my fingers in his. "I just need to find my new bag. It's Louis Vuitton."

"I'm sure that means something, but let's concentrate on you first, okay? The bag can wait."

I want to argue. I want to swear at him, which is my usual response to anybody telling me what to do – but I don't. Something about his calm, open face and his confident manner quells all of that. It's as if the fire that's normally raging inside me is being smothered by this good Samaritan with the bright blue eyes.

He double-checks the frame for glass, then uses the crowbar

as a lever to loosen the seatbelt. It's like he's been in this situation a thousand times before. He then tells me to reach out towards him. Being skinny is finally good for something, and I easily slither through the window. Simon scoops me straight into his arms, cradling me against his chest. He frowns as he looks at me, and says: "That's a nasty cut, Connie. Let's get you somewhere safe, shall we?"

Safe, I think, gazing up at those eyes. I can't remember the last time I felt safe – but right here, in this man's arms, I wonder if it might just be possible after all.

Spring, twenty years ago

I am sitting with Simon in the caves that are hidden off to one side of the beach. The little splash of turquoise that I'd seen from the car that first day turned out to be Starshine Cove, the place that I now call home.

A lot has happened in the last few years. I have abandoned my work in London. I have been sacked by my agent, and completely blown all chance of becoming a celebrity. I have ditched my Louis Vuitton bag, sold my flat, and donated all my designer duds to charity. I shed my skin, and disappeared from the world I'd known.

In return, I have gained more than I could ever have imagined. A husband. An extended family. A community. A beautiful little boy called James. Plus, to be honest, over a stone in baby weight that I suspect I might not ever lose. I am rounder and softer and happier than I have ever been in my whole life. This little village by the sea in a hidden corner of Dorset has brought me purpose and contentment. By slowing down I have filled up.

These caves, the place where I am now sitting on a blanket with the love of my life, are my favourite place. It's dark deep inside them, but it's magical. We have a torch with us, and Simon switches it on and sweeps it around the cavern.

As always, it takes my breath away – as the beam of light dances through the darkness and shimmies over the cave walls, they shine and glitter and twinkle. Apparently it's some kind of freak geological thing, but I don't care about the science – it's just so beautiful. As soon as the light touches, the place sparkles with reds and greens and blues and purples. The colours glimmer over our heads and all around us, ordinary on the surface but dazzling in the right light – it's like being surrounded by precious gems.

The first time Simon brought me here I'd been in Starshine Cove for three days. There wasn't much phone reception and hardly any internet either, so I'd decided the village was the perfect place to hunker down and get a grip on my life. I'd always intended to go back – to patch things up with my agent, to flirt with Zack the producer until he forgave me, to return to my night-time routine of screaming at my team in the restaurant. To keep running on and on and on, with not even fumes left in the tank.

Somehow, none of that happened. Simon's kind blue eyes and gentle humour distracted me. Then I met his family, and they welcomed me. And then he brought me here, to these caves, and they bewitched me. I'd stood in this exact same spot, looking around in astonishment as Simon revealed the shimmering rainbow that was all around us. It was one of those moments – ones so life-changing that even someone as pig-headed as me recognised it.

I'd looked up at his smile, and known – with absolute one hundred per cent certainty – that I'd found my place. That I didn't need the Louis Vuitton, or the fame, or the agent. I just needed this place, and time to heal.

I'm not sure I expected to stay forever, but that's what happened. I sold up in London, and opened my own business here. Not a swish restaurant where tempers boil as hot as the gas and where the pressure threatens to choke you every night. Just a café, perched on the edge of the world, with views to infinity and beyond. Just a haven, a heaven, a safe place filled with goodness. Like these caves – nothing special on the surface but made of pure magic.

Simon asked me to marry him right here in these caves, getting down on one knee with the starshine all aglow around us. We talked about having a baby right here in these caves. We made plans for the café, and for our future, and for our lives together. All right here.

And now, we are back – holding a flimsy scrap of printed paper and staring at it in disbelief.

"So, Constance Llewellyn," Simon says, using my full naughty name. "This is going to be fun, isn't it?"

My hand goes to my tummy with a sense of both wonder and fear. Just one more, we'd decided. One more baby. James is almost four, and he is the light of our lives. A little blonde-haired monster with a smile that shines even brighter than the jewelled walls of the cave. I didn't know it was possible to love someone as much as I love James, and I'd been worried that having another baby would be wrong – surely there was no way I could love anyone else as much?

"Don't be daft," Simon had said, giving me that lop-sided grin of his. "Love like this doesn't come with limits. You don't run out."

"Maybe. But I'll gain even more weight, and things will be even more chaotic, and how do you know that I won't run out?"

"You could stand to gain a bit more weight – there'll just be more of you to love. You'll always be perfect to me, Connie. You could double in size, shave your hair off and start wearing clip-on elf ears. You'd still be the sexiest woman in the world. And I know you won't run out of love because I know you. You're made entirely of love."

"And cake. I think I'm made of cake."

"Possibly a scone or two – but mainly love."

It is, as ever, unbelievable to me – that I literally crash-landed into this life. This place. Into the arms of this man, with his strength and warmth and never-ending laughter. I've been so very, very lucky – and now, here we are. Looking at that scrap of paper.

"You said just one more," I murmur, stroking the blurred black and white image. "One more."

"I suppose I lied. But how was I to know it would be twins? It'll all be fine, my love. It's our next adventure together."

Twins. Two babies who will come into our world later in the year. Two siblings for James. Two more grandchildren for George and Molly. Two more everything. I am excited, but I am also scared. Simon has a lot more faith in me than I do, which is one of the reasons I love him so much.

He takes the scan photo from my hands and puts it away in his wallet. He wraps me up in his strong arms, kissing my neck in a way that is both gentle and promising.

"Stop that right now," I say, not sounding very convincing. "It's behaviour like that that got me into this mess…"

"It's not a mess, Connie," he replies, stroking my hair back from my face. "It's our life. And I love it."

Autumn, last year

I am pathetic. Truly pathetic. I am a grown woman in her fifties, and I am sleeping in a single bed in a room that smells of dirty socks and sweat. The floor is non-existent, coated with an array of discarded clothes, gym equipment and a scattering of video game controllers and chargers. There's a mouldy towel bundled up in one corner, and a collection of used mugs beneath the desk that seem to be growing their own biosphere. I don't care about any of it, because it's all part of my boy.

Last night, I was also pathetic. Last night, I slept in a single bed in a tidier, more fragrant room: pale pink walls decorated with Taylor Swift posters and the scent of Marc Jacobs' Daisy lingering on the pillowcase. The only clutter was an overflowing jewellery box and a scattering of hair slides on the dresser. I'd spent ages picking them up and stroking the stray strands of long blonde hair that still lived in them, like I was about to steal them for a DNA test.

I look at my phone, see that it is not quite six a.m. I stretch and clamber out of the covers. My bare feet hit one of the plastic boxes for a game called Overwatch, the corner digging into my sole. I put on my slippers and pick my way across the obstacle course to the landing.

Downstairs, I make coffee on auto-pilot. I treat myself to a fancy pod-based mocha, and a dollop of squirty cream on top. I sit with it at the dining table and look around at the kitchen. It's tidier these days – the table is clear of everything other than the fruit bowl and a copy of *Hello!* magazine I was reading the night before. Guilty pleasures.

Not so very long ago, this table was always covered in stuff. Textbooks, chargers, notepads – the detritus of my wonderfully feral children. My eyes go to the huge fridge in the corner, the one I always used to call my external hard drive because it was covered in appointment cards and to-do lists and scraps of Very Important Paper.

If fridges could talk – and I kind of wish they could right now – this one would have a few tales to tell. When the kids were small, there were always brightly coloured invitations to parties at soft play centres, school letters, pictures they'd drawn. It was chaotic but joyous at the same time, the mess of our lives.

Now, there are some photos, a postcard from James, and a reminder that I need to go for a smear test. Not so joyous.

One of the pictures shows us all together – me, Simon, James and the twins, Dan and Sophie. The twins were fourteen, and the shot was taken at Disneyland Paris. They thought they were too old for Disney, but Mickey Mouse has a way of shaving the years off everyone. They lost their pretend cool as soon as they saw Sleeping Beauty's Castle, its towers looming behind us in the picture. We're all smiling, drunk on Disney, queasy from rollercoasters, all wearing giant mouse ears.

That was our last family holiday together. We didn't know that at the time – nobody ever does, do they? We take it all for granted – enjoy ourselves, and then start planning the next one. Always assuming that there will be a next one. That's probably a good thing. You can't go through life expecting the worst to happen – at least that's what I tell myself. Most of the time, I manage to trick myself – but underneath, there's always that layer of fear. Of waiting for a phone call that changes everything.

Simon died a few months after that photo was taken. My beautiful, beloved man – my saviour. The father of my children, the love of my life. My best friend. On mornings like this, I don't know how I have survived so long without him.

I have done okay, I tell myself. I have not only survived; I have lived. The café is doing well, I have friends, I have my father-in-law, George, and my brother-in-law, Archie. We're linked forever, because the car crash that claimed Simon also took Sandy, his sister. We've helped each other through it, and we've raised our children, and we've shared our strengths and our tears.

But now, everything feels so damn bleak. James is working in Jersey, which is a whole ocean away, and three weeks ago Sophie and Dan went off to start the next phase of their lives. Dan is studying medicine in Liverpool, and Sophie is at catering college in London. They have new friends and subsidised bars and fresh places to explore – they are living in big, brash cities instead of this tiny village where they grew up. They are loving it, and I am happy for them.

I'm happy for them, but right now I am sad for myself. Does that make me a bad person? Does that make me a terrible mother? Is it wicked that a tiny part of me hoped they'd want to come home? It is, I suspect – but I can't help it. I was okay when they first left – I was as excited as they were, and to start with they messaged and called all the time. My phone was forever pinging as a new photo landed. I suspect they were worried about leaving me, too, but now I've done too good a job of convincing them that I'm okay.

I'm not okay, I decide. At least I'm not okay this morning. This morning, I am brittle and sad and grey. My empty nest is closing in on me, and I am choking on how lonely I feel. I have been a mother for a very long time. I am still a mother, but my babies are all grown up, and nobody needs me anymore. I feel useless, a waste of space – a person without a point.

I know this will pass. I know it is not only the kids leaving – it is a combination of that, of missing Simon like I'd miss my own heart, and the sneaky joys of the menopause. A toxic brew, but one that I know will blow away like a cloud on a sunny day. Until the next time, anyway.

I stare at that photo from Disneyland. Simon's mouse ears are wonky, and his grin makes him look like a child trapped inside a grown man's body.

"I know what you'd say." I speak out loud. "You'd say 'Constance Llewellyn, stop feeling sorry for yourself, put on some Dolly Parton, and dance around the kitchen.' That was always your answer to everything."

He always used to say I looked like Dolly, which I take as a compliment. I nod, finishing my coffee. I have a squirty cream moustache on my upper lip that I decide to leave there. I open Spotify on my phone, and find *9 to 5*, smiling as the opening chords play out their familiar dum-dum-dum-dum-dum rhythm.

The music kicks in, or maybe it's the coffee – I've poured myself a cup of ignition, and suddenly I am full of energy. I dance and twirl and clap my hands, singing along at the top of my voice. I shimmy around the kitchen island, and use a spatula as a microphone, and play air piano on the dining table. My hair is flying, and my heart is pumping, and I am smiling.

I feel a million times better by the time I finish, and I make a solemn vow to myself: I will be more Dolly.

TWO

Spring, the present day

It is the second week in March, and the village is starting to come alive after its winter hibernation. The holiday cottages that skirt the edge of the green are booked, the Starshine Inn is getting busy, and the weather is playing with us all. Yesterday was grey and wet, but today is bright and sunny, the air filled with a hint of the warmth to come.

Once Easter arrives, it will get even busier, and I will be back to opening the café every day – but for now, I am making the most of my time off.

I got up early, and came down to the beach for a walk. Maybe, I think, as I gaze out at the glimmering blue waves, I should get a dog. My father-in-law, George, lost his Golden Retriever, Lottie, at Christmas, and I know he misses her. He's determined not to get a replacement, though, because as he says, he's 'knocking ninety and it wouldn't be fair'.

I could get one, though, for us all to share. Maybe another retriever, or a little spaniel, or a stray that needs a new home. I could take it to work with me, and have something to cuddle at night. I'd definitely be the kind of dog owner that lets their dog sleep on the bed, though with my current spate of nocturnal hot flushes and restless nights, any dog with half a brain would stick to its basket.

My friend Ella, the village GP, has a little dog called Larry. They found each other when she first arrived here, and they've been a double act ever since. He looks like a lamb crossed with a Wookiee that was shrunk in the wash. He is the kind of dog who makes people laugh just by existing.

It's gorgeous down here on the sand, the sound of the water hissing in and out, the seagulls calling, the sun reflecting from the sea. It would be even more gorgeous if I had a pal to throw sticks for, and I decide that a dog really would be a great idea.

I've adapted to the kids being away – them coming home for Christmas helped, and I've finally stopped sleeping in their beds. But it's still not great, if I'm being honest. I have a busy life; I am rich in friendship and family ties and community. I have a place here, a place where I am needed and liked and loved. I know all of this, but I don't always feel it. Sometimes I just feel lonely.

Maybe that will change with time – I hope so, because in an ideal world, my precious babies will finish their education and fly. They will spread their wings and take off, into their own worlds and their own lives. This is one of the ironies of parenting: if you do your job well enough, your children are confident enough to leave you behind.

I stroll along the bay, my only company a solitary mum carrying a baby on her chest in a papoose. I wave at her, and smile as I take in her unbrushed hair and tired eyes. Those days seem a million years ago now, but I do remember how hard it is – how it feels like the fatigue and the chaos are never going to end. Then in the blink of an eye, they're at little school, then high school, then gone.

When my eldest, James, went to uni, I still had the other

two at home. Now they've left as well, it's harder to deal with. It makes me feel weedy, which I don't like very much at all. It would, of course, all be different if Simon was still here. If I had a partner in crime. Someone to hold me at night, even if I was having a hot flush. Someone to go on these walks with, to watch Netflix with – it's the little things I miss. Our house was always noisy – despite Simon saying when we first met that he liked peace and quiet, he seemed to love the opposite as well.

The noise, the clutter, the mess – it might have driven other people mad, but I always loved it. Now, it's way too silent. Just me and Dolly, and my singing fish – one of those where you press a button and he comes out with a song. He's on the wall, and does *Don't Worry, Be Happy* for me several times a day.

That's good advice, I decide, as I make my way up the steps that lead from the beach up to the Cove Café. Archie, my brother-in-law, is also the village gardener, and he keeps the place gorgeous. At the moment he has an apprentice, Rose, who is blooming just as brightly as her namesake.

The steps lead up to a terrace, and troughs of flowers are scattered on the stone. Swathes of vividly coloured tulips dance in the breeze by my side – pinks, purples, reds. There are daffodils of every shape and size, more than I ever knew existed. The hanging baskets are trailing overhead, not quite ready to come out and greet the world just yet.

I pause, stroke the velvety curve of a tulip, and look back at the view. As ever, it is breath-taking. I have lived here for a quarter of a century, and I still never get fed up of it.

I walk around the building and onto the green. When I first arrived here, staggering out of Simon's car with a bleeding scalp wound and desperate for a G&T, I thought it looked like something out of a movie. One of those Hollywood versions of rural England – the neat green, the thatched cottages around it, the pub. It didn't look real. Too pretty to be true.

Now, it's very real. I know the people who live in those

cottages. I know the people who live in the homes built up into the hillside, and Trevor who runs the village shop, and Jake who owns the pub. I know them all, and I'm part of the fabric of the place. I am Connie who runs the café, and is the chair of the Starshine Cove management committee. I host meetings and formulate plans and raise funds for everything from the communal minibus to our regular cinema nights and our yoga classes. I like to be useful, and for the whole of my life I've always had an abundance of energy.

I'm one of those people always on the move, always looking ahead, always busy. In my London life, that often got me into trouble – but here it's been a blessing. Now, though, for the first time, I feel it ebbing away – I feel like I'm gradually deflating, like a tyre with a slow puncture. I don't know how much of this is down to simple aging, or if it's because of the kids leaving, or some toxic mix of both – but I feel like I'm in a state of flux. Everything's changing, and I'm not sure I like it.

Trevor waves at me from behind his counter. He calls his shop the Emporium, looks like Gandalf, and sells his own herbal teas that claim to help everything from heartbreak to negative auras. I should probably pop in and buy the lot. Maybe take a bath in it.

I wave cheerily back, because that's what people expect of me, and head into the former Victorian schoolhouse that is now our community centre. I have my office here, and it's the base for lots of the village activities. We've recently started running a crèche for the village parents, and I'm helping out this morning.

My eardrums almost burst as I walk through the doors. There's music playing, the kind that is the background to the lives of every parent with a small child – in this case *The Wheels on the Bus*. A small group of toddlers is sitting on a colourful mat singing along and following the actions, apart from one little boy who is hitting himself on the head with a wooden train and laughing each time. That's boys for you.

There's a TV set up in one corner, where the slightly older children are watching a show that seems to involve animals who are enlisted in the emergency services. Others are busily playing with blocks and dolls, and one has a plastic toy lawn-mower and is running around with it at breakneck speed.

It's a kaleidoscope of colour and sound, and when you're not used to it, it feels a bit like someone spiked your morning coffee with magic mushrooms. I head over to the area where the babies are, because why wouldn't I? There's Evan, who was born on Christmas day the year before, and is now a delightfully fat little man who has recently started walking. He still does more falling than actual walking, and I remember it so vividly, that stage – when the corners of tables become potentially lethal weapons as they stagger around.

His mum, Miranda, works at the Starshine Inn, and is a very close friend of my oldest son, James. I've never quite figured out if they're more than friends – he is almost twenty-five, and it feels inappropriate to ask. I decided he'd tell me if he wanted to. James was there for Evan's birth, and even when he was technically still living with me, he spent most of his time with Miranda and the baby. Now he's moved to Jersey for work, and I know how much Miranda must be missing him – because I'm missing him too.

Ella is sitting on a rocking chair, giving her five-month-old daughter a feed. Her GP surgery is in the same building, so she's already back at work – taking plenty of breaks to spend time with baby Caterina. She's named after her husband's Italian mum, but she is universally known as Kitty. So far she has Ella's blonde hair, and Jake's deep brown eyes, and she's going to be a heart-breaker when she grows up.

That is a long way off, though, and at the moment she is blissfully unaware of anything but the warmth and sustenance of her mother. Ella sees me approach, and gives me the weary smile that new mums always seem to have. The one that says they are happy, but also wondering what the hell they've done to their life.

I pull a chair over and lean in to see Kitty's sweet little face as she starts to drift off to sleep. Ella tidies herself up, sighs, and says: "I was going to whisper, but I reckon if she can sleep with this racket going on, she won't mind."

"Here's hoping," I say, holding up crossed fingers. "How are you?"

"Apart from feeling like a dairy cow, I'm fine."

I nod with an understanding smile, and bite back on the reply that all mothers of twins are tempted to make: yeah, try it in duplicate.

Ella studies my face, and I get a slightly prickly feeling on my skin. She's lived here for less than two years, but she already seems to have the ability to read my mind. I don't know if it's a doctor thing or an Ella thing. It's definitely an annoying thing.

"Why haven't you been in to discuss your medication?" she asks, frowning slightly.

"Ummm... I've been busy. And I'm feeling fine. And I'm sure Trevor has a special tea I can take instead."

"If you're planning to go into the Emporium and start talking to Trevor about the menopause, let me know beforehand so I can get the defibrillator ready. He'll have a heart attack."

I ponder this, and decide she is right – our Trevor is a gentle soul, and much as he might have a passionate interest in standing stone circles and fertility goddesses, a real-life woman describing her hormonal imbalance would freak him out. I might do it just for fun.

"You seem tired and sad, and I hate that – especially when there's no need for you to tolerate it," Ella says, shifting slightly so Kitty can snuggle more comfortably.

"Everyone is tired and sad sometimes, Ella. I'll deal with it. Stop pushing the drugs on me."

"I'm offering you HRT patches, Connie, not crack cocaine!"

"Well, maybe that's where you're going wrong... and thank you. I don't mean to be snippy. I know you're trying to help. And most of the time I genuinely am okay. HRT patches won't bring my kids back, anyway."

Or, I silently add, Simon.

Adding it silently, of course, doesn't stop the Incredible Telepathic Woman next to me from figuring it out.

"I was talking to Lucy the other day," she begins. Lucy is another recent addition to the village, the mother of Rose the gardening apprentice and partner of Jake's brother, Josh. "Her mum has joined a dating site! She's been single for decades, but now she's getting out there, meeting men for coffee and doing Pilates. And you remember Cally's mum – she met the new love of her life in her seventies!"

"Yes, I'm aware, and good on them. But I think I'd rather hit myself on the head with a wooden train than do that, Ella. I'm happy being single. Meeting new men for coffee is my idea of hell – never mind the Pilates. I'm just going through a period of... readjustment."

That, of course, is putting it mildly. When Simon died, I had three grieving teenagers to care for. I had to put them first, and I also suddenly had to do everything on my own. Put the bins out, unload the dishwasher, buy a stepladder so I could reach the top of the cupboards. Remember the car's MoT, find an accountant, renew the home insurance. Couples all have their different ways of divvying up the household tasks, a kind of domestic rota of responsibilities – and when one half disappears, the one left behind has to become an instant expert.

Between the practicalities and the kids and running my business, I never had time to even think about meeting someone new – nor the inclination. Simon was, and always will be, the one for me. Even the memory of him is better than the reality of someone else.

"Anyway, enough life coaching, Doctor. Don't you have any warts to look at?"

She grimaces, and says: "I'm due back on in a few minutes. But it's blood pressure and cholesterol checks today, unless there's a wart emergency."

"There might be, you never know. Could be an epidemic heading your way. Give me that baby and leave us be."

She shuffles Kitty into my arms, and I love the solid weight of her, warm and chunky against my body. It's a long time since mine were this age, but I've had a bit of practice with Miranda and Evan, and it all comes back pretty quickly. The baby makes a little squeaking noise and has a half-hearted snuffle at my boobs.

"There's nothing there for you, Kitty Kat, and I know you've just been fed," I say, rocking her gently until she settles again. Nothing on earth compares to a sleeping baby, with their tiny snores and the funny faces they pull, the way their chubby fists wave around. The lush milky smell of their tiny heads.

Ella stands up and stretches her arms into the air. She's already pretty much back to her previous self, weight-wise, which frankly disgusts me. It's almost as though eating sensibly and going on runs helps with that kind of thing.

"Hey," she says, as though she's suddenly remembered something. "Is it tomorrow that you're going to get Sophie from college?"

"The day after," I reply, unable to keep the glee from my voice. "Technically it's still term time, but the last bit of it is practical, so she's coming home to help out. I now get free slave labour and the chance to claim I'm doing it all for her education. She's bringing a friend, Marcy, to stay as well."

"Will they help out at your posh food night?"

The Cove Café is, most of the time, quite a simple place – fresh croissants from the village bakery, soup and sandwiches, ice creams, all the usual stuff. People come for good, home-made meals and the chance to enjoy the view and the ambience – which is, if I do say so myself, very welcoming.

But every now and then, usually once a season, I put on something special. I indulge the part of me that was once the head of a Michelin-starred restaurant, and plan gourmet nights. They're pretty popular – which is me being modest. In fact, they're always over-subscribed, and there is a waiting list of people hoping for cancellations. We serve three courses, and pair them with wines, and charge a small fortune – though it's nothing, of course, compared to London prices. It's hard work, but it allows me to express my creative side and brings in a lot of revenue – some of which is reinvested in the Starshine Cove fund. Those Zumba classes don't come cheap.

"They will," I say, grinning. "It couldn't have worked out better if I'd planned it – which of course I have!"

Finding staff in our quiet little corner of the world can be a challenge. My kids always helped out, as did a young man called Sam, who has also gone off to college now. This university lark has cut right into my workforce – I hope it doesn't catch on.

"So are you just driving to London, grabbing your free labour, and coming straight back?" Ella asks.

"No, sadly. I'm going up the night before, to have dinner with Marcy and her family. I suppose it's fair enough, they want to meet me before they let their precious girl come and stay. Probably want to check I'm not a nutter."

"They'll be disappointed, then, because you definitely are!"

"Is that a medical diagnosis?"

"One hundred per cent, yes. It sounds like fun, anyway – a night out in the big city!"

"I suppose so. But I lived there for years, and the charm wore off. Plus I'll have to find, you know, real clothes to wear. Ones that don't make me look like a clown."

I see her debating whether to dispute that or not, and she

wisely decides on not. I've always liked bright colours – pinks and yellows in particular – and when I was younger, those colours always came in the form of skin-tight dresses and other glamorous gear. These days, I'm more of a dungarees and jeggings kind of woman.

"Well, let me know if you want me to come shopping with you. I could do with some new bits myself. None of my old bras fit."

"That's because you're a dairy cow these days. And thank you, maybe I'll take you up on that. Now, leave me alone with this adorable baby girl."

She leans down to drop a soft kiss on Kitty's forehead and does exactly that. She looks back and makes a *moo!* noise as she disappears into her surgery.

THREE

I am in Sophie's tiny college room, looking around at the pictures on the wall and the potted plant Archie gave her and the scattering of make-up on the desk. This is her home now, I think, feeling a bit weirded out by that. It is like her room in our house, but in miniature – and it also smells of Marc Jacobs' Daisy.

"You look nice," she says, standing with her hands on her hips and frowning as she looks at me. Sophie has long blonde hair and is made mainly of legs.

"If that's true, why are you frowning?"

"Because you look nice, but you don't look like you! I've never seen you wear anything black in the whole of my existence!"

"I've become a goth in later life," I reply. "I've always wanted to do it, I was just waiting until you and Dan left. Now I only wear black and purple. It's the new me."

She surveys me and shakes her head.

"No, sorry – no self-respecting goth would have curly blonde hair. Epic fail, Mum. New dress?"

"I borrowed it from Cally."

Cally is my brother-in-law Archie's new partner, and she is also a more curvaceous lady. That's our word, and we're sticking to it. She's a bit taller than me, but the black wrap dress looks good enough. My boobs are on show, though, which I'm not really used to.

"Do you want me to do your make-up?" Sophie asks. Truthfully, I've already done it – I'm wearing more slap today than I have for the last few decades. By which I mean some tinted moisturiser and a lick of mascara.

"Yes please," I say, delighted to have the opportunity to do something fun with my girl. She starts by wiping off everything I already have on and applying approximately eighteen layers of different creams and primers. It makes me feel like an old cupboard; I'm slightly concerned she might sand me down as well.

We chat as she works, and I pick up snippets about her new world that I will treasure. It's very odd, this stage – for the whole of her life I've known her friends, dealt with her emotions, witnessed her triumphs. Mopped up the tears after her heartbreaks. Now, quite suddenly, she is here – in a place that I only have a peripheral knowledge of. It's all good, it's all right – but it does feel strange, this distance from her everyday reality. Everything she tells me – about new pals, about her course, about the college bar – is trivial, but I log it all to help me build a better picture of Sophie-land.

She stands back when she's done and admires her handiwork. She pins my hair up, sprays it with something that smells of chemicals, and nods.

"All done. You look gorgeous."

"For an old lady?"

"No, Mum – just gorgeous. Shall we go?"

We've arranged to meet Marcy and her family at a popular

restaurant nearby. It didn't exist when I lived in London, which isn't a surprise as a lot of restaurants come and go very quickly. As we walk through the bustling streets together, I realise that I am enjoying the atmosphere. The sun is still out, and groups of drinkers are making the most of it, spilling out onto the pavements. Delivery people whizz past us on bikes, and the familiar big red double decker buses crawl along the roads.

It's easy to forget the rest of the world when you live in Starshine Cove, and honestly I've never felt any real desire to leave it. My own time in London wasn't especially healthy, even if it was exciting – but a little visit like this is enjoyable.

"Where did you live?" she asks as we stroll. "When you were in London. You never talk about that part of your life."

"I lived in Kensington."

"Ooh, posh! What was that like?"

I ponder how much to tell her. I am a very different woman than I was back then, but she is technically an adult, and I don't suppose there's any harm.

"I never really spent much time there," I say. "I was really busy, working mad hours in the restaurant, and when I wasn't working I was usually doing something stupid."

"Like what?"

"Like going clubbing, drinking too much, and living my whole life like it was a competition. It was fun, but I burned out – I was exhausted by it all. None of it made me happy."

I see her slight look of surprise at this information, and know she is piecing things together in her mind.

"And that's why you ran away? Dad loved telling us he found you in a ditch. He always found it very amusing."

"It was amusing. It was also the best thing that ever happened to me, because I met your father, found Starshine, and had you guys. It was a more than fair swap."

She smiles as we pause outside the restaurant – a fancy

Italian place – and responds: "Well, I'm glad you did. You became a Michelin-starred mum."

This is such a lovely thing to hear that I am momentarily taken aback. Before we make our way inside, I give her a big juicy hug.

I have a weird relationship with restaurants, which I suspect is true of anyone who has worked in the business. I find it impossible to just relax and enjoy the experience as a customer. I remember Simon taking me to a fish place in Lyme Regis not long after we became a couple, and me spending the whole night commenting on the service, the food, the glimpses I got of the busy kitchens each time the doors swung open.

I wasn't an especially nice boss, I know. It's a high-pressure environment, and there's a reason Gordon Ramsay swears so much. It was my whole life, which made me less than empathetic with some of my staff – people who were sometimes also dealing with families and kids and the normal complications that I was unhindered by. I hope I'd be very different now – my priorities certainly are.

Still, as we enter and are greeted by the maître d', I find myself automatically surveying the place – how many covers, whether the team is smiling, if the specials board is visible.

"Stop it," Sophie says firmly. "You always do this. Just enjoy yourself, okay?"

I nod and give her a grin. I'll try my very best, but in honesty I am feeling a little tense. Being with Sophie is marvellous, and being in London has been less troublesome than I imagined it would be. But meeting new faces, in this swish little eatery, is well outside my comfort zone. I'm not shy – the very opposite in fact, I love people – but I am usually on my home turf. Here, it feels different, like a test I have to pass. I'm even dressed as someone else.

I'm keen to get to know Sophie's new BFF, Marcy, and am looking forward to having her stay with us – but the prospect of being thrown into a nuclear family set-up, even for one dinner, makes me wince a bit. I'm sure Sophie will have told her pal about her dad, and that is fine – but it always means that people have preconceived ideas about you. About being a widow, a single mum, and what that might say about you. There's always an underlying touch of pity, which is understandable but not something I enjoy. I really should have stuck with my own clothes – nobody pities you if you're wearing yellow dungarees. They're usually just a bit scared of you.

Sophie scans the room, then her face breaks out into a grin and she raises her arm and waves. Right, I tell myself – game time. Me and my boobs follow her through the pleasantly bustling, dimly lit room, the smells of garlic and basil fragrant in the air.

As we approach the table, I see two people – one is very clearly Marcy, who jumps to her feet and runs to embrace Sophie. They literally only saw each other a few hours ago, but I do remember what it's like with your friends at that age. It's a bit like being in love, without the messy bits – you hate being away from them. Marcy is tall, slender, with a super-cool pixie cut that she's dyed jet black. She looks like a modern take on a silent movie star, all pale skin and red lips and gorgeousness.

I notice that the table is only set for four, and that there is only one other person – a man with his back to us, sitting and looking at his phone. That's one of my pet hates, phones at the table, which I realise puts me in the minority – people seem to be obsessed with taking pictures of their food these days. At the risk of sounding about two thousand years old, it was much harder in my day – when I was growing up, if you wanted to do something similar, you'd have to take a picture, take the film to the camera shop, wait a couple of days for it to be developed, then go around to all your mates' houses and put prints through the letterbox with hand-written notes: Look, I had fish and chips for tea!

Sophie and Marcy disentangle from each other, and my daughter says: "Mum, this is Marcy – Marcy, this is Mum!"

She sounds a bit giddy and also a bit proud – though I'm not sure which of us she's proud of. Maybe both?

I give Marcy a hug, because I'm one of life's huggers. At least I am in Starshine Cove – here, in this bijou little place, I feel slightly awkward as I automatically go in for a cuddle. Marcy doesn't seem to mind and squeezes me right back.

"Told you!" Sophie says, smiling. "She'd hug a polar bear if she bumped into one on the street!"

"Polar bears are cute, who wouldn't?" Marcy says, her blue eyes huge and somehow innocent. She's almost twenty, I know, but despite the make-up and the stylish haircut, there is something almost childlike about her.

"Polar bears," comes a voice from behind her, "are apex predators. I wouldn't recommend hugging one, if you want to keep your arms."

Ah, I think. Still on his phone, but also listening in. Multi-tasking – a rare skill in a man, I've found over the years.

Marcy rolls her eyes, and says: "Yes, thank you, Captain Buzzkill – I was aware, and I promise I won't ever hug a polar bear if I encounter one on Charing Cross Road! Come and meet Sophie's mum! I'm so sorry, but my sister Amy cancelled on us – she used the excuse that she's still in France – pathetic isn't it? Has she never heard of the Eurostar? Dad! Get off your phone!"

Our table is in a back corner of the room, and although it is still light outside, the restaurant is deliberately shady – all about creating an ambience, I suppose. I don't see much of him until he stands up and turns to face us, by which time I've already decided he's a bit rude.

He's a good foot taller than me, which to be fair isn't hard as I'm vertically challenged. He's wearing a dark-coloured suit that I can tell is expensive, and he smells good, a subtle masculine scent that makes my nostrils flare in appreciation – this is the kind of sophistication you don't come across every day in a tiny village in Dorset. This is London glamour. I'd almost forgotten it existed.

I decide I'm not going to hug him, and instead hold out my hand. He takes it but doesn't shake – he just holds it. I realise that he is staring at me, completely silent, and that this is all suddenly a bit weird. Maybe it's the boobs – maybe I've broken him.

I meet his eyes and feel a flicker of recognition. It comes from somewhere deep, but it's there – I know this man. He's good looking, green eyes in tanned skin, hair that is slightly receding at the temples but otherwise thick and abundant, brown streaked with silver. Is he famous? Is he someone I should know from the telly? It feels like that – and he looks like he could be famous. One of those serious news presenters who looks grim as they report from outside the White House, or an actor who does a lot of Shakespeare.

He's still holding my hand, and he's still staring at me, and the girls are starting to exchange uncertain looks, wondering what's going on. Much like myself. Back home, I'd jump right in and ask something nosy and inappropriate, but I don't quite have my mojo in this place.

"Do I know you?" I simply ask, desperate to break the moment.

He starts to smile, and it changes his whole face – he suddenly looks younger, less stern. Way more amused.

"You do," he replies, finally letting go of my hand. It flutters to my side, unsure where to go next. "Well, you do if your name is Connie?"

"Her name IS Connie!" Sophie responds, confused. I'm too busy studying his face, trying to place it, to actually reply.

"It's been a while," he says, his eyes running over me, "but I'm quite disappointed you don't recognise me. I think we last saw each other about twenty-five years ago. You came into my office straight from a night on the town and left with the offer of a contract that you never signed."

Immediately, the ducks line up – I know who this is. I know who it is, and I feel totally freaked out by it. Like the floor is moving, and I need to hold on to the wall to steady myself.

"Zack," I say quietly. "Zack Harris."

He nods, and his eyes are on mine, and I feel suddenly faint. I have no idea why – maybe because that was so long ago that I'd forgotten it even happened. I've buried that version of me so deep that this feels like I'm being exhumed, one rotting limb at a time.

He looks slightly concerned, as the girls giggle in the background, trying to figure out what amusing thing the old people are up to. He puts his hands on my shoulders and draws me in for a hug. I let myself become wrapped up in his arms, my face against his crisp white shirt. He leans down and whispers into my ear: "Are you okay?"

I let out a sigh and stay where I am for a couple of seconds. It gives me the time to reconfigure myself, to breathe. To stem the strange sense of almost-panic. I nod against him, and whisper back: "Yes, thank you – just a bit weirded out. Blast from the past."

I pull away, and plaster on a smile as we all settle at our table. There are two bottles of wine – one white and one red to cover all eventualities – and I pour myself a glass, splashing a red stain onto the tablecloth as my hands shake. Zack has sparkling water, I notice, which probably means he's driving.

"So," says Marcy, leaning her elbows on the table, "tell us – how do you two know each other, then?"

Sophie looks just as curious, but also a touch concerned. She knows me well enough to spot the signs of nerves.

"Ah," says Zack, running his hands through his hair as he

talks, "well, that's a funny story. Basically, I was going to make Connie a star."

Sophie's eyebrows shoot up, and she stares at me in surprise.

"A star?" she says, frowning. "I thought you were a chef?"

"I was," I reply quickly, just in case she's starting to think I had a whole secret life. Which I suppose I kind of did. "I was a chef, but I was also... maybe a borderline celeb?"

"What?" she answers, looking impossibly befuddled. I suppose the idea of your yellow dungaree wearing, hug-obsessed café-running mum being a celeb, borderline or not, must be weird. If she'd ever googled me under my maiden name, she'd have found a few things – not as many as you would now but the internet certainly existed that long ago. I guess she's never done it, and why would she? Kids always seem to assume their parents are dull, and anything of note about their lives only started when they were born. As I basically said exactly that to her just minutes earlier, I can't blame her for it.

"A celeb?" she repeats, when I only shrug. "What kind? Like, the *Big Brother* kind, or the posh party in *Hello!* magazine kind?"

"It started with newspaper and magazine articles," I say. "Reviews for the restaurant, which was one of those places that proper famous people liked to dine out at, so there were often mentions in the gossip columns, that kind of thing. And that developed into profiles, because I was so young."

"Your mum was one of the youngest head chefs in London," Zack adds, filling up my glass for me. "She attracted a buzzy crowd. It wasn't just the food, it was her – she was fun and gorgeous and a party girl. When she walked into the restaurant to chat to guests, everyone was watching her, even if George Clooney was in the house. She was like the supermodel of the restaurant world."

I cringe as he says these things, because I recognise at least some of it from the way my agent Sal used to pitch me.

"That was a long time ago," I say. "I was a different person then."

A person who was maybe half the size she is now, I think, suddenly aware of my age and my weight in a way that doesn't feel good. I wasn't happy then, I remind myself, and I am now. It doesn't matter what I look like. I am a middle-aged mother of three, not the skinny adrenaline-fuelled wraith that I was back then.

"Were you, like, on the telly?" Sophie asks, wide-eyed, still clearly bursting with questions.

"Yeah. A few times. Interviews, and guest appearances – stuff to promote the restaurant and the recipe book I was writing."

"You had a book deal?"

"I did, but it came to nothing. Like I told you earlier, Sophie, that was a different life. Not one I even remember especially clearly, or especially fondly. It was... thin. It was unsubstantial. It was built on shadows."

This concept obviously goes over her head, because the next thing she says is: "But you were famous! That's really weird! So how did you know Marcy's dad?"

'Marcy's dad', I note, not Zack – strange how children do this. They see us only as those roles for most of their lives, not even giving us names. I have lived for a long time as 'Sophie's mum', or 'Dan's mum', or 'James's mum', and I've been content with that. I am not really enjoying the trip down memory lane back to a time when I was just me – at least the me that I was back then.

"I was head of content for a TV production company," he explains, "a couple of years before I started my own. We wanted Connie for one of our shows. A cookery show where amateur chefs competed for a job in a top London restaurant."

There have, of course, been many similarly themed shows since then – but I've never watched them. They hit a little too close to home, and even watching *Bake Off* can make me tense. I feel too sad for the contestants when their showstoppers collapse when they're taken out of the oven.

I have seen Zack's name pop up at the end of a programme occasionally, over the decades, but it never inspired anything other than a slight shiver at the memory of what might have been. I genuinely suspect that if I hadn't run away that day – if I hadn't crash-landed into the embrace of both Simon and Starshine Cove – that I wouldn't be sitting here now. I think being burned out would have led to something darker, something more destructive. I might not be a star – but I am very much alive.

"And that's what you ran away from?" Sophie says, shaking her head. "Fame, fortune, success? You swapped it all for raising a family in a village in the middle of nowhere?"

When I'd talked to her briefly about this earlier, she'd seemed to understand – but I guess a girl of her age will always be swayed by the allure of fame. This is the *Love Island* generation, and their motto seems to be I Am On Screen, Therefore I Am.

"It wasn't that simple, Soph. To put it into food terms—"

"Which you always do."

"Yes, which I always do – to put it into food terms, my old life was junk food. My new life has been superfood. I... I don't regret it. No matter what happened later."

Her eyes meet mine, and we share a look. She knows exactly what I'm talking about here. I'm talking about her dad. The thought of Simon floors me, and I feel raw with yearning. For his smile, for his humour, for his calm and steadying presence in my life. It's hard enough keeping my balance without him back home – here, in an alien place and being mugged by memories, it is even harder.

A waiter appears asking if we're ready to order, and I realise I haven't even looked at the menu.

"Are there any specials?" I ask, stalling for time. "And can you describe them in detail please?"

He does exactly that, and I smile and nod and pretend to be paying attention as he enthuses about lobster ravioli and slow-roasted porchetta. When he's finished, I thank him and order a lasagne. He looks a bit disappointed but perks up when Marcy gazes up at him and asks for the lobster. She is super-pretty, and he is clearly taken with her.

By the time everyone has finished and the waiter has gone, I am feeling calmer. This was an emotional ambush, I tell myself, and I can be forgiven for over-reacting. But now, it's time to Be More Dolly.

"So," I say, turning to Zack, "I suppose I should apologise."

I smile as I say it, because I don't want this to be serious – I just want to clear the air. Yes, it was a long time ago but his memories are probably also ambushing him, and maybe his are just as unpleasant. It was a big deal, that show he was putting together, and my disappearing act must have thrown a spanner in the works. It was unprofessional, and not at all grown-up, and I have to accept that.

"For what?" he says, leaning back and sipping his water. Lordy, I think, he is still a fine-looking man. There always was a spark, and even though I'm pretty flame-retardant these days, I can still appreciate the aesthetics. Back then I wouldn't have thought twice on letting that spark ignite, and I always got the sense that the feeling was mutual. Now, I am very much a look-but-don't-touch kind of woman.

"For running away without any explanation."

He shrugs, thinks it over, and says: "Well, I won't say it didn't sting at the time. I may have called you a few unflattering names. It was my idea to bring you in, and the bosses were all keen – thought you had star quality, that you'd be a ratings magnet. They were right, you would have been – and when you left, I got some stick for it. But life moves on, and I'm older and wiser now. I've thought about it occasionally over the years, and I came to the conclusion that you did what you had to do."

"I really did. And if it's any consolation, I never intended to stay away forever. I always thought I'd come back, do a bit of grovelling, and take up where we left off. But then… something else happened."

"What happened?"

"I fell in love."

His smile is big and genuine and warm, and he pats my still shaky hand on the tabletop.

"Ah. Well. Who can argue with that? Besides, things didn't turn out too badly for me in the long run."

Marcy pipes up: "He's being modest! He runs one of the most successful production companies in the entire world!"

"The entire world?" I echo, widening my eyes. "Really? Even without me?"

He knows I'm joking, and laughs before he replies: "Yep. Even without you. It's been… an interesting journey, to put it into reality TV parlance. One I must admit I'm getting a bit weary of."

Marcy makes a snorting noise and adds: "He's always saying that. He's always threatening to retire, or step down. Then he realises he'd be bored rigid and goes back."

Zack looks at her fondly. This is clearly a well-trodden conversational path. I glance at Zack's hand, see a gold band on the traditional finger. There is no 'Marcy's mum' here tonight, but that means nothing – she might be busy. She might be on the runway at Milan fashion week, or masterminding the hostile takeover of a multi-billion dollar corporation, or back at home with a litter of Afghan hound puppies. Who knows?

He glances at his phone again, and I wonder what is so urgent that he can't bear to put it away for even one meal. He looks up, catches me staring at him, and firmly sets the phone to one side.

"Sorry," he says, "that was rude. It's supposed to be me telling the young people off for that isn't it? Anyway, Connie, it's wonderful to see you again, and Sophie, it's great to meet you at last. Now, let's enjoy our night out together!"

He raises his glass in a toast, and we all clink in the middle of the table. He still looks distracted, but who can blame him? All we can do is try and make the best of a very strange situation.

FOUR

I wake up the next morning on the inflatable mattress on Sophie's floor. Or, to be precise, my legs wake up on the inflatable mattress. The rest of me seems to have scuttled off on an adventure in the night, and my head is underneath her desk, right next to the bin and a stray trainer sock. A classy start to the day.

I don't sleep especially well anymore, and it was impossible last night. I'd had a confusing evening, drank slightly too much wine, and London is so noisy I kept getting woken up by shouts and shattering glass and sirens. The urban lullaby of the city never used to bother me, but after so long in Starshine Cove, it is all brain-shreddingly loud.

Even now, as I slowly come to, I can hear a lorry outside, making that bleeping sound they make when they're reversing. I rub my eyes, surprised when my fingers come away smudged with black from my mascara. Yeah. I probably should have taken that off, I think, as I try to decrust myself.

I look up at the bottom of the desk and spot a lump of chewing gum wedged up in one corner. Nice. I do the little stretches I've found I need to do in the mornings these days, just to get my body ready for proper movement. Naturally enough I also knock over the bin, and a pile of used face wipes spills out onto my head. Sophie, it seems, actually took her make-up off – clever girl.

I wriggle my way back onto the mattress and look up at her. She's still asleep, one pyjama-clad leg hanging off the edge of her bed, blonde hair strewn over the pillows. I lie still for a bit and simply enjoy the moment – the guilty pleasure of being able to look at my baby girl. I know she's technically an adult now, but she will also still forever be my baby girl. I can still see the outlines of her younger self in the curve of her cheeks, the gentle flutter of her eyelids. Even that one dangling leg – she's slept like that since being a toddler, perfectly at rest but almost as though she's getting ready to spring out of bed and face the day ahead.

I roll onto my side, the mattress squeaking beneath my weight, and realise it was stupid of me to insist on sleeping here instead of the bed she'd offered. I'm going to have to get up from the floor now, which will be a complicated manoeuvre involving getting on all fours first, then working my way back upright. I am fit and healthy enough for my age, and I lead an active life – but I am also carrying some extra timber, and my knees have noticed.

Not quite yet, I decide, staring at Sophie a little bit longer. I grab the bottle of water I'd thoughtfully left out for myself, and check my phone. Just after eight. We didn't get back here until gone midnight, as our dinner turned into drinks, tucked away in a cosy bar a black cab ride away. I'd enjoyed it as much as I was capable of, and certainly played the part that was required of me – chatty, engaged, open.

Beneath that, I was still bewildered. Nothing personal against Zack, but I found being around him again disconcerting. He is from the past, and the past, as someone once said, is a foreign country. Everyone has a past, obviously – but most people's are a little more linear than mine. Mine had a great big schism in the middle of it – a fault line left by my emotional earthquake. There was Before Me and there was After Me, and never the twain shall meet.

It's a freakish coincidence that Sophie's new friend is Zack's daughter – but they do happen, I know. A pal of mine once bumped into a long-lost cousin while he was climbing Machu Picchu, and once, while Simon and I were showing one of his work colleagues our holiday snaps, he spotted his ex-wife standing behind us on the Spanish Steps in Rome. But they were freakish coincidences that happened to other people, and this one is happening to me – therefore, as human nature dictates, it's more important.

I sip my water, realising I have so many questions. The chat stayed light last night, the girls full of youthful energy and excitement, Zack and I both making an effort to maintain the same level. He didn't push to talk about the old days, and I appreciated it – I think he could tell I was struggling and showed me the courtesy of discussing nothing I might find challenging.

I needed that last night, but now I am curious – about his life, his career, his daughters (the older one works in France), his wife. I'm curious, but not curious enough to ask him – I'd just quite like to do one of those remote snooping sessions, like you do on Facebook sometimes when a name from the past emerges. You don't want to actually engage with them, but it's fun doing a gentle cyber-stalk.

He is, I think, a bit older than me, but he is aging disgustingly well, in that way that some men do – Pierce Brosnan, George Clooney, Liam Neeson. His eyes are still that gorgeous shade of forest green, and the hair... well, the hair is begging to have fingers run through it. He's clearly done well with his career; he has the golden skin of someone who takes regular skiing trips and winters in the Caribbean. Being around him made me feel two things – slightly fizzy, and even more frumpy. The frumpy outweighed the fizzy, even with Cally's dress and the boobs and the make-over. I rarely worry about the way I look – it seems irrelevant compared to the way I feel – but last night I was aware. Aware that when he last saw me, I was in a skin-tight pink mini-dress and could be described – in the over-egged words of an agent – as the supermodel of the food world. Now I'm just... me.

That's always felt enough, but I now have a niggle of discontent chewing away at me. A little flurry of what-might-have-beens. I made the right choice, leaving that life behind – but at the same time, I suppose I can forgive myself a little self-indulgence.

Sophie starts to stir, flinging one hand across her eyes.

"Are you staring at me while I sleep?" she mutters, making me laugh out loud.

"Yes."

"Well, it's creepy. What time is it? And do you have any ibuprofen?"

"Just after eight, and of course I do."

Even now, with all of them living away, my handbag is a cornucopia of delights – painkillers, blister plasters, safety pins, antiseptic cream. When you've raised three kids, it seems almost irresponsible to leave home without them. These days I've added my own – antacids, and a little battery-powered fan to help if I suddenly go nuclear.

I do my admittedly quite comedic clamber back to my feet, to the encouraging backdrop of my daughter's giggles.

"Yeah, laugh it up," I say, as I locate my bag. "Nobody ever believes this when they're nineteen, but one day this will be you!"

I pass her the pills and go for a quick shower. The bathroom is obviously basic, a bit like a hostel, but it gets the job done and I feel a lot better when I'm clean and don't have a clown face. I feel a sense of relief as I put my own clothes on, cropped jeans and a bright pink T-shirt with an acid house smiley face on it. I give my hair a little upside-down shake – it's naturally curly and will dry however it chooses that day – and add some hoopy earrings. Yes, I think, giving myself a wink in the mirror – looking a whole lot more like me, and that is a good thing.

When I come back into the room, Sophie is hopping around on one leg trying to get her leggings on, so I take the opportunity to laugh back at her. Fair's fair.

Once she's dressed, we finish off her bits of packing ready for the journey home. She doesn't have to empty the room, so it's just a matter of gathering what she'll need for the next few weeks. Most of it was already done – she is an organised kind of girl – but she does a final check for last-minute toiletries, chargers and her coursework files.

I briefly wonder how Dan is getting on in Liverpool. Nowhere near as organised as his twin, but he gets where he needs to get in his own way. I was worried when he left – he had meningitis the summer before last, and it took a lot out of him. It took him ages to fully recover, and I wouldn't have minded him having a year off – but he worked his arse off, got his grades, and disappeared up north.

Cally, Archie's partner, is originally from Liverpool, and she came back up with us when we dropped him off. She showed him her favourite pubs and a nightclub called the Blue Angel, and his eyes were shining with excitement for the whole day. Small-town boy in the big city. I rarely hear from him these days, which is probably a very good sign.

Sophie stuffs her teddy bear into her bag, and I try not to smile. I love the fact that she still has her teddy bear, not going to lie. She sits on the edge of the bed and checks her phone.

"Mum," she says, looking up from the screen, "would it be okay if we call off at Marcy's house on the way? Her dad's invited us for breakfast, and she says she wouldn't mind collecting a few bits and bobs."

Ugggh. I can't think of anything worse.

"I don't know, Soph – it's already a long drive and I could do without the detour."

I could also do without seeing Zack again, especially wearing my acid house T-shirt and looking like Grandma Glastonbury.

"Please! It's in Wimbledon, which is southwest London, and we live in southwest England, so it's practically on the way... plus I've never been there and I'm nosy!"

"Why haven't you been there? In fact, why doesn't she live there and commute to college? It'd be a lot cheaper."

Sophie pulls a face and replies: "She said both she and her dad thought it'd be good for her to live in halls, at least for the first year. And we've been busy, and it's miles away, and *please*? I'll do some of the driving on the way back."

I think about it, and find that there's something about seeing Zack again that intrigues me, and I am also a bit nosy. Well, if you ask anyone who has ever met me, they'll say I'm a *lot* nosy – and I suppose I have the time. The café is in safe hands – or at least in hands – for the rest of the day.

"Okay," I say. "But the deal is we swap at Basingstoke, after which I will get drunk on Prosecco in the back seat, then sing along to Katy Perry songs as loud as I like. Deal?"

"Deal!"

We rendezvous with Marcy in the lobby of the halls, and she looks fresh-faced and eager. She and Sophie are thrilled to be in each other's company again, and another round of hugs is dispensed. The two of them chat away as I plug her home address into my phone for directions, and we stroll to the side street where I'd managed to park the car.

I can't say that driving in London is even remotely pleasurable, and I have to concentrate hard to avoid smashing into a kamikaze cyclist or an especially determined pigeon. By the time we enter the pretty tree-lined streets of Wimbledon, I'm ready for an hour or so in a sensory deprivation tank.

I've never been to this part of the city before, and all I know about it is based on watching tennis. It turns out to be rather lovely, very green, with lots of cute shops and cafés and some grand houses tucked away behind neatly trimmed foliage.

"Have you always lived here?" I ask Marcy, as I make my way down slightly more civilised roads.

"Uh, yeah," she says, sounding uncertain. "Well, I think when I was born we were in central London, but then with two kids, Mum wanted to move somewhere with a bit more space. It's way too big for Dad now. Especially since Mum died."

I almost crash the car through the front of a Polish artisan bakery as these words come out of her mouth. I grip the steering wheel, and say: "I'm sorry, Marcy. I didn't know."

It would, I think, glancing at Sophie through the mirror, have been useful information. She pulls a little face back at me and mouths the word 'Sorry'.

"That's okay," Marcy responds with a sad smile. "Why would you? It's one of the reasons me and Sophie get on so well – shared trauma, etc. etc. But I don't tell people as soon as I meet them, because then they go all misty-eyed and start feeling sorry for you, you know?"

"I do know, yes. When did you lose her?"

"Ten years ago. Ovarian cancer. I was eight when she was first diagnosed, and it always makes me sad that when I imagine her, she's always sick. I mean, there was a time before that, but I can't always find it in my mind. Anyway. Next left."

For a moment I'm disconcerted, then realise she's giving me directions and hit the indicators. The wheels of the car crunch on the gravel driveway, and I park up outside a beautiful home. It's a big Victorian villa, all ornate red brick and big bay windows. The front garden has apple trees, and the door is draped with a bough of wisteria that hasn't as yet come into bloom.

The car next to me – Zack's, I presume – is a sleek Audi saloon in metallic grey. My own car is a bright pink Fiat 500 with stick-on eyelashes, which makes for an amusing contrast. They look a bit like they're out on a date.

I clamber out, pulling the seats forward so the girls can follow. I need to catch my breath, to recalibrate, to let this sad new strand to Zack's story sink in. I can't believe Sophie didn't mention this – and yet, I can. She is wrapped up in her own little world. Her squirrel brain is always dashing from one thing to another. Lots of times when she's forgotten to tell me something and I ask why, she simply looks confused and replies: "I'm sorry, I really thought I had!", or "I just assumed you knew."

I'm still feeling flustered as the front door opens, and the man himself is standing on the steps. And yes, I do now see him differently – even though I hate it when people react like that to me.

He waves, and is almost knocked over by a supremely fat black Labrador shoving past him to greet Marcy. She crouches down to stroke him and he washes her face in kisses, his tail wagging so hard that his whole body shakes. Even the dog is different – I'd pictured something fancy like Afghan hounds, and here is this tank-sized creature making happy snorting noises as he receives his adoration.

Funny how just a few pieces of the puzzle can change the whole picture. Last night, I imagined Zack as this uber-glamorous London dude, with an equally glamorous wife. I imagined a life of corporate lunches and flashy dinners and them living in the kind of apartment that comes with a pool and a doorman.

Now, here I am, faced with a completely different version of him – he is a widower who lost his wife when she was tragically young, and who has raised his daughters alone since then. Plus, he lives in a family home with a fat black Lab.

I look up from the slobbering dog as Zack walks towards us. He's dressed more casually today, in jeans and a short-sleeved white shirt that shows off his tan. His thick silver-streaked hair almost touches his shoulders, and the only slip from his 'effortlessly stylish off-duty' look is the fact that he's also wearing a pair of giant slippers in the shape of Christmas elves.

"Dad, I only got you those as a joke!" Marcy says, pointing at them and laughing. "You look ridiculous!"

He grins at her, shrugs, and replies: "They're comfortable, and they were a gift from you, so I don't care if I look ridiculous. Come on in. I ordered from the café on the high street, so nobody's at risk of being poisoned. Normal Lab rules apply – do not feed him, no matter how sadly he looks at you. He's on a diet."

The dog gazes up forlornly, as though he understands every word. I give him a quick rub on his broad dome of a head and follow the rest inside.

It is, as I'd suspected from the outside, a gorgeous house. Everything is painted in pale colours, and sunlight pours through every window. The hallway is lined with art and photos, and it smells faintly of lemons and lavender.

Zack leads us into the kitchen, which is a huge extension across the whole rear of the building. Skylights are open, and patio doors lead straight out into a long, lush garden. I spy clumps of bluebells and pots of daffodils, tables and chairs, and a wooden summer house that's painted completely black.

"That was from my vampire obsession days," Marcy says, seeing me look. "I'd sit in there in the dark, convinced that the sunlight would kill me."

She does have very pale skin, almost translucent, so I can see where she was coming from. I wonder how much of it was normal teenaged girl stuff, though, and how much of it was laced with loneliness. I have no idea if she's close to her sister or has cousins and aunts and uncles. She might have been raised in a clamour of noise and love despite the loss of her mum – but once the image takes root, I can't quite shake it.

I'm brought back to reality by both Marcy and Zack crying out: "Bear! Get down!"

The dog, predictably enough, is attempting to scale the kitchen table and reach the summit of Mount Breakfast. I can't say that I blame him – there's a gorgeous spread laid out for us. Fresh croissants and pastries, a platter of deli meats and smoked salmon, cheeses, bowls of strawberries and cherries, big slabs of some kind of chocolatey traybake topped with almonds. There are jugs of orange juice, a pot of coffee, and a bottle of chilled Champagne in an ice bucket.

Zack follows my gaze and says: "Buck's fizz?"

"I'm tempted, but no, thank you. I have a long drive ahead of me and I'll need all my brain cells functioning."

He nods, and I'm sure I see a flicker of relief on his face. I'm confused at first, but then I put it together. I suddenly realise that this isn't just about seeing Marcy one last time – it's about making sure that his daughter is safe.

I can't blame him. The last time I saw this man I was a wreck, a burned-out party girl running on attitude. I had more alcohol in my veins than blood, and I was clearly reckless. I sashayed into our business meeting wearing last night's clothes, stinking of booze, and skating by on winks and innuendo. It wasn't pretty, and even less so when I followed up on that by doing a runner and leaving him with egg on his face in his professional life.

I hope I don't give off those vibes anymore, but he has no real clue what my world has looked like since then. Yes, I still like a drink on a night out. Yes, I still like to party – but the party is usually held in our local pub, which is hardly a den of iniquity. I'm guessing that last night, he had similar thoughts to mine – wondering what I'd been up to for all these years. Wondering, perhaps, if I was still that same woman – a self-destructive lunatic who should have been checking into rehab, not running a restaurant and building a media career. And if I was, perhaps he wouldn't be quite so happy to let his baby girl come and spend the next few weeks with me.

I suspect the Champagne was a test, and the look of relief suggests that I passed. Go me. I'd like to be annoyed, but I'd be exactly the same in his shoes. And as Simon died in a car crash, the last person likely to drive while drunk is me.

I help myself to a plate of food and wonder if I should just talk to him about it, honestly. Assure him that all will be well. I decide that I will, once the girls are out of earshot – they will undoubtedly disappear up to Marcy's room at some point.

Bear stares at me soulfully as I slice some chilled Brie, and I can totally understand how he got to be so fat. He's too cute. Plus, I'd guess he's an older dog, still energetic but with greying fur around his muzzle – it's likely that Bear arrived as a puppy after their mum died. He's undoubtedly been spoiled rotten.

"Sorry, pal," I say, carefully keeping my plate high. "It's for your own good, honest."

He lets out a little whine and slides to his belly, his tail making one sad thump against the tiled floor.

As I'm pouring a coffee, I hear Marcy giving Sophie a verbal tour of the room. That's the yucca plant that Bear once peed on, she tells us. That's the hob where she made her first French onion soup. That's the chair she used to stand on so she could reach the high cupboard, where the chocolate biscuits were kept. That's the skylight that once had to be replaced when her sister Amy was practising hockey indoors on a snowy day and rocketed the ball right through the glass.

I smile as she does it and notice that Zack looks similarly amused. It's nice – a run-through of family memories, the legends we build, the stories we tell. You'd never guess from all of this that Marcy has spent years without her mum, and I hope the same is true of Sophie about her dad. Me and Zack? Probably we're just a whole lot better at hiding the pain.

She skitters around to a cork notice board on the wall, and I see Zack grimace.

"Marcy," he says firmly. "There's no need for that!"

"Oh but there is, Daddy dearest," she says, looking devilish. I look at the board to see what all the fuss is about, and I see several photos of women, clearly printed off at home, possibly from social media profiles. They're all young, but not super-young – like maybe in their thirties. They all look different but the same – totally gorgeous.

"This," Marcy announces with some glee, "is my dad's wall of shame! I know he wants to take it down, but I've told him he mustn't. He needs to face up to his mistakes, like he always told me when I was little. Like he told Amy when she smashed that skylight. So, these are the women he's dated in the last, what, two years?"

Zack swipes his hands across his face, then shrugs in resignation.

"About that, yeah," he says.

"So, after Mum died, he stayed single for ages," Marcy continues. "Understandable, especially with us two hanging around. Then when Amy went to France, and I was eighteen, he went on his first date for... how long was it, Dad?"

"It was my first date since I met your mother. So, since the first of October, twenty-three years ago."

He looks mortified, but all I can think is that it's sweet he remembers the exact day they went on their first date. After all this time, it's still embedded in his mind.

"That was Francesca," Marcy says, pointing at a glossy brunette with perfect teeth. "He dumped her because she'd never heard of *Tiswas*, whatever that is."

I have a brief image of Saturday morning chaos – the kids'

TV show that dunked celebs in goo and smashed people in the face with custard pies. It makes me smile just thinking about it.

"That's fair," I say, sipping my coffee.

"This," Marcy continues, showing us a pretty blonde, "is Lola. Her crime was that she thought the musical *Wicked* was better than the original version of *The Wizard of Oz*."

"Not quite," Zack interrupts. "It was because she decided that was the case even though she'd never even *seen* the original *Wizard of Oz*. I mean, who hasn't seen *The Wizard of Oz*?"

"Lola, apparently," I reply, leaning against the counter and enjoying his discomfort. It doesn't come as a surprise that Zack has dated beautiful women who are younger than him, given the world he works and moves in, but it is fun to see him skewered by his daughter.

"What about her?" I ask Marcy, gesturing at a stunning redhead with glittering green eyes. "What was wrong with her?"

"She didn't know the Lord of the Rings films were based on books."

"Right – and this one, with the dimples?"

"That was Elodie. That was going okay until he went to her flat and discovered she had a Pokémon collection."

"This one?" I say, looking at an athletic woman in a yoga pose, hating her already. Bet she doesn't have to clamber onto all fours to get off the floor.

"Simone. Actually, I think she dumped you didn't she, Dad?"

"Yes. She pitched me a concept for a show where overweight people did yoga, and wanted to call it *The Biggest Poser*. I wasn't keen, and she lost interest in me pretty soon after that. To be fair I was relieved – she was a weird combination of way too limber and supremely competitive. It wasn't good for my back."

I guffaw at that one, and accidentally dribble coffee on my chin.

"None of them lasted more than a few months," Marcy says. "And none of them were serious enough for us to meet them. I keep their pics here to remind him that he needs to up his game and find someone better, or he's going to end up as a sad and lonely old man watching clips of *Tiswas* on YouTube and living off multi-packs of crisps. All alone with his sense of superiority."

"Thanks for the pep talk, darling," he replies, sounding amused but actually looking a bit sad. Sophie and Marcy have known more grief in their young lives than most people their age have known – but they haven't got a clue what it's like to find your soulmate and then lose them. It is devastating, and Zack is doing better than me even if none of it has worked out. I suppose I only lost Simon five years ago as opposed to ten, but I've not been on a single date since.

"You're welcome, Dad! Sophie, do you want to come up to my room?"

Of course she does. They both grab more pastries and disappear off up the stairs in a thud of feet and a gust of giggles.

Zack looks at me, and I feel the intimacy of the moment. He looks raw, exposed, waiting for me to comment. I understand that sense of vulnerability all too well.

"My husband died as well," I blurt out. "Five years ago. I admire you for getting out there again."

A cloud of surprise appears on his face, and it's obvious that Marcy hasn't told him that either. Maybe we're just not interesting enough to talk about when you're their age.

"I'm sorry," he says simply. "It sucks, doesn't it?"

I laugh a little at that. It sounds like something my son Dan would say, not this sleek, successful man standing before me in his expensive cologne and his elf slippers.

"Yeah, it really does! I turned up last night expecting to do the widow dance, you know? That thing where everyone else is in couples and they're a bit too awkward to ask you about anything?"

He grimaces, and it's obviously not an alien concept to him.

"I know it well. It's a bit like having leprosy, isn't it? People are fascinated but also worried they might catch it. Look, they might be a while – do you want to come through to the living room where we can sit down? Then I can close the kitchen door and put poor Bear out of his misery."

I take my coffee and a pastry on a small plate, and we head out. I'm conscious of the fact that I am back wearing my clown clothes, no make-up, and that I've probably got crumbs on my face. But really, I decide, what's the point in being concerned about that? I could be at my most well-dressed and alluring and still look like a bag lady next to the beauty show of his ex-girlfriends. I'm not in the same league, and it doesn't matter anyway. I am who I am.

The lounge is as bright and airy as the rest of the house, walls lined with bookshelves, framed posters of some of his TV shows, potted plants, family pictures. I see one of a pretty dark-haired woman with two little girls, and say: "Is that her? Your wife?"

"Yes," he says, nodding. "Rowena. She was a food stylist. I met her on a photo shoot, where she was making everything look delectable even though it was actually cold by that stage."

I remember those days – vaguely. The days when I was front of house, getting the shots done for our website. The strange world of food showbusiness.

Rowena is, like I say, pretty – but she is not by any means glamorous or beautiful. She looks like a mum, with a gorgeous smile.

"What was she like?" I ask – because nobody ever does. Sometimes you desperately want to talk about them, but everyone is too scared to ask in case they make you cry.

"She was surprisingly blunt. Bearing in mind my work, I was used to people saying yes, people trying to curry favour. She, to put it frankly, took no shit at all. She told me off, called me out, and didn't care if she did it in public. She was from Dublin originally, and she swore like a trooper, which always surprised everyone because she looked so petite and meek."

"So you were hooked?"

"I was! She loved her work, but she loved family life more. She was a great cook herself, so I'm not surprised both my girls have gone down that route – Amy works at a restaurant in Paris. She was a great mum, a great wife, a great home-maker. Just an all-round great human being. I miss her every day, but now at least I can smile when I think about her, not just grieve."

"I get that. I'm starting to feel the same. Depends what mood I'm in, and I'm always amazed at how unpredictable it is – one day laughing at some nice memory and feeling lucky I ever had him, and the next day hysterical tears because I miss him so much. People assume after five years, I've moved on – but it's not that simple, is it? I was so busy after he died, raising three teenagers on my own, that sometimes I wonder if I ever really processed it all properly myself. There was just this raw, gaping hole in my life, and all I had time to do was slap on an emotional plaster and get on with making the packed lunches. It must have been the same for you."

"Yep," he says, looking thoughtful. "I've been considering that lately. There are all these stages of grief you're supposed to go through – you know, denial, anger, all that. Supposedly working your way through to acceptance. I think I stalled at anger, and went straight into sorting childcare, managing a demanding job, and trying to make it to as many school events as I could."

"Is it still there?" I ask gently. "The anger?"

"Sometimes, yes. She was so young, and so good. It felt unfair. I still find myself sometimes watching the news, some report about some awful crime or whatever, and raging that scum like that are still walking the earth and she isn't. Makes me sound like a psycho, doesn't it?"

"Not at all. It just makes you sound honest. It's even worse when you have those thoughts about perfectly normal people. Like when you're walking around the supermarket and see some happy couple, and think, why do they still have each other? Why was he taken away and not one of them? Then feel yucky about it, because of course you don't actually want someone else to die! It's complicated. I don't think it's something you can judge, and it changes every day anyway. Sounds like you're at least trying to move on though?"

He laughs and runs his hands through his hair. I've noticed this is a thing he does – maybe when he's nervous, or maybe when he's unsure of what to say next. It's an attractive emotional tic and doesn't help dampen down my Zack's Hair fascination.

"Not really. I mean, yes, I did date those women. The girls were independent, and I felt like I should at least try, you know? But as you'll have gathered from Marcy's little performance, I'm not exactly taking it seriously. They're too young. They're too different. They're too everything, except right for me. Partly it's just the kind of women I meet in my world – but partly, if I'm being honest, it's deliberate. I know from the get-go that it's not going anywhere. I'm playing a part, and I pick women who I know won't offer me anything real. I might be ready to move on to a bit of fun, but I'm not sure I'm ready to move on to anything real."

"Maybe you won't ever be," I reply, because exactly the same thought has occurred to me. "Maybe something real would feel like too much of a betrayal."

"That's exactly it. Now, enough of this morose conversation. Isn't it strange, though, Connie? That we haven't seen each other for such a long time, and end up having this awful thing in common?"

"It is strange, and I wish for both our sakes we had nothing to talk about. But now we're discussing the past, just let me reassure you that I am no longer the train wreck you used to know. When you last saw me, I was young, dumb, and full of Jack Daniel's. Now, I'm a very respectable, very boring mum-of-three who lives in a remote corner of Dorset and runs a little café. Marcy will be perfectly safe with us."

He gives me a grin that tells me my earlier suspicions were right.

"Ah," he says, "you noticed my sneaky little sobriety test, did you?"

"It wasn't that sneaky – and I don't blame you. I was a basket case last time you saw me. Don't worry. She'll be fine."

"Good. I do worry – as I'm sure you know. Once something that bad has happened, you never feel quite safe again. Maybe we could swap numbers, so I could check in with a grown-up occasionally?"

"I don't know about a grown-up, but you can definitely have my number."

We're in the process of doing this when the girls come racing down the stairs again. Marcy has an extra bag to cram into the tiny boot of my car, which will be fun. I hope she doesn't have any Fabergé eggs in there or it could end badly.

"We were thinking..." says Sophie, glancing at her friend.

"Oh no. Did you hurt yourself?"

"Ha ha, very funny. No, we were thinking that maybe Marcy's dad could come and visit for the Spring Feast night?"

The two of them are the picture of innocence, but I am not fooled for a minute. I suspect they've been discussing their poor old mum and dad, and how sad their lives are without their babies at home. In my case they may be right, but I'll never admit that in a million years.

My mind quickly races over all the potential pros and cons of this scenario, and I realise that I don't feel especially comfortable with Zack being in Starshine Cove. It's nothing personal – he seems like he's become a very nice man – but he is from that other country. The Past. Starshine is my present and my future, and I have a completely illogical fear that the two won't mix. Or that they will in fact curdle.

If I'm being brutally honest with myself as well, I also find him unsettling to be around for other reasons. It's been so long since I've felt attracted to a man that I almost didn't recognise it at first, this fizzy feeling. Now I do recognise it, it's not entirely welcome.

"It's sold out, Soph," I say sadly. "You know it always is. Besides, I'm sure Zack has better things to be doing."

"I don't actually," he says, frowning. "I'd booked a fortnight off to go and visit Amy, but she says she's too busy to manage more than a weekend. But I totally understand if it's not possible. I'll make it down for the next one."

"Couldn't you squeeze an extra table in?" Sophie pleads.

"Not really. People don't pay that much money to be squashed in like sardines. I can let Zack know if there's a cancellation, though?"

I'm really hoping there isn't. Zack is looking at Marcy, deep in concentration, as though he's trying to solve a problem.

"How about this?" he asks. "How about if I come down to help out? I've been around food shows enough to know the basics, and I did years waiting on tables while I was uni. That way I don't need a table, and Connie, you get an extra set of hands."

"Brilliant!" says Sophie, giving Marcy a high five like it was all their idea to begin with. "We're always desperate for more staff, aren't we, Mum?"

I nod, and plaster on a smile. She's right, we are – but I still feel unsettled at the thought of those hands belonging to Zack Harris.

FIVE

I am out in the woods with my brother-in-law Archie, foraging for wild garlic. It's not exactly hard to find – the woodlands here are old, and the floor is carpeted in swathes of the tell-tale little white flowers and pointed green leaves.

You'd be amazed how much food you can forage for if you know where to look. Fruits, vegetables, mushrooms, herbs, nuts and seeds, several different types of seaweed. It's fun to forage, and somehow the food can taste better when you've found it yourself – maybe it's a throwback to hunter-gatherer times.

I take small amounts – never more than nature can easily replace – and add them to the more traditionally sourced foods on my menu. The wild garlic is a favourite, and it also means a trip to the woods.

I love the woods. I mean, I love the beach as well – but something about the trees is so soothing. It's a sunny day, and the light is striping through the canopy, dappled gold falling through the green. The air is alive with birdsong, and the only scents are those of nature – the thick, rich soil and the plants that grow in it. You could literally be in a different century out here, and I think that's one of the reasons Archie loves it too –

he loses himself in the ancient rhythm of it all. He'd fit right in as a hunter gatherer, I think, as I watch him crouched down working with his knife, slicing a few leaves and adding them to the harvest already in the basket.

He is a very big man, my brother-in-law. Kind of like a grizzly bear in human form. If this were a shape-shifting fantasy film, he would morph into a bear. Marcy would be an otter. Ella would be a lion cub. Me? A yellow Lab, at a guess. Maybe a manatee, on a good day.

Until relatively recently, Archie had the fur to go with his bear-like appearance – a big beard, long hair, sideburns, his face all but obliterated by the fuzz. Then he met Cally, who happens to be a hairdresser, and everything changed. She didn't just give him a short back-and-sides – she gave him a whole new lease of life.

The car crash that claimed Simon also claimed his sister – Archie's wife, Sandy. Simon was driving her to hospital because she was in labour with their second little girl, Meg. In the end Meg survived, but her mum didn't. It fills me with joy that Cally is here now, because she is one of the most maternal women I've ever met. She's kind and jolly and funny, and Archie is a different man now – and those girls have a second mama. Not one to replace the first, but one to help them grow up and turn into young women with a bit of feminine guidance. I've done my best but it's just not the same.

We've always been close, me and Archie – we've clung to each other like life rafts in the last few years. We're a tag team – stepping in to help when one of us feels overwhelmed. I had three teenagers on my hands, which wasn't easy – but he had a motherless newborn, which was off-the-charts demanding. It's been tough, horrendously tough, but I like to think we've helped each other through some very dark times.

Now, strolling through these woods, Archie in his element as he points out various plants and signs of insect life, I let the familiar and gentle music of our relationship soothe my rough edges.

"You okay?" he says, gazing up at me, shielding his eyes from a patch of sunlight. "You seem a bit out of it."

I settle on a lichen-coated tree stump, and he joins me.

"I'm worried we've taken too much," I say, looking at the basket. I'm worried about all kinds of things, of course, but that seems like a good place to start.

"No, it's fine – there's masses of the stuff, and we've cut the leaves so they'll grow back. The bulbs are all still in place."

"Right. Good. And how is the rhubarb coming along?"

"Great. There'll be plenty for you to use. I've been growing sorrel as well."

Archie is the gardener for the whole of Starshine Cove, but he also has a huge greenhouse, and a patch of land where he grows his own produce. Since Rose became his apprentice, he's had more time to plan his empire, as well as provide fresh food baskets for local people who can't get out and about too easily. The man is never happier than when he's uprooting carrots or watering his rows of lettuce.

"Brilliant. So. Everything's okay, then," I reply.

"If you say so, Connie." He's looking at me curiously. "Feeling stressed because of the Spring Feast?"

The answer to that is, of course, yes – but the stress is part of the package. I've been in far more high-pressure situations than my little gatherings, where I only serve for about forty people, and anyway, I enjoy it. I thrive on that feeling of balancing a million little details at once, getting the timings right, the myriad moments that go into something like this. It's pretty much the closest I get to an adrenaline rush these days.

It's not just that bothering me, though, and he knows it. I look up at him, and he nudges me playfully with his shoulder. His shoulder is so big he almost knocks me off the tree trunk and laughs as he grabs hold of me to settle me back in place.

"Come on," he says. "After all these years I can tell when something's on your mind. Is it having Marcy to stay? Is she not settling in?"

"God, yes – I think that girl could settle in on Mars, she's so bloody enthusiastic about everything! I offered her James's room – it's not like he uses it anymore. I should really clear it out a bit, maybe decorate it... but anyway, she said no, and she has a camp bed in Sophie's room. I hear them giggling and chatting all night long. It's actually really nice, having that kind of energy in the house again. They're like Meg and Lilly, but they talk about different things. At least I hope so, because last night there was a *lot* of laughing about the boys they'd snogged on their last big night out in London."

"Yikes," he says, shivering. "I know that's going to happen with my girls at some point, and I'm not looking forward to it."

"Well, they're only five and nine, Archie, so I think that's a while off. Sophie's had boyfriends before, as you know, so this kind of thing isn't exactly a shock. I know what I was getting up to at her age... which now I come to think about it isn't very reassuring! Anyway, they're fine. Also, I'm making them work – this is technically part of their course, it's not a holiday. I have to fill in logbooks and everything, almost as though I'm a grown-up."

I've planned out tasks for them, some of which will be helpful for me but also good stuff to learn – food prep, cleaning, appliance checking, stock control, boring stuff. I've given them jobs in the café, which Sophie is an old hand at because I've been using her as child labour for years now, but also added in extra responsibilities like ordering from suppliers and going over our allergen information.

The fun bit, the bit they're enjoying the most, is that I've also put them in charge of the daily specials – they come up with the idea, cost it, make it, sell it and serve it. It's been highly entertaining watching them try to talk customers into ordering whichever dish they're pushing, then waiting breathlessly for a response. You can learn a lot at catering college, I'm sure, but this is the magic – the moment when a meal you've created and lovingly cooked goes out into the wild. It's like a little part of you, and you desperately want people to love it.

"Where are they now?" Archie asks. "Thought they'd want in on the wild garlic collecting."

"Yes, Archie, because that is the stuff of dreams for all teenage girls, isn't it? Actually I've got them back at the café after hours – I told them they need to go through a basic food hygiene inspection. I've set some deliberate booby traps, like putting raw chicken on the shelf above an open packet of ham."

"Is that a bad thing?"

"Good Lord, man, how are you still alive?"

"Dunno. Cast-iron constitution, I suppose. Is Marcy's dad supposed to be coming soon?"

And just like that, he whacks the nail on the head. I nod, but don't add anything. Zack has been in touch a few times since we left London, initially in a bit of a panic because he hadn't heard from Marcy.

I explained to him that we have extremely dodgy wifi and phone signals, and that only a few places – the inn, specifically the fire escape outside the inn, and the offices in the community centre – have decent reception due to dongles. Also, I will never, ever be able to say the word 'dongles' without laughing.

Zack was a bit taken aback at the slower pace of communication, which doesn't surprise me – he seems to live with a phone glued to his hands, and he works in the media in London. That's a very different, very quick-fire rapid-response kind of environment. Ours is more of a 'we'll get back to you a week on Monday' kind of vibe.

Annoyingly, there was a cancellation for the feast, and a matching one for the room they'd booked at the Starshine Inn. I'm not entirely sure I'd have informed him if not for the fact that Sophie took the call, so I was all out of choices. I suppose it's better than the alternative – him staying at our house. I'd planned to make him use Dan's room, which is not for the fainthearted.

Despite the cancellation, which means he could just visit, enjoy the night and leave the next day, he is still insisting that he's going to come and help out, plus stay around 'for a while' if the mood takes him. I'd guess that he's not a man used to having time on his hands – he has been busy for decades and has an empire to run – and the fact that his plans to head to France to see Amy have been derailed have left him at a loose end.

I, of all people, completely understand that feeling – he doesn't want to spend his weeks off sitting around in the home he made with Rowena, alone apart from a chubby dog and his memories. He would probably find it hard dealing with the solitude and the lack of occupation – and I get it. He needs something to keep him busy, something that makes him feel connected to his family and to a world outside work.

That, it seems, is where we come in, and he is determined to come and visit. Why he can't just dial up another stunning temporary girlfriend I don't know – it's not like he seems short of options on that front.

I have absolutely no right to be bothered by this. I have absolutely no reason to be bothered by this. I have absolutely no clue why I am in fact so bothered – but I definitely am, and as Archie is here with me, a human boulder by my side, maybe I should at least try and talk it through.

"I'm a bit weirded out by it all," I say simply.

"By what?" Archie asks. "By Marcy's dad? Sophie told Rose you used to know him, back in the day."

"Yes. Back in the day. I think that's the issue – I don't really have many fond memories of back in the day, or my life when Zack and people like him were involved in it."

I see Archie turning this over, obviously exploring a few options before he speaks.

"Right. Was he a dick to you? Do you want me to rough him up?"

"No!" I say, laughing. "Nothing like that at all – in fact if anyone was a dick it was me! You know I was on the verge of signing all these various deals, I'm sure I've told you – recipe book based on dishes from the restaurant, a signing tour, a TV show?"

"Yeah. I find it hard to imagine all of that, but then again, you probably find it hard to imagine me as a lawyer in London. We both kind of shed our skin when we moved here, didn't we? Found things that made us happier."

"Exactly. Well, Zack was the guy producing the TV show. I left him in the lurch so I do feel a bit embarrassed about that, but it was years ago and water under the bridge – he's not holding grudges. It's just... I suppose when I shed my skin, I basically burned the old one. Not just burned it – I burned it, locked the ashes in four different boxes, and buried them. It was different for you – you didn't mind being a lawyer, and you had a life in London you were okay with. It was just that meeting Sandy brought you here and showed you something even better."

"So how is it different for you?"

"It's different because I hated everything about myself back then. I hated the way I behaved, the way I looked, the way I treated people – including me. I don't even like thinking about it, it gives me chills. And then Zack bumbles back into my world, and it's like everything feels a bit raw – like my old skin is still out there, looking for me."

"I think you're going a bit far with the skin thing – it's starting to sound like a horror film."

"That's kind of how it feels."

Archie shakes his head and says: "I think you might be overreacting – and yes, I know, a man saying that to a woman usually earns himself a slap on the chops – but in this case I think it's true. Look, you might like to think that there was this one big turning point, and that the Connie you are now bears no resemblance to the Connie you were then – but you're wrong. Life can't be neatly sectioned off like that, into the before and the after. You wouldn't be who you are now without who you were then."

"Archie, you're at risk of sounding like some kind of zen master!"

He grins. "I am. I am the guru of the woods. So, let's figure this out – tell me one of the things you didn't like about yourself back then."

"Well, for a start, I was a chef but I never ate. I was so skinny."

He gently pokes my admittedly 'womanly' thighs, and replies: "I'd say you've sorted that out."

"Gurus aren't supposed to body shame."

"I'm not body shaming – you're gorgeous and you know it."

I shrug, as if to say well, yes, I'm not too bad.

"What else?" he pushes.

"Okay. I was mean – I was a mean boss, and a bitchy person."

"You are neither of those things now. You are the kindest woman I know, with the biggest heart."

He gives me a little smile, and I take the compliment.

"I was selfish," I go on. "Everything was about me. I never gave a damn about anyone else. I worked hard, and thought the whole world was mine."

"Well, these days you're the opposite. You organise all those little things that make people's lives better – the food deliveries, the minibus, all the events that bring us together. You donate a portion of your earnings to the village funds. You are a mother, a daughter, a friend – your door is quite literally always open. You can't do enough for other people. In fact, you're practically a saint!"

"True. Or at the very least a minor angel. But... look, you see what I mean? Things are different here. I'm different here – and I like that."

"I do see, but I also think you're being deliberately dense. The life you led before, and the way it made you feel – that's all fed into the life you lead now. Your experiences then built the foundation of what you are now – even just as an example of what you *didn't* want your life to look like. You have a way of seeing beneath the surface of people, Connie, and figuring out what they need before they do – except when it comes to yourself. Then you're just really, really thick."

"Oi, you! You're the worst guru ever!" I say, laughing at his mock-serious face. "I choose to accept the nice things you said about me and ignore the rest. Anyway, you're not one to talk – you almost messed things up with Cally because you were so thick about what you really needed!"

"I did, you're right – and you're one of the people who made me realise that and sort it out. So, stop being so hard on yourself, and stop worrying – one face from the past isn't going to bring everything you've built here crashing down on you. It's too solid for that."

He wraps me up in his arms and gives me a big bear hug, and I nod into his flannel shirt. He's right, I think – I'm definitely being over-sensitive. It's been such a transitional time, both with my own body and the kids starting out on their own journeys, that I suspect I'm feeling less stable than usual. That doesn't mean impending doom – it just means change.

"Thank you," I say simply. "You're right, and I needed that."

"It's okay, you can repay me in scones."

"Sorry, Cally's banned me from giving you guys scones. She's on a diet again."

"Don't worry, it won't last!"

We gather up the basket, and I breathe in the fresh woodland air. I feel better for our chat, refreshed and ready to take on the world. Or at least my part of it.

We're on a slight hill, looking down at the path that leads from a quiet road to the village. As we make our way towards it, Archie puts a gentle hand on my arm and draws to a halt.

"There's someone on the path," he says, peering through the trees.

For any normal path, of course, that wouldn't be anything unusual – but this one is usually quiet and secluded. The road on the other side ends at the cliffs and is literally the road to nowhere. It is rarely used, even by hikers doing the nearby coastal route towards Lyme Regis.

We pause, and I find an opening in the branches to look through. Sure enough, a solitary figure is ambling along, a slightly confused look on his face. He pauses frequently, taking pictures and maybe video on his phone. A fat black Lab is bumbling along behind him, sniffing and peeing in time-honoured canine tradition.

"Is that him?" Archie whispers. "Is that Zack?"

"Yep," I reply quietly, watching as he crouches down to look at a patch of wildflowers. "That's him."

Archie grins, and answers: "You didn't tell me he was a silver fox, Connie. Now I've seen him, I've got my suspicions about why you feel so stressed about him being here. You bloody well fancy him! Was he an ex? Was there more to your relationship than the professional?"

"No! No, there wasn't – and no, I do not fancy him!" I bleat, sounding unconvincing even to my own ears. "And anyway, he only goes out with supermodels and influencers. I'm more of a binfluencer – everyone looks to me when it's bin day and they're not sure which one needs to go out..."

"Binfluencers are important – I never remember when it's recycling day. Anyway, come on – I'm starting to feel creepy lurking up here looking at him."

He bounds down the hillside, his long legs confident, and I follow at a more sedate pace. I don't especially want to greet Zack by sliding down a hill and landing at his feet on my backside.

"Ahoy there!" booms Archie, giving Zack a bit of a shock. He recovers quickly, and his face breaks into a smile as he sees the two of us approaching. God, he looks so good standing there, the sun dappling through the trees onto his hair. It's like Mother Nature staged him just to make my tummy fizz.

"Ah," Zack says, "I am in the right place after all. I got lost – did you know this place isn't even on the map?"

"Yes," I reply. "It's actually an imaginary village, populated entirely by imaginary friends."

He quirks an eyebrow, considers this, and says: "I wouldn't be surprised. What's with all the fairies and dinosaurs?"

"What fairies and dinosaurs?"

"Ha! Nice try, but I have them on video."

"They're my work," says Archie, offering his hand to shake and introducing himself. "My little girls love them – you'll see the fairies all over the village."

Zack's face breaks out into a warm smile, and he answers: "They're cute. I look forward to meeting more of them. So, I've left my car parked up on the side of the road back there – is that right? I mean, there was no other traffic, but I was told there was a car park at the inn."

Archie takes the basket of wild garlic from me and says: "I'm heading home. Connie will go back to your car with you and take you round. Welcome to Starshine, Zack!"

I try not to scowl at Archie's retreating bulk and concentrate instead on stroking Bear's velvety ears.

"Come on then," I say. "Let's get you sorted. This fella looks like he needs a bowl of water and a lie-down."

"The same could be said of me. It's really warm for March."

We wander back along the path through the woods, Zack

intermittently stopping to take more photos and video. I get it – this is a beautiful place, and I suppose given the nature of his job, he always has one eye on the visuals – but I always think people who spend so much time on their phones capturing the image of something often miss out on simply experiencing it. He's a grown man, though, so it's none of my business how he behaves.

We emerge onto the road, and Bear obediently clambers into the back seat of his car. I tell Zack to go back the way he came, and talk him through the slightly tricky route back around to the other side of the village. It's hidden away, tucked between other routes but invisible from them – our own little secret slice of heaven.

We chat about how Marcy is doing, and what I have planned for the Spring Feast, and it's all pleasant and harmless enough – but lurking in the back of my mind is Archie's comment about me fancying him.

As I glance at his profile while he drives, I can't deny that he might be right. Don't get me wrong, I appreciate a good-looking man – Jake, Ella's husband who owns the inn, looks like a god in human form, and his brother Josh is just as gorgeous. But appreciating that and fancying them are two different things. I don't think I've actually fancied a real-life man since I met Simon – setting aside the holy trinity of Daniel Craig, Chris Hemsworth and Henry Cavill, of course. I have life-size cardboard cut-outs of them in my living room, left over from Ella's hen night, and they are fantastic company.

Now, though, I can't help noticing the way Zack's jeans fit snugly against his thighs, and the width of his shoulders, and the tiny gold flecks in his green eyes. I don't want to notice these things, but I do, and it is unsettling. I keep imagining what it would be like to put my hand on those thighs, or wrap my arms around those shoulders. I think I'm managing normal conversation, but my mind is feeling decidedly abnormal. By the time we reach the inn, I am feeling hot and bothered and wishing I had my little fan with me. Hormones are absolute bastards.

I get out of the car as quickly as I can, scrambling for fresh air and hoping I don't look as hot as I feel. Bear tumbles after me, and immediately pees on the wheel arch of Jake's new car. He used to have a fancy Audi but he's swapped it for something more boxy and big-booted since baby Kitty arrived. It never ceases to amaze me how much gear one tiny baby needs.

Zack is looking at me with slightly narrowed eyes, and I wonder what he's thinking. Does he remember that spark we used to share, or was it all too long ago? Has he ever wondered what might have been? Or is the explanation much simpler – I've gone bright red.

"Would you like a quick tour of the village before you check in?" I ask, forcing myself to be welcoming even though I'd quite like to go home and stick my head in an ice bucket.

"Yes please," he replies. "Will my gear be okay in the car? I've got my luggage, plus some quite expensive cameras."

"Zack, your gear would be okay if you piled it up in the middle of the village green with a sign saying 'steal me please'. I know it takes some getting used to when you've lived in London, but nobody is going to do anything like that. I was exactly the same, don't worry – these days I've forgotten what keys are actually used for."

"That must be nice," he replies, walking by my side as we make our way across the car park. "And not exactly a long commute to work, either."

"Nope. I could fall out of bed and roll there in my duvet. Anyway, as you can see, this is the Starshine Inn. It's owned by Jake, who also owns several of the holiday cottages in the village. He's married to Ella, who is the local GP, and they have a baby called Kitty, and a dog called Larry."

He nods and says: "Okay. Just checking, will there be a test on this later?"

"Absolutely, and if you get anything wrong, we'll tie you to a stake in the bay and let the crabs eat you."

"Yikes. What a terrible way to go – sounds very Greek. What do I get if I pass the test?"

"A pint in the inn, and a crustacean-free night."

He nods to accept the terms, and I lead him through to the village green. He actually pauses and sighs out loud when he sees it, and I feel the familiar lick of pride that I always get when somebody sees Starshine for the first time.

The central green is lush and neat, the bedding plants around it starting to blossom in clusters of spring pinks and purples. The homes that surround it are an interesting mix – chocolate-box thatched cottages, little terraces built of mellow golden stone, the old school that houses the community centre. Trevor's shop, the bakery, my café – it all adds up to an impossibly pretty blend of old-world country charm.

"I feel like I've just stepped onto a set," he says, predictably enough getting out his phone to frame some shots. "This would be an amazing filming location…"

"Ah. But then our secret would be out, and everyone here is pretty much happy being one of those places that get called a hidden gem. There is a tourist trade – the cottages are always booked, the inn too. People who know about us come back year after year, but it's never too much. It doesn't overwhelm us or take away from Starshine's identity. I'm not sure we'd enjoy it if we started getting coach parties."

"But wouldn't that be beneficial, for the economy?" he asks as we stroll along the side of the green. "Help people make a living? I know it can be hard in rural areas, with the decline of traditional industries…"

I laugh out loud and shake my head.

"I'm guessing what you actually know about rural areas is based on reading articles or watching TV, because that sounded exactly like a quote you've picked up while you were sitting in an office in central London! And yes, of course, some places depend on tourism – but this place is a bit different. We have a real mix of people and they all do different jobs. It's not just yokels desperate for cash and running moonshine across county lines – assuming that is a little bit patronising!"

He looks horrified at the accusation, and replies: "I'm sorry if it came across like that. And you're right – it was my big city privilege talking. What do I know?"

"Nothing, when it comes to Starshine Cove. So, you see that bakery over there? That's owned by the Betties. They don't just churn out a few loaves for the locals – they supply high-end grocers all across the UK. They're actually pretty famous."

I see him processing the information, nodding thoughtfully. "Yeah... okay, I think I've heard of them – or at least seen their cakes on the shelves. Do they have a logo like two letter Bs covered in seashells?"

"Yep, that's them. And up there, over the rooftops and halfway up the hill, there's a studio that belongs to a jewellery maker called Daisy, who isn't here right now but is also really successful – as in, international shows successful. Jake, who owns the inn? He used to be one of the leading property developers in the UK. And Trevor, who runs the shop—"

"Let me guess, he used to be the CEO of Amazon?"

"Don't be silly – he's just a nice old hippie dude who likes selling herbal tea and occasionally sleeps overnight in the middle of a stone circle. But anyway – I'm just making the point that this place isn't hurting. It doesn't need publicity, or to be a filming location, or any of that. I've noticed you getting everything on video – don't be scheming away to make some kind of reality TV show about us, all right?"

I smile to take any potential sting out of my words, and he holds his hands up in surrender.

"Okay, okay – you caught me! I suppose I've just been doing my job for so long that my brain is trained to see potential. Are you sure, though? It'd be a great spot for a rural dating show, or one of those life-swap programmes where city slickers learn how to milk cows..."

"No. Absolutely not. Switch that part of your brain off and just enjoy yourself. Do you think you're capable of doing that?"

"I'll try my very best," he says, sliding the phone into his jeans pocket. "I shall attempt a digital detox."

We continue our walk, and I lead him around the green to the Cove Café. It's early evening now and the place is closed, but I take him inside so I can get Bear a bowl of water. There's no sign of Marcy and Sophie, but the place is spotless. I smile as I check the big fridge and find that all the fresh meat products are now correctly stored – looks like they didn't fall for my cunning booby trap.

Zack stands and looks around, taking in the pale wood and the white walls and the pretty seaside relics on shelves. He holds up a large conch shell and smiles as he puts it to his ear.

"I can hear the sea..." he says, grinning. Something about a shell to the ear tends to bring out the child in all of us.

"That's because the sea is right outside."

"I know, but I choose to believe it's magic! This place is lovely, Connie."

"Thank you. I think so myself. It might not be a Michelin-starred restaurant, but I love it here."

He nods and makes his way to the back of the room, where sliding glass doors open onto the terrace. Bear slurps down some water and follows him.

"Wow..." Zack says simply as he looks down at the bay. "It really is perfect."

It is, I think, looking on as the sun starts to slide towards a horizon made entirely of shining blue sea. Maybe, while he's here, I'll show him the caves – no phones allowed.

I get us both some water as well, and we wander down the terrace steps, settling on the very bottom one and gazing out at the view. He seems engrossed, distracted, his eyes narrowed against the sun, deep laughter lines creasing around them as he loses himself in thought. He looks slightly sad, and I wonder what some of those thoughts might be – I know even now, when I encounter something new and wonderful for the first time, I inevitably wish Simon was there to share it with me. Maybe he's thinking about his wife, and missing her.

I realise as I sneak peeks at him that despite his surface glamour, beneath the veneer of success, he is still a wounded man who needs to heal – and that just happens to be Starshine Cove's speciality. I feel petty now for the way I resented him coming here, because I am beginning to suspect that he needs to be here. The others laugh at me – especially Ella, with her I'm A Scientist vibe – but I've genuinely always thought that this magical place somehow invites the people who need it most.

"You okay?" I ask, briefly touching his arm.

He looks at me as though he's surprised to find me there, and nods.

"Yeah. Just... stuff on my mind, that's all."

"Well, we can't have that – you're on holiday! What's the name of Jake and Ella's baby?"

"Um... Kitty?"

"Congratulations! You win – come on, let's go to the pub."

SIX

Zack is submitted to some pretty intense local scrutiny as we sit in our corner seat in the Starshine Inn. Ella and Jake live here in an apartment at the back, at least for the time being, so she pops out to say hello. Jake himself is serving, and greets him with a drink on-the-house before he checks him in. Archie arrives, with Cally and the little girls in tow, and brings them all over to introduce them.

Cally, it turns out, is a huge reality TV show fan, and she's a little bit star struck meeting the man who was behind several of her favourites.

Zack handles it all with a calm and friendly manner, but looks a little tired by the time he's also been introduced to Rose, Archie's apprentice, and her mum, Lucy.

"Is that it?" he says quietly, as he sinks back into the red-velvet booth. He's only on cranberry juice, which is a waste of a free drink in my opinion.

"Nope. Plenty left – and one of them is George, my father-in-law. He's awesome. Don't worry, nobody actually expects you to remember names – and you've already dealt with the nosiest one of the lot."

"Who's that?"

"Me. The Inquisitor General of Starshine Cove."

"Self-appointed?"

"No, we had a ceremony in the woods at midnight. I have a pointy hat and a cloak back at home... the girls have apparently gone to Dorchester for the night, by the way, according to the message that has only just landed, and will be back later."

"Oh," he says, looking a bit deflated. I'm guessing he was desperate to see Marcy, who has with typical teenage daughter flair decided to dump him for the night. "Will they be late, do you think?"

"Oh yes. Possibly as late as midnight."

"Ha! That's probably when they normally go out in London. How is Marcy adapting?"

"Really well actually. She's great."

He looks suitably pleased by this, as we all are when someone compliments our offspring. I mean, we had something to do with it, didn't we?

He sips his juice, and says: "Do you worry about them? Your kids?"

"Of course I do. And they give me plenty of reason. James, my oldest, still doesn't seem settled. He works in IT and moved to Jersey for a job, but I'm not sure it'll stick. Dan... well, he's fine now, but he had meningitis the summer before last and it was touch and go for a while. Sophie, so far, hasn't presented me with any huge concerns – which is a concern in itself, because it will definitely happen at some point or another!"

"I'm sorry about Dan," he says. "That must have been hard, on your own."

"Well, I don't think I'm on my own in the same way most people are. Yes, I miss Simon – obviously and desperately – but this place, as you might have gathered already, is pretty much like a family anyway. A big, messy one with a rude sense of humour. Ella was by my side, and George, and everyone else rallied around to keep the café going and make sure the sky didn't fall in."

"So you don't feel lonely? You don't feel, I don't know, isolated?"

He's looking at me with quiet intensity, and I know it would be easier to lie. To simply smile and say it's impossible to feel lonely when I'm surrounded by such a cosy community – when the truth is that you can feel lonely anywhere, can't you? In a crowded room, at a party full of friends, in a busy café. Loneliness isn't just external, it's internal as well.

"Yes, sometimes," I reply, feeling slightly guilty for admitting it. I have so many blessings, and admitting to someone that I'm not perfectly happy feels like I'm disrespecting that. "It's not my default setting, but yes – every now and then, I feel like I'm the only woman on the planet."

"Detached from everyone else – like you're just pretending to be part of that world, when inside you feel very different?"

I nod. "I suppose that's exactly it. It's been more noticeable since the kids left – or maybe I've just had more time to pay attention to the way I feel, you know? Which I'm not sure is actually a good thing!"

"I know what you mean. And I'm sorry to pry. I just... thankfully, I suppose, I don't know many people in our position, and it's good to talk to someone about it."

"I get that. I have people to talk to here – sad story, I'll tell it to you one day – but it's not always easy. I'm worried about upsetting them – imposing my pain when they could do without it. And anyway, like I said, it's not all the time – mostly I'm okay. I have a great life here, great friends, family, everything I could ever wish for."

"Everything?" he says, raising one eyebrow, the corner of his mouth quirked up in a grin. I can't look away from his eyes, and I actually feel my heart rate speed up, a small boom echoing around inside my chest. Maybe I'm about to have some kind of cardiac event. This man is dangerous to my health.

"Everything," I reply firmly, sounding a lot more sure than I feel. "Except for another G&T. My glass seems to be empty."

I rattle the remaining ice in front of him and pull a sad face. He shakes his head in amusement and heads off to the bar.

I lean back against the wall, and use a beer mat to fan my face. Am I having palpitations? Yes, a little bit. I take some deep breaths, close my eyes, and let the moment pass. Okay, so Archie was definitely right. I do fancy Zack. I suppose I always did – but back when I first met him, that wasn't unusual. I fancied loads of people. Now, though, not so much – in fact not at all. I tell myself it's fine, it's normal, it's human – and it's certainly nothing to panic about. Fancying him doesn't mean I'm going to do anything about it, and besides, it's probably not mutual.

He returns with more drinks, and I suddenly find myself noticing every little detail about him. I notice the golden hairs on his tanned arms, and the length of his fingers. I notice the way the sunlight sparkles on the silver in his hair, and the fact that he has unfairly thick eyelashes for a man. I notice the scent of that cologne again, and the way his T-shirt moulds to a body that looks to be in superb shape. I notice it all – it's as though now I've admitted this evil fancying thing to myself, a tsunami of the stuff is crashing over me.

He tears open two bags of crisps and spreads them out on the foil like a makeshift plate. Bear immediately goes on high alert.

"I like what you've done there," I say, helping myself to one.

"Well, it's all in the presentation, isn't it? And I know I said I wouldn't think like this, but Jake, who owns the inn? He's... well, he's..."

"Really hot?"

"Yes! He's exceptionally good-looking. He'd make the perfect Fred Sirieix for that rural dating show..."

"Ha! Good luck with that. Jake doesn't even like having his photo taken, never mind being on telly."

We concentrate on the crisps for a few moments, then he says, out of the blue: "What about real family? I mean, blood family – not real, because I totally get what you're saying. You don't have to be related to someone for them to be your family. But even back when I first knew you, I never really found out anything about your past."

"That's because my present was so big it blotted out the sun."

"Yes, exactly – you were a force of nature. These days, I'm less naïve – we research everyone before we use them in a show."

"In case someone turns up a tweet of them having a racist rant later, or finds out they used to run an illegal cock-fighting ring?"

"Sadly more common than you'd think – at least the first one. But we never really did that with you, did we?"

"Well, I never ran an illegal cock-fighting ring, and I certainly never had a racist rant. As to your original question – about family – I don't have any. My parents died when I was eleven, and I was raised by my grandmother. She was pretty old school working-class London, lived through the Blitz and took no shit from anyone – she'd had a tough life and it made her a tough woman. She passed away when I was seventeen."

He takes this all in and nods. I rarely talk about that part of my life – yet another chunk of the past I don't enjoy thinking about – and I'm starting to realise Archie was right about yet another thing. I have a tendency to chop my life up into sections, rather than seeing it all as part of a whole.

"And you were out on your own then? At seventeen?"

"Yes. I had a home – the little terrace she'd lived in her

whole life – so I wasn't under the arches in a cardboard box or anything. I'd been working in pubs and cafés for a while, and then I managed to blag my way into the kitchen at one of the bigger restaurants, pretty much without any qualifications apart from an A in home economics and a winning smile."

"Ah, the eighties – things were different then!"

"Yep. Rah-rah skirts were cool, and Spangles were still on sale in the corner shop. All was well with the world. How about you – do you still have family?"

"Not really. My parents aren't around anymore, and my brother lives in New Zealand. Rowena's family is pretty big, but they're in Ireland. I suppose it's always played on my mind, since I lost her – worrying that if anything happened to me, the girls wouldn't have any parents. Every year they get older, I feel a bit more relieved."

"I understand that. I always knew that mine would always have people here, which is comforting, but yes, there is that underlying worry isn't there? Even now, when they're technically adults – I know I was independent at their age, but I still worry. But look – we're both fit and well, Zack, living on our extremely healthy diet of booze and crisps. I don't think either of us is going to be shuffling off any time soon."

He glances away for a moment, seeming to think that through, then nods firmly. "You're absolutely right. Now, tell me all about your Spring Feast."

"I can go one better than telling you. The actual event is the day after tomorrow – but tomorrow night, as is Starshine custom, I'll be having a trial run in the café. I hope you weren't lying about your waiting experience."

SEVEN

I stand in front of the small crowd in the café, and run through the menu. On the actual night, I'll do this before each course, explaining what the guests are about to eat and why I chose it. The dry run is a lot less formal – not least because every single person in front of me is wearing a brightly coloured paper crown and making a racket with plastic whistles and party blowers. Trevor found a job lot of Christmas crackers in storage and brought them with him.

Tonight, the tables aren't dressed, and they're scattered with a variety of different types of booze – it's bring-your-own, and they're all getting stuck in to cans of beer, bottles of plonk, and in the case of the Betties, a decanter of port. I laugh as I try to talk over the noise, my own paper crown perched on top of my unruly hair.

"Okay, okay," I say, holding my hands up in defeat, "I can see none of you are taking this seriously – but are you hungry?"

There is an eardrum-splitting round of whistles and party blowers rippling out into the sky, and some stamping of feet to accompany it.

"Right. First course – sorrel and wild garlic soup, served

with parmesan and rosemary croutons! My glamorous assistants will be around shortly."

I turn back to my team behind the serving counter. I don't need all of them tonight, as the guest list only includes George, Archie and Cally, Jake and Ella, Trevor, the baking Betties, and Jake's brother Josh. All of their offspring, human and canine, are being looked after for a few hours by Rose's mum, Lucy, and Miranda – it probably explains why some of them are especially riotous, enjoying a rare night off.

I could probably manage this lot on my own, but it's good to practise – and more importantly it's a lot of fun. It'll give me the chance to make sure all my dishes are working, and to smooth out any wrinkles before the main event. Tomorrow night, there will be fancy white linen tablecloths, paired wines and absolutely no party blowers.

Marcy, Sophie and Rose are wearing their Cove Café T-shirts, along with big grins. Marcy is clapping her hands together, looking like she's about to float off into the stratosphere with excitement.

Zack hasn't even turned up yet, which is not the best of starts to his short-term unpaid employment in Starshine Cove. I try not to let it bother me – I don't really need him. In fact he's only here as a favour – so what if he's changed his mind and decided to give it a miss? Like I said, I don't need him.

As I bustle around with the girls, I know that I'm not quite as unbothered as I am trying to appear. I feel disappointed, sad that he has let me down, even this tiny bit. It's unreasonable, but I am not a creature of logic at the best of times.

We've just finished serving the soup when he finally turns up. He missed the memo about the dress code – probably because I didn't issue one – and is wearing a smart black suit and crisp white shirt, looking every inch the posh maître d'. He looks good enough to eat, and it's troublesome that I can still notice that even though I'm annoyed with him.

He dashes over to me, running his hands through his hair, and says: "I'm sorry! I'm so sorry I'm late – I had a call that I needed to take."

"It's okay," I reply, smiling. "I'll just dock your wages."

"I'm getting paid?"

"No. So you now owe me £12 an hour."

He grins, and I see the worry melt from his face at my light-hearted tone. He doesn't know me well enough to spot that I'm faking it – not many people do.

"Right. That seems fair. What can I do to help?"

"We'll be clearing in about twenty minutes, until then maybe just go and mingle? Make sure everything is okay? I need to start on the mains."

He nods and takes a deep breath – gathering his game face, I realise. He heads over to introduce himself to George, who he hasn't yet met, and I see my father-in-law stand up to shake his hand. George is not far from ninety, but still hale and hearty, with a shock of white hair and the brightest blue eyes I've ever seen. Exactly the same eyes as Simon, to the point where I sometimes find it hard to look at them.

I head back to the kitchen, grateful for the breakneck speed of our work. Work is good. Work keeps you busy, and I like busy. We all know what the devil does with idle hands, and in my experience idle minds are even worse.

The main courses come in three options, although nobody here tonight has ordered the veggie dish so I've made it for the girls to try later. Tonight, I have locally sourced lamb with garlic-and-thyme-infused fondant potatoes, purple sprouting broccoli fresh from Archie's vegetable patch and a rich red-wine gravy.

The fish is fresh Dover sole, with more to be sourced for tomorrow's guests on the day. That comes with a delicately flavoured lemon-and-mint risotto, salsa verde made with home-grown herbs, and spring greens wilted in butter. If I do say so myself, it's pretty darn good – real food, cooked well, and served in portions designed to satisfy the stomach as well as the eyes.

I wait to see that everyone is happily enjoying their soup, and head back into the kitchens. The next half hour is the usual mix of chaos and calm – minor burns from boiling water, swearing, heat from the ovens and people bumping into each other. It's all the usual clamour of a busy kitchen, and I love it. Marcy and Sophie are fantastic additions, and I wonder how I ever did this without two assistants in the past.

Zack starts clearing as soon as people are done, and joins in with serving. To give him his due, he does it with style – he clearly has done this before, even if it was many years ago.

All of the dishes are delivered without incident, and I lean back against the serving counter and look on as my friends tuck in. Even now, after doing this all of my adult life, I still get a thrill from watching it – seeing the happy faces, hearing the sighs of pleasure as the first forkful hits the taste buds. I know I could have served up fish and chips and this lot would have been happy, but it's a relief to see them all enjoying it.

As they near the end, I clink a fork against a glass to get their attention, and all of their party-hat-wearing heads turn in my direction.

"Okay, people – before we bring out the pud, a reminder that usual rules apply. You are my guinea pigs, and I need feedback. Let me know if anything didn't work, or you think anything could be done better."

There are rumbles of chatter at this, and most of them just shout out compliments and tell me it was perfect. George holds up a wooden paddle with the number 10 painted on it – it's an old ping-pong bat, one we used when we did a *Strictly Come Dancing*-themed party a few years ago.

I see the Betties taking it more seriously though, their heads bent together as they discuss things. They're professional bakers, and they get what I'm asking for – fine tuning.

The Betties are in their seventies, and one of them – Big Betty – is tiny, and the other – Little Betty – is amazonian. They've been a couple as long as I can remember, and got married as soon as they were legally allowed to. When they're not baking, they're usually to be found watching action flicks that involve sub-machine guns and heavily muscled men fighting their way through enemies of indeterminate nationality. Like most things in Starshine, they're not quite what you expect.

They nod over to me, and I know they'll give me their advice later. It will be valuable, and I will not take it as a criticism.

We clear the tables, and emerge with the desserts. Both options are rhubarb based, because of Archie's bumper crop – nothing quite beats food that is fresh from the earth. There's a traditional crumble with vanilla and lemon custard, and a rhubarb and ginger sorbet with dark-chocolate shavings.

I head first to Cally, who is slumped in her seat holding a glass of wine, her party hat all askew.

"Cally, I know you ordered the sorbet because you're on a diet," I say, placing dishes in front of her, "but I also know you actually want the crumble. So I've brought you both."

She looks up at me and grins, saying: "You're an evil genius. Do you want me to do your hair tomorrow?"

I usually just bundle everything up into a wonky bun and hope for the best, but there is something to be said for having your own personal hair stylist on tap. She does some kind of magic thing where she straightens it, and it flows in a smooth curtain instead of looking like a bird's nest.

"That would be lovely," I say. "Yes please."

"Great. I'll see you whenever suits you, assuming I haven't gone into a pudding coma..."

I laugh and leave her to it, heading into the kitchen to start on the clear-up. The girls are ahead of the game, putting away produce and sanitising the surfaces, and Zack is standing behind a cloud of steam as he opens the dishwasher.

I notice that he has a red-wine gravy stain on his posh shirt, and fight the urge to go and clean it off for him. I'm sure Zack has many other shirts.

"What happens now?" he asks, as the steam cloud swirls around him. The effect is a bit like a rock music video for middle-aged people.

"Now," Sophie replies as she carefully hand-dries the mezzaluna, "we all go to the pub!"

"Though to be fair," Marcy adds, "since I've been here, it seems like that's the answer to 'what happens now' on most nights!"

"Not true," I say, taking the mezzaluna from Sophie. I still feel nervous about any of my offspring handling especially sharp objects. "Sometimes we go to the community centre and watch a film, or meet up at one of our houses, or..."

"Go to the pub?" Zack suggests helpfully as I trail off.

"Well. Yeah, I suppose there is a fair bit of that – it's a sociable place, what can I say?"

Before long, we hear chanting from the main room, along with the sound of party blowers and slow handclapping.

"Co-nnie, Co-nnie, Co-nnie!" the chant goes, making me grin.

"I think your public wants you," Zack says, looking amused. "See? You're still the supermodel of the restaurant world."

I throw a tea towel at him, and walk through. The dessert plates are still out, but I can deal with those tomorrow. I'll be up at the crack of dawn anyway, off to the fish market, so a bit of final cleaning is no big deal.

As soon as I'm back, I get a round of applause and a standing ovation. They are easily pleased. Ella gets to her feet and raises an empty glass at me, announcing: "Three cheers for Connie!"

Once the hip-hips are done, everyone starts to make a move towards the inn. It's still only eight p.m. – we made an early start in deference to the fact that people had children to tend to, or were, as George put it, "too old to be out of my bed until midnight".

It's just about dark outside but the air is still warm as we spill onto the patio. Spirits are high, and as we move across the green, Archie grabs hold of me and hoists me up onto his shoulders. Everyone cheers and claps, while I desperately cling on.

"Archie, put me down!" I protest. "We're not at Glastonbury!"

He ignores me and starts to jog towards the pub, making me scream like one of his little girls. This, I think, is definitely one of those things that is fun when you are five and torture when you're fifty-five, and I'm hugely relieved when he deposits me safely back on the ground. I punch him in the chest and he pretends I've wounded him.

Everyone settles down in the inn, some way more drunk than others. I have a small glass of wine, but limit myself to that because I have a busy day tomorrow. I don't fancy facing the fish market with a hangover, because who would?

Cally puts some Wham! on the jukebox, and an impromptu dancefloor immediately forms between the tables and chairs. The Starshine Inn is one of the oldest buildings in the village, and its walls and beams slope at strange angles – as does the floor. It makes dancing an amusing challenge, as I've discovered many times.

Marcy, Rose and Sophie join in with a spirited routine to *Wake Me Up Before You Go-Go*, and George and the Betties do an almost as lively sitting-down dance. As ever, I feel a sense of warmth roll over me at everybody's antics – mad as a box of frogs, the lot of them. But they're my mad frogs, and I love them for it.

I see Jake and Zack chatting at the bar, and then Zack spots me and comes over to sit by me.

"Were you an Andrew Ridgeley girl or a George Michael girl?" he asks as he puts his pint down.

"Neither. I was Spandau Ballet all the way – I fully expected to marry Martin Kemp, and I was devastated when he got together with Shirlie. I do love a bit of Wham! now though – I mean, you'd have to be weird not to, right?"

"Absolutely. Timeless classics. When I was a teenager, I pretended to be into much cooler things like Pink Floyd and Jimi Hendrix, and the cool-adjacent 80s bands like The Cure and Echo and the Bunnymen. But at home I secretly listened to a-ha, and used to dance around my bedroom pretending I was Morten Harket."

"Well, that's understandable. Morten Harket was very hot. I'd definitely have climbed into that comic book with him. Why don't you wear your glasses anymore?"

He looks temporarily confused by the change in subject, as am I – I have no idea where that question came from.

"I had laser treatment. Why?"

"Dunno. I just always remember you having them on, and thinking they looked cute..."

He grins and says: "Aha! You thought I was cute?"

"That's not what I said. I said I thought your glasses were cute."

He pretends to be crestfallen and replies: "Nothing else? I'm disappointed. Maybe I'm remembering this wrong, but I always thought there was something there, between us? I used to look forward to our meetings so much. You'd always look great, always be so fun, always do or say something outrageous... and you definitely winked at me more than once!"

He is, of course, totally right – but that description of me is not something that fills my heart with joy. The truth is I considered dragging him off into a broom cupboard on more than one occasion, and the idea of it is still appealing.

"Hmmm. No," I reply. "That doesn't sound like me at all. Maybe I just had something in my eye? It was just the glasses, Zack. I always liked a man in glasses."

"Well, I'm sure I can always find a pair with plain lenses if that floats your boat?"

"My boat floats just fine as it is, but thanks for the offer."

Is he flirting with me? I think he might be, and I'm not used to that. I'm not used to men who look like him paying any attention to me at all. I'm feeling a little hot again, and quickly sip some wine. Do not get drunk, do not get drunk, do not get drunk, I remind myself – the fish market knows no mercy.

"I'm sorry I was late," he says, politely ignoring the fact that I'm rooting around in my handbag for my handheld fan. "Today I mean."

"Yes, that's what I assumed you meant. It's no big deal."

"Maybe not, but I don't like being that guy – the one that says he'll do something and then doesn't."

"Oh. What guy do you like to be? Apart from Morten Harket I mean?"

"I like to be the guy who's reliable. Especially to you."

"Why on earth especially to me?"

He shrugs, and genuinely seems to think about it. That redwine gravy splodge on his shirt is driving me nuts now – I'd really like to ask him to take it off so I can get some stain remover on it, but that could be interpreted the wrong way.

"I think I'm going to go with your very eloquent 'dunno' here," he says. "Maybe because I've known you for so long, but still feel like I'm getting to know you? Maybe because I feel comfortable with you in a way I'm not used to? Maybe just because I like you and don't want you to think I'm a prick."

I laugh out loud into my wine, and answer: "Look, don't

worry about it – you were only a bit late, and anyway, you're not that important."

"Wow. Thank you. That was good for my ego."

I laugh. "I'm sure your ego will survive. I just meant tonight – tonight was a practice run, and we'd have been fine without you. Tomorrow night though..."

"I'll be there bright and early, Scout's honour. Do you need any help in the day?"

"I can offer you a 5.30 a.m. wake-up call and a trip to the fish market?"

"Sounds enticing. Will it take long, though, because I don't want to leave Bear on his own for hours, and a fish market really isn't an appropriate place for a greedy Labrador. He'd run amok."

"George will look after him," I say, after a moment's thought. "He's always up bright and early, and he misses having a dog – his lovely Lottie died last year. But again, I don't really need any help – it's nothing I haven't done a thousand times before on my own."

"Well, just because we've done something a thousand times on our own before doesn't mean we always have to, does it?"

I nod and choose not to examine that one too closely. Instead I focus on our daughters, who have stopped dancing and are staring across at us, whispering to each other.

"Don't look now but we're being watched," I say, nodding towards them. "Nothing good can come of this..."

I wave at Sophie, and she walks towards us. She and Marcy sit on the stools opposite, both clutching bottles of Becks.

"You two look cosy," Sophie says, giving me a raised eyebrow. "Talking about how fantastic your offspring are?"

"Yes," I answer. "We're talking about how fantastic Dan, James and Amy are, but decided the other two were a bit suspect."

She makes mock horrified noises, and I notice Zack

sneaking a glance at his phone while we chat. It must be driving him mad having hardly any signal here.

"Have you ever thought about dating again, Connie?" Marcy asks, all innocence.

"No, I'm planning on joining a convent once the kids move out for good."

"No you're not, Mum! Besides, no convent would have you – you're too loud! But maybe you should."

"Should what?" I say, wondering if the alarm I'm feeling inside shows on my face. This is not a conversation I even want to have with myself, never mind my daughter.

"Consider dating again. I know it's not been a possible thing when your house was clogged up with us lot, but what about now? You could sign up for an app. All the old people are using them these days – Zack, what did you use?"

Zack and I share a look and realise that she doesn't even know she's just insulted us. Ah, the joys of youth.

"Umm... well, mainly I met people through work, or got introduced to them at parties and events. I didn't really use a dating app."

"Well, I suppose it's different for you," Sophie replies, frowning as she thinks about it. "I mean, you probably go to the BAFTAs and dinners at Keira Knightley's house, don't you? Mum just mooches around Starshine Cove singing Dolly Parton and feeding the hungry masses. The only new people she meets are tourists, and they're usually in couples or family groups. Zero dating potential."

I throw a beer mat at her just to remind her that I am actually here, sitting right in front of her, and she says a quick: "Sorry!"

I'm hoping that's the end of it, but Zack tilts his head to one side and says: "She might have a point, Connie. You're an attractive woman. You're still young. Why don't you sign up?"

I narrow my eyes at him, and I see him fighting back laughter. It's nice to be called attractive, but I could do without a united front of people trying to force me back into the dating pool. It sounds stupid to say I'm not ready after more than five years, but, well – I'm not ready. Not to go on dates anyway. I can't deny that having Zack around has woken up a few nerve endings I'd thought were long dead, but that's different – he's not a stranger, and besides, nothing is going to happen between us.

"I could set you up a profile?" Sophie says, whipping out her phone. Her face falls as she sees she has no wifi – I suppose living in London has lulled her into a false sense of security. "Come on, Marcy, let's go hang out on the fire escape – we'll get it done there."

I'm about to issue a very firm 'no', but before I can get the word past my lips they're gone. How is it that teenagers can move at the speed of light when they try, but take three hours to walk from one room to another when you've asked them to do the dishes?

I scowl at Zack and say, "If I end up going on a date with an axe murderer, I'll come back and haunt you."

"I'd expect nothing less. Look, don't worry – you don't have to use it. But why not? I mean, I know how hard it is to take that step – but I meant what I said. You're too young to write off that part of your life forever. Wouldn't you be even the tiniest bit interested in meeting someone? It doesn't have to be serious – it could just be fun."

There are many flippant answers I could give him, and there is the very honest answer too – that he is the first man I've harboured such thoughts about since I lost my husband. That he is the first man I have looked at and imagined waking up with. Neither of them seems appropriate, so I settle for somewhere in between.

"I've never really considered it," I say truthfully. "Life has indeed been very full, and Sophie actually has a point – this isn't exactly a hotbed of social activity. I know everyone here, and I certainly wouldn't want to snog any of them."

"Snog! I love that word – makes me feel young again! But, if that's the case, then maybe a dating app isn't a bad idea. There are some really nice ones out there now."

I scoff at the idea, hoping he'll drop it. "How would you know? You apparently collect your women straight off the red carpet!"

"That doesn't mean I haven't looked. I have a profile on one, I just never engage with it. If you like, I'll help you check it all out. Also, if you go on a date while I'm here, I could sneakily sit on the next table and make sure he's not an axe murderer."

"I'm not sure you can tell by looking. He might be one of those axe murderers where afterwards, everyone says they're really shocked because he seemed so nice and volunteered at a dog shelter."

"Well, okay – I can at least rescue you if you look really bored. Look, just give it some thought. You've told me about your friends here, and how much you've enjoyed seeing them get their happy endings – why don't you think you deserve one yourself?"

He looks disgustingly sincere, and I hate the fact that I can't poke any logical holes in what he's saying.

"Aaaagh, shut up!" I say. "This is all too deep and meaningful, and I need to be thinking about Dover sole, not my love life!"

I slap my thighs and stand up. I leave him behind as I march over to the jukebox and scoot through the various playlists written on the paper cards. I find what I'm looking for and hit play.

I turn around, and watch Zack's face as the opening drum beat of *Take On Me* flows through the room.

"Come on then, Morten!" I shout over. "Let's see what you've got!"

EIGHT

The Spring Feast goes off without a hitch, which is a big relief. People seemed to love the food, the wine, the whole event. I have a lot of repeat customers, but there were also some new faces – including a couple who got engaged on the night.

The young man took me to one side when they arrived and asked permission to propose, and I made sure there was some Champagne handy for when she said yes. He did the whole thing – down on one knee while the sorbet plates were still on the table. There was, obviously, a brief moment where I held my breath – it'd put a real dampener on things if she'd said no!

She didn't, and they both seemed thrilled as the entire room broke out into applause and cheers. Zack had filmed the whole thing, as well as a few different moments during the evening when we were quiet. He had also asked permission, telling me he'd send whatever he got for me to use for marketing and social media.

I didn't break the news to him that I don't bother much with either, because I don't really need to – I have a mailing list that is already thousands long, and these events could sell out ten times over every time. That seems rude and borderline smug to boast about, so I just say thank you. He is in his element when he's doing that, but he's also a dab hand as a waiter, and having him here does turn out to be useful.

By the time everyone has left, back to their drive home or their accommodation, it's almost midnight. I've stayed behind to finish the clean-up, because I always have an adrenaline rush after one of my events. It is, in its own way, a performance – and I am left with excess energy to burn off. Handy when you have a whole café to clear.

Zack stays with me, and we work in companionable silence apart from the music on the radio. Late night Motown classics, perfect to sing along to. By the time we've both belted out an off-pitch but enthusiastic version of *The Tracks of My Tears*, we're both laughing. I close down the kitchen, switch off the lights, and we head outside. The girls have already gone back to the house, claiming exhaustion. You can't get the staff these days.

It's a clear night, a spring chill in the air but not even a flutter of a breeze. Zack stands on the patio and looks up at the sky. I follow his gaze, wondering what's up there – but I soon realise it is the usual gorgeous display of stars. I forget, sometimes, how different it is here to London. There is so little light pollution that the stars seem to number in the thousands, shining like jewels.

"Wow," he says eventually. "That is amazing. I'm not even going to try and take a picture of that."

"Good. Just file the image in your mind instead."

I realise as we stand there together, gazing at the constellations, that I am not tired enough to go to bed. If I go home, I'll just end up sitting downstairs on my own, watching TV with the volume so low I can barely hear it. There is a way to put subtitles on but I can never figure it out – without my teenagers around, I am remote control challenged.

"Is the pub still open?" he asks, obviously thinking the same.

"I know it's almost one in the morning but for some reason I'm not tired enough to sleep yet."

"Technically the inn isn't open now, no, but you are a resident, and Jake won't mind if we help ourselves and pay up tomorrow."

"Will the door be locked? I only have a key to my room, not the building..."

"Ah, ye of little faith – of course the door won't be locked! Just a little nightcap, maybe? I still feel a bit wired."

"Me too, and it wasn't even my event. Do you think Bear is okay?" he says, his brow furrowed. I'm beginning to recognise the little flash of concern that crosses his face when he worries about his dog and it's very endearing.

"Of course Bear's okay. George fried up a load of extra crispy bacon bits for him!"

"Oh Lord. That dog is on a diet..."

"He's on holiday. Get him on the Slimfast when you're back home."

We cross the green, no lights on in any of the cottages, and let ourselves into the Starshine Inn. There are piles of glasses on the bar waiting to be washed, and the tables and chairs are askew from a night of merriment. The scents of beer and whisky still lurk in the air but the place is entirely empty, lit only by the glow of the jukebox and the fridges behind the counter.

I'm just about to head to the bar and write Jake an IOU for a bottle of wine when I hear footsteps coming down the corridor that leads to Jake and Ella's apartment. Ella appears, her hair in disarray and wearing mis-matched pyjamas. She's holding a crying Kitty in her arms and looks like she's sleepwalking. Larry, the dog who looks like a lamb, trots along behind her.

"I'm sorry," I say sheepishly. "Did we wake her up? We tried to be super quiet..."

"No, don't worry – she's been awake for ages. I was just

bringing her out here so Jake could get some sleep. He did it last night."

I smile, my mind going back to those days – the mind-numbing combination of fatigue and boredom. Wandering through the house at all hours, feeling like an extra in a zombie film. Babies turn all their parents into the cast of *The Walking Dead*.

"Can I help?" says Zack, striding over. "Let me take her for a few minutes while you have a rest?"

Ella seems to turn this over in her mind, then nods and passes the fretting baby over to him. He immediately nestles her against his chest and starts to do the little half-dance, half-shuffle that your body never seems to forget. He murmurs comforting words, rocking her lightly, and she stares up at him in fascination. Maybe it's just the change of scenery, and an unfamiliar face to stare at, but she soon stops crying and instead gazes up at him, her pudgy hands waving in the air.

"This is one of the reasons I got the laser treatment on my eyes," he says, smiling down at the precious bundle in his arms. "The girls were forever grabbing at my glasses."

Ella slumps down onto one of the seats, and watches gratefully as Zack continues his patrol of the room. I sit next to her and pat her thigh.

"It gets easier, I promise," I say quietly.

"Oh, I know, but living on the promise of tomorrow being easier doesn't make today any less hard. I can't remember what life looked like before she arrived."

"Simple, fun, full of selfish pleasures?"

"Something like that, yes."

"And would you swap it?"

She follows her baby around the room with tired eyes, and then breaks out into a grin.

"No. I wouldn't. What are you doing here anyway? Are you robbing the place?"

"Yes. I plan on stuffing all your Rioja into a swag bag and selling it on the black market."

"I thought as much. Did the event go well?"

"It did," I reply. "And somehow we found ourselves still wide awake and in search of a nightcap. I'm sorry again if we disturbed you."

I clearly recall the absolute fury that anyone making a noise can provoke when you're trying to keep a baby asleep. You'll just have got them off, and then someone will invariably step on a squeaky dog toy or slam a door.

"Again, you didn't – and at least I've had ten minutes' respite while Zack is on duty. He's a natural. I might see if I can hire him as my manny."

I look over at Zack, who has managed to settle Kitty off into the land of nod, and have to agree. For all his surface glitz, he looks completely at home with a little one.

He walks towards us, and smoothly hands the baby over to Ella. She squalls for a second and we all hold our breath, but then settles down for a snooze.

"I'm just going to chill out here for a bit, guys," Ella says. "Help yourself to booze – call it a babysitting fee. But if you're going to chat, would you mind going up to Zack's room? I don't want to risk the Wrath of Kitty."

I catch Ella's eye, wondering if she is playing matchmaker here. That is exactly the kind of thing I have done in the past – to her and Jake, to Cally and Archie, to Josh and Lucy. I am an incorrigible rogue when it comes to matchmaking.

She looks completely innocent, though – clearly too tired to scheme. Zack raises his eyebrows at me and I nod. Yes, I think – one drink, and then home.

We select a bottle and swipe a couple of glasses, and when I turn to say goodnight to Ella I swear she winks at me. Ah, I think – not too tired to scheme after all. She has learned from the master.

Zack's room is in the top of the building and is the same one Ella stayed in when she first arrived here. I know that by day it has a spectacular view over the bay, and even at night it's not too shabby; the moon is reflecting off the dark horizon of the sea, and the stars are putting on quite a show.

I mooch around the place as Zack uncorks the wine. He only pours himself a thimbleful, topping it up with water a bit like French parents do for their teenagers, but glugs out a full glass for me.

I take the glass, nosing at a pile of papers on the dressing table he is using as a desk. It seems to be some kind of plan, an outline of camera shots and filming locations.

"What's this?" I say, pointing at the sheets as I sit on the chair. I'll let him have the bed, I decide. "Work, while you're on holiday? What happened to switching off?"

"Oh, that – would you believe me if I said it's not really work? Or it doesn't feel like it anyway. It's a new concept for a show about refugees. Helping them track down lost family, telling their stories – it's a bit of a passion project to be honest. The world feels like it's exploding at the moment, and I wanted to try and do something different. I barely have anything to do with the day-to-day stuff now, and I miss it. One of my interns – originally from Syria – came to me with this concept, and I'm just fleshing it out. He said he wanted to show refugees as real people, not as saints and not as villains. I thought it had some potential."

I nod and look again at the outline. I don't understand some of the abbreviations, and the technical stuff is beyond me, but I can see the shape of what he's trying to do – each person gets an introductory narrative on camera, and an in-depth look at their home nation and its culture, as well as why they left.

"That sounds really great," I say after a few sips of wine. "Bit different than some of your stuff, though."

"I know. Nobody will be wearing a bikini or have veneers,

for a start. But like I said – passion project, and early days. I was serious when I said I was considering retiring – well, not retiring, but maybe just slowing things down. Handing over some of the responsibilities and making the most of what time I've got left to pursue things that I actually believe in."

"The time you've got left?" I say, smiling. "You're not exactly old, Zack!"

"Well, I'm fifty-seven, which according to Marcy is round about the time I should start looking into mobility scooters and stairlifts."

"I suppose she has a point. You're two years older than me, and clearly ready for the knacker's yard."

He snorts out a laugh, and switches on his phone. I know this room gets pretty decent wifi, unlike the rest of the village, and I anticipate losing him for the next twenty minutes as he catches up on vital emails and cute kitten videos.

"I was checking out your profile," he says after a moment. He looks up and gives me such a fabulous grin that I feel a flutter in my tummy. I am alone in a bedroom with a man who gives me butterflies. What could possibly go wrong?

I gulp down some more wine and wonder if I look as confused as I feel.

"What profile?"

"The one the girls set up for you on the dating app."

"Oh. Right. I'd completely forgotten about that – and I can't believe they actually did it! Crikey, what have they said about me…"

He scoots over and I sit next to him, my mind filled with disastrous possibilities. I expect something utterly embarrassing, and I'm quite taken aback when he shows me the screen. There's a really nice picture of me, if I do say so myself, from the night we all met in London. To be fair, I look a lot more glam on it than I usually do, but it's definitely me – I wouldn't be catfishing anybody. My profile name is Connie666 – thank you, Sophie – and all the information is correct, and makes me sound fun and interesting. I'm not sure about her describing me as 'pocket-sized' though – I may be short, but it'd still need to be a pretty spacious pocket.

"See?" he says. "It's not that bad, is it? You *are* a fun-loving woman who enjoys cooking, socialising and short walks on the beach."

"Isn't it usually long walks on the beach?"

"Yes, so this is better – it shows you have a sense of humour."

"Do men on these kinds of apps like a good sense of humour? Aren't they more into, you know, boobs?"

"Well, most straight men are into boobs, there's no denying it – but this isn't just a hook-up thing. It's for making friends as well as dating. A lot of people use it when they move somewhere new, or if they find themselves single, lots of reasons. I suspect your views might be a bit out of date, Mrs Llewellyn."

"I suspect you might be right. Hang on, I'll get into it on my phone. Sophie will have set it up with my usual password."

"Which is?"

"None of your business, but it does involve a combination of animal noises and ice cream flavours."

I fish out my phone and find that Sophie has also downloaded the app for me. She knows I'm not someone who pays much attention to such things – apart from occasionally messaging the kids, I mainly seem to use my phone as a watch. She's obviously swiped it at some point and installed the Incredible World of Dating. I remind myself to be annoyed with her – once I've stopped being amused, at least.

"What does that little symbol mean there?" I ask, once I'm in.

"It means you've got messages!"

I make a whooping sound and punch the air with a celebratory fist. I didn't want this – in fact I specifically told the girls I wasn't interested – but now I've seen it I feel slightly curious. Plus, if someone puts you on a dating app behind your back, it's at least nice to see that someone has liked you enough to respond, isn't it?

I click on the icon and feel my eyes widen in surprise when I see that I have eleven messages. Wow. Go me.

Zack looks along with me, and I soon realise that of the eleven only a few are actually viable. One of them lives in Edinburgh, so I have no idea how he thinks that could work.

"This guy has a fake photo," I say, pointing at one of the profiles. "Unless he actually is Cristiano Ronaldo."

"Yeah. Maybe ignore that one. And some of them are really far away, so you'd have to get to know them online first and then see if you liked them enough to make the effort."

I nod, then realise that I am getting carried away – this is all nonsense.

"It doesn't matter how far away they are," I announce firmly, as much to myself as him. "I won't be getting to know any of them."

"Why not? It could be fun – what have you got to lose?"

"Self respect, dignity, and in the case of Ronaldo there, possibly my life savings?"

Zack shakes his head, takes the phone from me and scrolls through, studying the potential candidates.

"What about these two? Both of them live within striking distance, and neither of them gives off an axe murderer vibe. Come on, humour me – take a look."

"You only want me to do it so you're not the only one getting stick about their love lives, don't you?"

"That would certainly be an added bonus – but I also want you to do it for you. Connie, I completely understand where you are right now. I completely understand how hard this is – how scary. How even the thought of it feels like a betrayal of Simon and everything you meant to each other."

I feel tears sting the back of my eyes at this, and bite my lip to stop it wobbling. I manage a small nod, and he continues: "But it's not. Simon would want you to be happy, just as Rowena would want me to be happy."

"I am happy!"

"Yes, I know – but I'm sure you could be even happier. Even if it comes to nothing, maybe it's worth a try? Plus, I think it might go down well with Sophie. It was actually one of the reasons I started dating again – the girls wanted me to. I had zero interest, but they held an intervention, told me they were worried about me. Told me they wanted me to start living again."

"God, that sounds awful," I reply, turning away from the screen and looking at the man next to me. He smiles gently, and those disgustingly cute laughter lines crinkle together.

"It was. It was the last thing I wanted to hear – that I was worrying them. It's supposed to be the other way around, isn't it? I decided to give it a go, for their sake at first – Marcy was moving on with life, and Amy was planning her move to France. I didn't want them sitting around holding meetings about their poor old dad, when they should have been enjoying the most carefree time of their lives. And once I'd been on a few dates... well, I suppose then I started doing it for me instead."

I think about what he's said, and wonder if my own children feel the same. They've never really said anything about it, but it could be true – am I casting a shadow on their lives because they think I'm not living mine to the full? Sophie did seem awfully keen on the idea – she's gone to the trouble of setting up this profile, installing the app, everything. Maybe, like he says, I should give it a go – even if only to set her mind at rest. To reassure her that she doesn't need to be concerned.

I go back to the messages, and study the profiles with a bit more of an open mind. Two of them, he's right, look nice – and they both live within an hour's drive, which by countryside terms is pretty much on your doorstep.

"Maybe one of these," I say, pointing them out to Zack.

"Why not both?"

"Isn't that a bit... icky?"

"Not in this universe, no. It's not like you're agreeing to marry them, is it? Nobody goes on a date expecting it to turn into something real – hoping, maybe, but not expecting. Nobody will think you're immoral if you go on two dates, Connie. It's how this works. Imagine it's like the olden days, when you were in a bar or a club – you'd maybe chat to three or four guys before you found one you liked."

"Right. I suppose. And for someone who doesn't really use these apps, you seem to know a lot about them, by the way."

He also seems very keen for me to get out there and meet new men, which I confess is slightly disappointing.

"Cultural osmosis," he replies. "I have friends who use them, plus they featured in one of our shows so I did my research. And I wouldn't rule out using them anyway, when the time is right."

"Can I see your profile?" I ask, curious as to how he is presented to the online dating pool.

He grimaces, but finds it on his phone. The main picture is gorgeous – him side-on, at sunset in a place that looks a lot more exotic than London. He's wearing a loose white linen shirt, his skin is even more golden, and his hair is lifted slightly in the breeze.

"Bloody hell," I proclaim. "You look like the poster child for Saga holidays! Very glamorous."

"Thank you, I think. That was taken on a trip to the Amalfi Coast. The others are more mundane."

I flick through, seeing a carousel of pictures. He is being modest, because he looks great on all the rest as well. I glance at the mail icon, and raise an eyebrow. He clicks on it, and we see that he has over two hundred messages.

"And here's me," I say, laughing, "feeling like a sex goddess because I had eleven!"

"Well, to be fair I've not logged on for a while. Some of these are probably really old, and some of them might be from the female version of our close friend Cristiano Ronaldo. Plus I'm in London, and London is a lot different than Dorset. Dorset is a pond, and London is an ocean."

I shrug and accept his protestations, but I know it's more than that – he is incredibly attractive, and I suspect he'd be flooded with offers even if he lived in Timbuktu. Wherever that is. I do a quick google while I have a signal and find that it is an ancient city in Mali. Now I know. It's not surprising I felt a little flicker of attraction for him too, and maybe I shouldn't take it too seriously. Me and two hundred women agree that he is a very handsome man.

"So, okay," I say, "what happens next? Do I message them and arrange to meet up?"

"Usually you'd chat a while first, get a better idea of whether you're a good fit or not."

"I don't have much time for that – plus as you may have noticed, it's not exactly easy to keep on top of anything World Wide Web related in Starshine Cove."

"Nobody calls it the World Wide Web anymore."

"They do here. We still call cars a motor carriage. I think... I think I'll just ask them both if they want to meet up for coffee."

Even as I say the words, I can't quite believe they're coming out of my mouth. What has happened to me? Have I suffered a head injury without noticing?

"Sounds like a plan," says Zack. "Here's to you, Connie!"

He raises his glass, and I clink mine against it. My hands are a little shaky, and liquid sloshes over the side.

What the heck have I just agreed to?

NINE

I am having coffee with my father-in-law, George. He lives literally seconds away from me, and I try to call in every day. This house used to belong to Archie and the girls, and George lived in a much bigger thatched cottage on the front of the green. Last year they simply swapped, because it made sense – more room for the growing family, and a cosier space for George. I'm still getting used to walking in here and seeing George's things instead of Archie's. I'm also still getting used to there being no Lottie, his old Golden Retriever. Every time I walk in, I expect to hear her tail thumping on the floor.

"So," George says, sitting across from me at the little table, "I have something for you."

As ever, there's a twinkle in his eyes, and I wonder what might be coming next.

He reaches into his pocket and produces a whistle. It's on a string, the kind a referee might use during a football match – in fact it's probably exactly that, as George used to be a teacher and oversee a lot of sport.

I pick it up and give it a blow. Still going strong.

"Okay. Thank you. It's a very nice whistle. I shall treasure it."

"I thought you might wear it this afternoon, when you go on your dates."

"Ah. I see. Are you worried about axe murderers too?"

"Not really, but it pays to be cautious, doesn't it? Any problems, three sharp puffs on this and the cavalry will come running. Or at the very least you'll have eyes on you."

I nod, and know it will put his mind at rest if I accept this wisdom. I put the string over my head, and tuck the whistle beneath my top.

"Are you okay with this, George?" I ask, reaching out to hold his hand on the table. He is, after all, Simon's father, and for years now he's been my surrogate dad as well. He lost two of his children in that car accident, and I can't even imagine the agony of that – I don't want him thinking that he might lose me as well.

"Of course I am! I was happy when Archie met Cally, and I'll be happy to see you find someone, my lovely – you're much too young to give up on love. Simon wouldn't want that, and neither do I. No, I'm fine with it… It's just the technique I feel a bit uncertain about."

"I know," I say, giving his fingers a final squeeze, "me too. I knew you didn't mind really, I think I was just looking for an excuse to cancel. I feel… guilty."

"You really mustn't. He wouldn't want that, and you know it. It's been a long time. You'll always love him, and he'll always be part of you – but he wouldn't want you to put yourself in cold storage, would he?"

"No. No, he wouldn't. Maybe it's not just guilt, though, George – maybe I'm also a bit nervous. It's been a long time since I've put myself in a position where someone can judge me."

"Well, what could they possibly find lacking in you? Any man would be lucky to have you."

George has a shock of silver hair and blues eyes that put Daniel Craig to shame. Even at his age he's a good-looking man, and I suspect he'd be a hit on a dating app himself.

"Thank you, George, but I think you might be biased."

"Not at all, I'm speaking as an objective observer! Anyway, what's that thing you always say – be more Dolly? Would Dolly be nervous about going on a date?"

"She might be – but she'd hold her head high, plaster on a smile, and stride forth to dazzle the world."

"Exactly! So that's just what you should do, Connie. Stride forth and dazzle."

"But take an emergency whistle just in case?"

He nods approvingly. "That's right. You never know when you might need an emergency whistle. Will I see you later, so you can tell me all about it?"

"Of course. I suspect there won't be much to tell. If it's really boring, I'll just make something up, okay?"

"I'd be disappointed if you didn't. Right, off with you, madam – time's ticking and you don't want to be late!"

I pull a face as I get up to leave. I kind of do want to be late, actually. In fact I kind of want to abandon the whole idea, because I wasn't lying – I am strangely nervous.

I head home and realise that I also have no clue what to wear, or what to do with my hair, or if I should bother with make-up. These are all issues that usually have little relevance to my life, and I start to suspect that I have lived for so long in my cosy little bubble that stepping outside it feels terrifying. Part of me knows that this is a good thing – stepping outside my comfort zone – but part of me also thinks it's stupid. I mean, why would you want to step outside a comfort zone? Comfort zones are nice – the clue is in the name.

I head upstairs and start to go through my clothes. Before

too long, my bed is covered with tried on then discarded outfits, and my wardrobe looks like it's been ransacked, empty coat hangers rattling as I've pulled out various dresses, tops and skirts. None of them feel right.

I decide that I will start from the bottom up and have in mind a certain pair of sandals that I haven't worn for ages, but always make me feel good. I root around in the bottom of my wardrobe, but they're not there. Next I run downstairs in case they're in the dumping ground of footwear that lives in the porch. Also a bust. I go back up to my room, and pull out the storage boxes I keep under my bed, rummaging through the contents.

"What are you looking for?" Sophie says, as she ambles into my room. She's in her pyjamas still and stifles a yawn as she clears a space on the bed.

"My sandals!"

"Which ones?"

"The ones with the low cork wedge. My favourites."

"Well, they can't really have been your favourites, because you gave them to the charity shop before Christmas."

"Did I? Why would I do that? I loved those sandals!"

She joins me on the floor, and picks out another pair from the debris.

"Wear these. They're almost exactly the same."

She has a point, I think. Okay. That's good – one thing at least has been decided.

"Your room looks like someone threw a hand grenade in it," says Sophie, looking around at the chaos.

I am a messy person, and my room is never what you'd call minimalist, but this is, I have to agree, a whole new level of mess.

I shrug and say: "To be honest, Soph, I'm a bit freaked out at the thought of these dates. Even simple stuff like what to wear is making me feel a bit bamboozled."

"That's a good word, bamboozled. And this is supposed to be fun, you know – not an ordeal!"

"I know it is, but it doesn't feel much like fun at the moment. I mean, what *do* I wear? And what should I do with my hair? And should I put make-up on? I don't want to seem like I've made too much effort, but at the same time it seems rude not to make *any* effort..."

I'm rambling, and shoving shoes back into the storage box as I do it. Why do I own stilettoes, I think, staring at the pair in my hands. I never wear them. I put them to one side to take to the charity shop – which means I'll probably have a desperate need for some high heels in the near future.

Sophie helps me with the tidy-up, then says: "Look, Mum, you don't have to go on a date. It was just an idea. Now me and Dan are away and you have more time, I just thought it'd be... well, like I said, fun."

I glance up at her, and see that she is frowning. Ah, I deduce – Zack was right. She has been worrying about me, and I hate that. I need to reassure her. I need to do what all us grown-ups do, and fake it till I make it.

"It will be, I'm sure, love – it was a great idea! I'm just nervous, that's all. It's been a long time, and I'm blowing off steam. It doesn't mean I don't want to go – ignore me."

"No, I'm not going to ignore you," she replies. "I'm going to help you. Come on, let's get you sorted. You'll feel better once you've got your casually stylish glad-rags on. I told Dan you were going out on a date, by the way."

"Right. Did he make vomiting noises?"

"He did! But he also thinks it's a good idea."

Everybody else in the whole world, it seems, thinks that this is a good idea. I am very much in the minority thinking that it's a spectacularly bad idea.

Within minutes, Sophie has selected my outfit. Cropped jeans and a pretty pink peasant-style blouse that I'd forgotten I owned. It looks nice, and is also flowing enough to hide my emergency whistle. She puts my hair up with combs, leaving a few tendrils loose, and hands me a pair of hoopy gold earrings to put in. We settle on very light make-up, and a spritz of my favourite perfume.

Once we're done and I look at myself in the mirror, I realise that Sophie was right – I do now feel a bit better about the whole thing. I am a middle-aged woman who has had three babies and loves cake, so I can't expect to look like a supermodel. But, I have to admit, I look okay. Better than usual, but still recognisably me. Surely that's good enough? And if not, then I'm not on a date with the right person.

"There," she says, grinning at me, "job done. You look great. And you are great – just be yourself, and you can't go wrong!"

"Ha! People always say that: 'just be yourself'. Then you spend ages wondering what that is."

"Well, in your case, it's super-nosy, always hungry, and ready to do karaoke at the drop of a hat."

"Hmmm. You're right. I suppose the being nosy bit might help."

"Exactly – it's not like you'll ever run short of conversation is it, Mum? You and silence are mortal enemies."

"What if I talk too much though?" I say, suddenly gripped by yet another fear. "What if I just don't stop, and words keep flooding out of me in a stream of consciousness rant? What if I come across as a lunatic?"

"Then that would be pretty accurate. Look, don't get so stressed – and remember they'll be nervous too."

I hadn't even thought about that, but I know she's right. It makes me feel marginally better. It's not like I'm going to an audition or a job interview – I'm going to enjoy a pleasant social interaction with a couple of new people. When I think about it like that, I feel calmer. I like pleasant social interactions. In fact I am the queen of pleasant social interactions.

"Thank you. For everything. How did you get so wise?" I ask her. "Actually, if the answer to that is 'because I am on a million dating apps and hook up with strangers all the time', then don't tell me."

She stays ominously quiet, and I remind myself that she will be twenty this year. Of course she's on dating apps.

"Thank you anyway," I say. "I think I might have been on the verge of exploding before you came in."

"I know. I'm amazing. You can repay the favour by making me and Marcy some pancakes."

I nod eagerly, and head downstairs. I put on my apron, and get to work. As I whisk up the ingredients in a big bowl, I feel even better – soothed by the familiar actions of cooking, comforted by doing something that comes so naturally to me. In fact, I have a sneaky suspicion that that's why Sophie asked for pancakes, now I come to think about it – she knew that it would help. My daughter, the benign manipulator.

I am pouring the batter into the pan when there is a knock on the door. The traditional mode of entry into my house is to knock, shout something like 'it's only me!' and then walk straight in. The fact that nobody does this after the knock means that it is either a delivery person, or Zack. Or, you know, an axe murderer, because I seem to be thinking about them a lot these days. Though I'm guessing they don't knock on the front door, so maybe not.

I dash to the door, open it, and run back into the kitchen, jumping over random piles of shoes and boots as I go. They were casualties in the Great Missing Sandal War, and I tell myself I really must get around to tidying them back up again. Famous last words.

"Sorry!" I say as Zack follows me through, looking amused. "I was at a critical point in pancake-land!"

He leans back against the island, and I see him gazing around. I wonder what this place looks like from another person's view, with its clutter and organised chaos. I don't suppose it looks organised to anyone else, though, just chaotic.

I flip the pancakes, managing a spectacular catch, and he applauds. I give a little bow and carry on. Bear looks incredibly disappointed each time I flip and catch, and if he wasn't on a diet I'd have deliberately dropped one just to cheer him up. He follows my every move, nose twitching in excitement, tail swishing against the tiles.

I clear a space on the table, and lay out a big stack of pancakes, adding bowls of strawberries and sliced bananas, along with some home-made blueberry compote and a jar of Nutella. Pancakes aren't complete without Nutella, in my professional opinion. I fetch some cream from the fridge and decant it into a pouring jug, knowing that Sophie likes hers drowned in the stuff.

"This looks good," Zack says, gesturing to the spread. "And so do you. I especially like that flour smudge on your face."

I realise as he compliments me that hearing those words makes me feel warm inside. And it strikes me all of a sudden that all the time I was trying on outfits and looking for shoes, it wasn't just my dates' reaction I was thinking about – it was Zack's.

I give myself a rub, and say: "Did I get it? The flour?"

"No. Allow me."

He closes the distance between us, and gently smooths his thumb across my cheekbone. It is unexpected, the feel of his hand on my face, the closeness of his body, and I just about stop myself from gasping out loud. I am so surprised I wobble a little, and instinctively put my hand on his hip to steady myself.

I rally, trying to look cool, calm and collected, but the intimacy of the gesture, the touch of his skin on mine, is enough to turn my heart into a jackhammer. His fingers linger a little longer than they need to, and our eyes meet. He looks as surprised as I am, and I wonder if he felt the same kind of zing – the same little jolt of electricity.

Of course he didn't, I tell myself. I've seen the kinds of women he goes for, and they ain't me. He's the one who is encouraging me to see other men, talking me into going on dates. If he was at all interested in me, he wouldn't have done that, would he? I am an idiot to have even imagined there was more to that touch than friendship.

"There," he says, finally taking his hand away. "All gone."

He's still standing close, though, still gazing down at me with a look of... well, I'm not quite sure what it is. Curiosity, maybe – combined with a touch of surprise? What the hell is happening here?

I return his look, and manage what I hope is a casual 'everything's fine' smile – but inside, I am fighting a raging battle with my own urges. What if I reached out and placed my palm on his chest? What if I pulled him closer? What if I wound my fingers in his hair? What if I emptied a full packet of flour all over myself, so then he'd have to wipe smudges from the whole of my body?

The moment is well and truly broken by the dainty sound of our two hungry daughters galloping down the stairs. Zack and I immediately pull apart, putting a table between us for safety.

I'm glad they didn't come a few seconds earlier, and I'm equally glad of the distraction. Zack touching me like that was perfectly innocent, I'm sure, but my reaction to it was not. I'm still tingling where he made contact, and I go and open the fridge door for absolutely no reason other than I want to stand in front of it and cool down. Phew. It's getting hot in here, in all kinds of ways.

I let the cool air flow over my face, and listen in on Sophie and Marcy's chatter. The café is closed today, and they're planning a trip to Bristol on the train, staying overnight in a cheap hotel. Apparently they're suffering from Big City Withdrawal Syndrome, and need to up their quota of inhaled traffic fumes and angry people in queues. Zack came down here to spend time with his girl, but he is left picking up scraps – something most parents of teenagers have to accept early on in the process.

"So," he says, as we all sit down to tuck into our feast, "I have a proposition for you, Connie."

I'm embarrassingly mid-chew with a mouthful of pancake, so I simply nod. I'm still a little befuddled by the flour-on-face incident anyway.

"Both of your dates are in Lyme Regis, and I'm really keen to see Lyme Regis. I went there as a boy with my grandparents, and remember it being magical. So, why don't I drive us? That way, I get some company for part of the day, and you get less stress."

"You can also drink," Marcy points out helpfully. "You might need a G&T if things don't go well... or even if they do!"

If this was Archie or Jake or Ella offering me a lift, I wouldn't hesitate – it would be a whopping big 'hell, yes'. But it's Zack, and I'm not sure that spending time alone in a car with him will do anything positive for my stress levels. I take my time while I try and come up with a way of saying no that doesn't sound rude – 'I'm sorry, you're just too hot to be around' somehow feels wrong.

"Go on, Mum," Sophie says. "You know you always hate parking in Lyme."

She does have a fair point, and I have to concede.

"Okay," I finally say. "Sounds like a plan. I have an emergency whistle, Zack, so if you hear me blowing on it, come running."

"An emergency whistle?"

"Yep. George gave it to me as a safety precaution. I think he's worried I might get taken."

I pull the whistle out from my blouse and give it a light toot. Sophie laughs and points at me.

"See how it feels?" she says. I know what she's talking about but the others don't, and she explains: "When I first moved to London Mum bought me three different attack alarms – one for my pocket, one for my keychain, and one for my bag!"

"I was just covering all the bases," I reply, refusing to feel embarrassed. "I wish I'd got you one on a string around your neck as well now. Plus I assumed you'd lose at least one of them."

She has nothing to say to that, so I assume I was right.

"So, when should we leave?" Zack asks. Bear has his big head rested on his thighs and is gazing up at him with adoration. Possibly because he has a Nutella-coated chunk of pancake on his fork.

"I'm pretty much ready. I'll just clear this stuff away, then meet you at the inn in half an hour? We'll get there early, but that suits me."

"Perfect. It's a date."

Ha, I think. As if I need another one of those.

TEN

The Day of Dates turns out to be what you could only describe as a mixed bag.

The drive to Lyme passed without incident, and because we were early I got to take Zack on a little walking tour of the town's higgledy-piggledy old streets and pretty gardens. It's a bit of a showstopper, is Lyme – perched around a glorious bay, lined with pastel-coloured beach huts, a thriving and bustling little place packed with cafés and shops lining the promenade. It's a sunny day, the sea sparkling blue, the sky streaked with circling gulls. It's not yet the main tourist season, but there are already plenty of visitors.

We walked Bear down on the beach, and Zack said it was all exactly how he remembered from his childhood. He has vivid memories of eating fish and chips from newspaper wrappings, and going crabbing with his grandad. I could tell he was feeling wistful, in a way that seems to get more frequent with age – when you realise that you have less time ahead of you than you have behind you. It's all the circle of life, of course, but it's still a bit weird when you feel your circle start to shrink.

We parted ways just before my first coffee date, and now

we're back where we started – in the car park by the harbour. I wave as I see him, and Bear snuffles at me affectionately when we're reunited. Zack unlocks the car, saying: "So? How did it go? The suspense has been killing me!"

"Well," I reply, as we drive out of town and head back to Starshine, "I didn't need my emergency whistle – but I don't think I've met the love of my life either. Do you fancy calling off for a drink before we get back to base? I feel a bit hyper and wouldn't mind decompressing. Downside of being of a close-knit community – they'll all be waiting for me to get back so they can quiz me, and I'm not sure what I even think myself yet!"

"Absolutely. I'm your slave for the day – just give me directions."

I take us to a little place near the coast in Charmouth, and send George a quick text message saying I am safe and well before we go inside. Fingers crossed it lands.

The pub is quiet, and we bag a window seat with killer views out across the sea. Bear finds a stray crisp under the table, staying true to his proud retriever heritage. Zack gets us some drinks, and when he settles back down he says: "Okay. Spill."

"Right. Well, I met the first guy in the coffee shop where you left me. That was Eric. I'd quite liked the look of Eric – plus his name. It's a bit Viking, isn't it, Eric?"

"Not as Viking as Bjorn Bloodaxe, but definitely more Viking than Clive. Is Eric the one who was a retired fireman, now living in Devon? The one who posted pictures of his artwork?"

"Yeah. I thought that was a pretty good combo – a fireman for the hunky factor, and an artist to appeal to my sensitive side. He looked just like his photos, too. But the problem was his wife."

"His wife? He's *married*?"

"Technically no – he's divorced. But he talked about his ex

literally all the time. He ranged between furious and on the verge of tears whenever he mentioned her. I felt more like a counsellor than someone he was on a date with, and at the end he wanted to take a selfie of the two of us together. I thought it was harmless enough until I realised he only wanted it to make the ex jealous, and I wasn't up for that at all."

Zack makes a little whistling noise, raises his eyebrows, and says: "Wow. That's not great. I assume you didn't arrange to see him again?"

"No way! And it kind of made me glad that he doesn't know my full name or have my actual phone number. Poor Eric – he has a broken heart. I suspect it might be terminal."

"Poor Eric indeed. Well, what about the second one – you went for lunch, didn't you?"

"Yeah. I was still a bit freaked out by the first date to be honest, and I was worried Eric might follow me and see me with someone else. I mean, I know that's stupid – I was completely honest with him. Plus I wasn't his ex-wife so therefore he wasn't really invested – but it still felt odd. Like I was sneaking around. Anyway – date number two was Laurence. Laurence with a 'u'. He was... better."

"That wouldn't be hard. What was his deal?"

"He's also divorced, but amicably and apparently without regret. Three kids and two grandchildren. He confessed that he'd lied on his profile, and said he was fifty-nine when he's actually sixty. He thought that made him sound much older – and as he confessed it straight away, I forgave him. He said it was a bit like shopkeepers making something ninety-nine pence instead of a pound – a psychological advantage!"

"He sounds like he has a sense of humour at least."

"He did. He's a GP as well, which is always handy. We had a nice time together."

Zack looks at me over his pint, and says: "I feel like there's a 'but' coming."

I sigh, and lean back in my seat.

"I feel like an absolute cow for saying this, Zack, but I just didn't fancy him! I hate myself for even thinking like that – it's not as though I'm a teenager is it? I'm old enough and ugly enough to know that there are far more important things in life than fancying someone. Laurence was lovely – he was funny and open, a good conversationalist, an interesting guy. But there was just no spark. I could imagine being friends with him, but I felt nothing beyond that. It's so stupid!"

"No it's not – why are you beating yourself up about it? You're in your fifties, you're not dead. Of course you need a spark. It doesn't even have to be a big one – just enough that you think it might kindle a fire at some point down the line. But if you literally felt nothing at all for him, then it probably wouldn't be fair to him to get his hopes up anyway."

"I know. We left it that we'd stay in touch. I'll message him and explain, but possibly say it a bit more diplomatically than 'soz, I don't want to snog you.' And I'm not assuming he's into me either, I'm not that arrogant – he might also just be happy to have a new pal."

Zack nods, and remains silent for a moment. He has the look on his face that I already recognise as signifying him having more to say on the subject.

"What?" I ask. "Out with it!"

"You might not like it."

"Since when has that stopped you? It's your bloody fault I'm here anyway – you're the one who convinced me it was a good idea to start dating again!"

I'm smiling as I say this to take the sting out of it. Even though it is true.

"Okay – well, do you think that maybe you're being extra fussy because deep down, you don't *want* to meet anyone?"

"This from the man who dumped a woman for not knowing about *Tiswas*?"

"Fair point, well made. But that's what I mean. The women I've dated – I've known they weren't right from the start. Yes, they were attractive, and yes, I'm a man so I noticed that – but I knew none of those relationships were going anywhere long-term. You say you don't fancy Laurence, but is it possible that you've just... I don't know, switched off from that side of life? Is it possible you wouldn't fancy anyone?"

I gulp down some G&T, and look past him at the view. I'm finding it especially fascinating right now. Zack is wrong, of course – I haven't switched off from that side of life, I now realise. And it is possible for me to fancy someone. The problem is, he's sitting right across from me, intent on counselling me on how to find another man. That's pretty messed up.

Maybe I should just say it. Maybe I should simply tell him how I feel and ask him if he'd be interested in some afternoon delight while the girls are away. It's been a long time since I had that kind of delight, in the afternoon or any other time, and I feel a little thrum inside me as I imagine it. It's been a long time since I felt a little thrum as well.

I turn back to look at Zack, and can't help grinning as I imagine how shocked he'd be if I propositioned him. Probably horrified too.

"What's so funny?" he asks, frowning in confusion.

"Everything, don't you think? Life in general? It's a very silly thing. And to answer your question, no – I don't think that's true, Zack. I just didn't fancy Laurence, it's that simple. Nothing he'd done wrong, I just didn't."

"Right. Well, in that case, keep on trying I suppose – the right person will be out there for you somewhere, Connie, I'm sure."

"Maybe – but I'm not convinced I'm into the idea of kissing a million frogs before I find my prince. I genuinely am quite content with my life as it is. Anyway – what about you?" I ask, turning the tables. "You've admitted you've been deliberately going for the wrong type of woman. You know you've sabotaged yourself. Is the right person out there for you as well, or do those rules only apply to other people?"

He smiles and shakes his head, looking a little sad as he speaks.

"I don't know. Maybe they are – but I'm taking a break from looking. This isn't the right time for me."

"Why not? It's a bit hypocritical to be pushing me off the cliff without a parachute while you stay on the top and wave at me as I fall. Why don't we find you some dates, too? You might find love in a little corner of Dorset, not in London!"

Even as I say it, I realise I hate the thought. I know Zack has an ocean of options when it comes to women. I know he has hundreds of messages in that dating app. I've seen an actual notice-board full of pictures of his gorgeous exes – it is not a secret that if he chose, he could be out with a different person every night.

I know all of this, but I still hate the idea of him setting off from Starshine Cove and going on a date. He'll probably end up meeting some ultra-glamorous retired fashion model who lives on a chic boho houseboat in Cornwall. The kind of woman who looks skinny even in a kaftan, and listens to opera while she writes her memoirs about life on the Paris catwalks in the eighties. I'm not sure a woman like that lives around here, but if she does, Zack is sure to find her.

I hate it, but I still seem to have suggested it. What can I say? I'm a complicated person. Messy inside and out.

"Would that make you feel better?" he asks, looking amused. "If I also threw myself off the cliff?"

"Maybe," I reply. Definitely not, I think.

"Okay," he says, pulling his phone out and navigating to the app. "Let's see who's out and about, while we have decent wifi..."

"Good point. The wifi I mean."

I message all three of my children, telling them I love them and celebrating the decent internet connection with a string of emojis that involve hearts, clapping hands and party poppers. I add a video clip of Dwayne 'The Rock' Johnson dancing to a lip-synch version of Taylor Swift's *Shake It Off* as well, because some things simply never lose their shine. I could watch Dwayne Johnson dance all day long and not get bored.

Once that important business is done I scoot over to sit by Zack, who is changing the settings on his app to make his search more localised instead of in London. I peer at the screen nosily, seeing that he's got age at between forty and sixty-five. That seems annoyingly reasonable.

"You can't date her," I say, pointing at one of the possibles.

"Why not?"

"Because I know her. She's Becky, and she runs a wedding dress shop near to Starshine. She's lovely, but it would just get weird."

"Okay, fair enough. What about this one? She looks okay."

"No, that's Maggie Jones who works in the Post Office. She and her hubbie Geoff are constantly on-again, off-again – too complicated."

"Right. Do you know every single woman within a hundred-mile radius?"

"Don't be silly – maybe twenty miles?"

He laughs and goes back to his scrolling. I'm secretly delighted at the lack of viable options, but then he stops and studies one of the profiles in a bit more depth. The picture shows a slim, attractive woman in her middle years, holding a spaniel puppy on her lap. She has a lovely smile, and warmth seems to radiate from her blue eyes. She has one of those super-sleek bobs where not a single hair is out of place, and she runs her own accountancy firm. Damn – brains as well as beauty.

"She looks nice," I say, taking in the information provided.

"She does," he replies. "She's in Poole."

She would be, I think. Poole is full of beautiful people and millionaire homes and luxury yachts. It's still in Dorset, but it's a lot more glamorous than Starshine Cove – just like this woman is a lot more glamorous than me.

"That's just under an hour away on a good day. What do you think?"

He still looks undecided, and puts the phone down on the table before he speaks again.

"I don't know," he replies. "I'm not sure it's fair. I'm not in a position to really make a go of anything right now."

"What do you mean? Why not?"

"Well, I'll be going back to London for a start. Some kind of time warp seems to have occurred, and I've already been here a week."

"Ah, yes. Time does move differently in Starshine. They should really set an episode of *Doctor Who* here."

"Realistically, I can't stay for more than another week because of work, and Marcy's placement with you ends in a few days, so I was hoping to spend some time with her."

I nod, deciding not to tell him that I've already overheard at least two conversations where the girls were discussing heading somewhere cheap and cheerful for a bit of beach-based R&R before they start the next term at college. That is very much for her to discuss with him, and at some point I'm sure Sophie will do me the same honour. Probably when she realises she has £2.50 left in her bank account.

"Right. Okay. But – look, this is Dorset, not Timbuktu – which by the way is in Mali! And like you said to me, nobody really expects to find true love right away, do they? You could just be honest with her and say you're in the area for the time being. And if it did turn out to be something worth pursuing, then I refer you to the aforementioned 'not Timbuktu' comment. There are even direct trains from London to Poole – we truly live in an age of wonders!"

He is starting to look convinced, and I have no clue at all why I am arguing in favour of this. I think it's partly to cover up how I'm starting to feel, because it's embarrassing to have a crush on someone when you're fifty-five. And partly it's simply because I suggested it, and therefore I have to stick with it now. Funny how we never really grow up, isn't it? I'd have expected to be mature and sensible by my age, and here I am – still a complete knob.

"Okay, you have a point," he says, starting to type a message. He does it fluently, clearly used to writing extended communications on his phone. I'm one of those people who still stabs at the screen with two fingers and gets everything auto-corrected to weird alternatives.

"She'll probably hate the look of me anyway," he says once he's done, looking pained.

I let out a bark of laughter before stealing a glance at his silver-streaked hair, his golden skin. The bright green eyes. "Yeah. You are a bit of a minger. Maybe she'll just feel sorry for you?"

"I live in hope. Anyway, can I show you something?"

"That very much depends on what it is."

"It's just a little side project of mine."

He pulls up a document on his phone and shows it to me. It's similar to the outline I saw in his room about the refugee TV show idea – except that this time, the places, names and suggested filming locations are all a lot more familiar.

I see the Cove Café mentioned, and the inn, and notes about me and my friends. Little pen portraits that combine potted bios with ideas for shots – like Archie being interviewed in his greenhouse, and Jake behind the bar at the inn. Me, predictably enough, on the terrace of the café with 'views down to bay'.

I frown, and feel a little flicker of worry uncurl in my stomach. Worry, and something more – a burgeoning sense of betrayal. I trusted this man, and thought I'd made my views clear when I said nobody here was looking for fame. That nobody here would want this kind of intrusion. I've noticed him constantly taking video and photos on his flashy phone with its hundred million giga-pixels or whatever, but I never thought he was doing it for work – I thought he understood that wasn't welcome.

It's not a decision I made unilaterally – I did float it very tentatively and half-jokingly with the other members of the Starshine committee at our last meeting, just in case I was over-reacting. I mean, I hate the idea, but I wouldn't want to make that kind of decision on everybody else's behalf. I was super-relieved when they were all horrified at the very idea, and I could stop worrying about it.

Now, though, I'm wondering if Zack has ignored our wishes – ignored me – and it doesn't feel nice. Maybe my instincts were right that first night I saw him in London – he is from the past, and the past was not great. He is from a world more ruthless than mine, a world where people maybe don't count for more than profit and success. You probably don't get to build the kind of career he has built by being sensitive to other people's views.

"What is this?" I ask simply, trying not to show how upset I am. "I told you no. I told you we were off limits – no TV shows welcome in Starshine Cove. What are you up to?"

I'm clearly not doing a very good job of hiding how upset I am, because he immediately puts his hand on my arm in what I assume is supposed to be a reassuring way. If the next sentence out of his mouth dares to involve the words 'calm down' I may well chuck my G&T in his face.

"It's not for a TV project," he says quickly, obviously sensing danger. "You told me nobody was interested in that, and I respect that decision. It would be impossible to do without co-operation anyway – you can't do these things by stealth."

That's true, I realise, suddenly feeling a bit silly. The whole show would consist of very short interviews with nobody at all, and shots of people's backs as they walked away.

"So what is it then?" I ask, still not feeling completely settled.

"It's just something I was doing for you. For the village. You've all been so welcoming, not just to Marcy but to me, and I wanted to give something back. I'm always taking video – occupational hazard – so I had this idea that I'd pull together a little Starshine special. Nothing at all intended for public consumption outside the village, I assure you."

"No farmers looking for wives? No psychics heading in to suss out where all the positive energy comes from?"

"No, but that's a fun idea. No, honestly, Connie, nothing at all like that – just a little gift. I don't have any real skills outside this. I can't bake you a cake – not one you'd want to eat – and none of you seem to need anything. This was just a way of saying thank you. I thought maybe you could screen it at one of your community centre film nights..."

I am swamped with relief as he explains, and as I start to believe him; there is no sign of deception, no indication that he has been playing with me. He really does just want to put Starshine on screen for us, and us only. I'm delighted – not only that I won't have to physically kick him out of the village, but that he hasn't betrayed me at all. That I was right to trust my judgement.

"Maybe," I say, starting to turn the idea over in my mind, "we could have a premiere. We could have a red carpet, and paparazzi, and Champagne. We could invite celebs."

"Like who?" he asks, sounding amused now.

"Like Jolly Ged and the Funky Farmhands. They do a comedy strip routine that involves a lot of vegetable-based innuendo. They're going down a storm, and they've even got their own calendar out where they look muscular on tractors, and ride horses with their tops off."

"I see. Well, I suppose they would be celebs then. And yes, you could do all of that – just promise me you'll invite me down for the screening, all right? If you like the idea then I'll get the rest of the footage while I'm here, and I can do the editing when I'm back in London with all my equipment. I'll definitely come back down for the premiere, though."

I smile, but I am sad at the thought of him leaving, I realise. Not just because of the crush thing, but because it's actually been nice having someone to hang around with like this. Apart from my father-in-law, George, pretty much everyone else in Starshine is part of a couple – which is lovely. I have in fact been instrumental in forming some of those couples, and I am never made to feel like an outsider. I know I am loved, I know that I'm never the third wheel – but I'm only human, and sometimes I feel like I am. While Zack's been here, that feeling has faded. If nothing else, I've had a pal.

"You're quiet," he says. "I find that unnerving. Are you planning your outfit for the red carpet?"

"Ha! Well, maybe there'll be some actual carpet left over, and I could just wear that – glamour isn't exactly my thing these days!"

"Well, glamour is vastly over-rated. Besides, you looked really nice that first night in London." I raise my eyebrow at him and he hastily adds: "And, of course, every day ever since then..."

"Don't worry," I reply, grinning. "I'm just messing with you. I can scrub up okay, but I prefer the day-to-day me. I know it's not your type of glamour, but it'll do for me."

I realise that I mean it, which is nice. It's all very well feeling good about yourself when you're dolled up for a night out or a date, but isn't it even better to feel good about yourself all the time instead? Just like Dolly?

"You don't really know what my type of glamour is," he says. "Maybe I'm secretly really into... whatever it is you call this particular look."

He gestures to my hot pink peasant blouse and my now tumbledown hair.

"I call it Beach Chic for Dating Days. My other looks include Dazzling Dungarees for Doing the Dishes, Bright Blues for Big Boobs, Knock-Out Knitwear and my personal favourite, Fun With Primary Colours. It's what you might call a playful palette."

"I like it. It works for you. Everyone in London wears black, all the time. It's like some kind of style uniform. You always look great, no matter what you're wearing – you still have that thing you had back when I first met you."

"What thing?" I ask, frowning. I don't see any similarities between me back then and me now. "That thing that made you think I might be up for a one-night stand or a quickie in the stationery cupboard?"

"I never said such a thing – though yeah, maybe I thought it at the time. But it was always more than that with you. You just have this energy. That light that seems to shine from the inside. That little bit of extra that makes you irresistible."

"Irresistible, ha! That makes me sound like a cream cake!"

"It does, doesn't it? I don't know, I'm not expressing myself very well. I'm making it sound weird. You just have a quality about you, Connie, that makes people want to be around you. That draws people in. You had it then, and you still have it now."

"Oh," I reply, taken aback. "That... well, that's very nice of you to say. Maybe I'll pack in this café lark and become a cult leader instead."

"If you do, you really have to let me make a TV show about that!"

ELEVEN

A few days later, the population of Starshine Cove increases by three.

Dan comes homes from university at Liverpool, as does Cally's son, Sam, who is studying marketing in Manchester. My oldest, James, has also returned from Jersey to spend a week with us. Or, more accurately, a week where he mainly sees Miranda and Evan and pops in to say hi to us lot every now and then.

It's the first time I've had all of my children around me for a while, and I have to say it feels good. I'm surrounded by them in the Starshine Inn, and James is taking a selfie. I'd tried to do it myself, but they'd all got frustrated with me as I repeatedly failed to fit everyone in. This is, apparently, 'classic Mum'. I can't help it if I have freakishly short arms, can I?

James takes several shots, and even manages to get one where none of us are gurning. Miraculous.

"What a handsome bunch you are," I declare, staring at the screen. All three of the kids are varying levels of blonde – Sophie's is very light, like mine, and James's settles at the darker end of the spectrum. Dan is in the middle, but is also currently growing his way out of some misadventures with box dyes so he looks a bit stripey.

"Dunno," says Dan, pulling a face. "Reckon we look a bit like Children of the Corn. Or the creepy kids from *Village of the Damned.*"

"Oooh," says Sophie, poking him in the ribs. "Guess who's dating a film student? You'll be quoting *Citizen Kane* and pretending you like French New Wave next. Those of us who've known you for more than five minutes know your favourite ever film is actually *How To Train Your Dragon.*"

"This is true," Dan concedes. "But if you meet her, never mention that, okay?"

"Maybe Julia secretly loves it too," James says. "Maybe you could role-play Hiccup and Astrid together. That would be so romantic!"

Dan doesn't rise to the bait, which tells me he definitely likes this girl. Instead, he just smiles and says: "I don't care what you think. And I will avoid any possible complications by simply never letting her come here."

"Ah, don't be like that!" I reply. "I'd love to meet her! I have so many questions..."

All three of the kids groan and pull horrified faces, and I feign a moment of hurt feelings.

"What?" I ask. "What do you mean?"

"We mean, Mum, that you're so nosy you scare normal people!" Sophie replies on their behalf.

"I'm not nosy. I'm just... interested."

"You're NOSY!" they all say at once, with some intensity. Huh. I suppose they're right. Some people do find it intrusive. Ella, when she first landed here, was extremely cautious of me – took me ages to break down her resistance, which was of course futile. Cally was the complete opposite – she's as 'interested' as me, and always happy to answer any questions with a complete lack of reluctance. My kind of gal.

Exactly at the moment I think about her, she walks through the door to the pub. Just in case I actually have magical powers, I close my eyes and imagine any of my holy trinity – Daniel Craig, Chris Hemsworth and Henry Cavill – doing the same. None of them appear, so sadly it looks like it was mere coincidence.

She gives us a wave and walks over to join us, sending Sam to the bar for drinks. Sam is much taller than his mother but has the same thick dark hair and lovely smile. He's dressed in a pair of red-and-black tartan trousers and a top that seems to be made from leftover scraps of net curtain and extra-large safety pins. As ever, Sam manages to make it look stylish.

"Isn't it a joy?" Cally says, sliding into the seat opposite me. As if choreographed, all three of my kids move along a bit, so they can talk amongst themselves.

"Isn't what a joy?"

"Having them back? Even more so for you I imagine – at least I have Lilly and Meg knocking around the house. But still, I've missed him so much."

"I know what you mean," I say, in a half-whisper. "But I'm trying to keep it quiet so I still look cool."

"Good for you! I think I left cool behind a long time ago. In fact, never even had it. I'm just thrilled to have him back for a bit."

Sam spent the summer before he started uni travelling with his then-boyfriend Nathan, and only had a few days back here before he headed north again.

"Dan's in love, by the way. It's a new look for him. Any romance on the horizon for Sam?" I ask, as he walks towards us with a bottle of Prosecco in an ice bucket, carrying just the one glass. He nips back to get his own G&T, and I laugh at Cally's expression.

"I didn't ask for a whole bottle all to myself, honest," she bleats, staring at the bucket. "I just asked for 'a Prosecco' – I meant a glass!"

"Looks like he knows you better than you know yourself."

"Ha! As for romance, nothing serious from the sounds of it. I think he's just enjoying the buffet rather than choosing a main course, if you know what I mean."

"Are you talking about me?" Sam says as he rejoins us. "Of course you are! Connie, I believe you've invited a super-glamorous showbiz hit-maker into the sleepy community of Starshine Cove..."

"Um. I'm not sure that's what's on his CV, Sam, but I suppose I have."

"Marvellous. I can't wait to meet him. I have some ideas..." Cally groans and holds her face in her hands. He rolls his eyes and adds: "She's worried I might embarrass her. Little does she know that I am a showbiz genius. When can I meet him?"

I glance at my phone and see that it is nearing seven p.m.

"Pretty soon, I guess. He's been out for the day with Marcy and they're due back soon."

As soon as the words are out of my mouth, the door to the inn opens and Marcy and Zack walk inside, followed by Bear.

"What are you doing?" Cally asks a moment later. "Why have you got your eyes closed and why are your lips moving? Are you praying?"

"I was trying to conjure up Henry Cavill. It seems to work when I think about other people – this just isn't fair!"

"What isn't fair?" asks Zack, sitting next to me. He's sent Marcy to the bar – this is one of the most useful aspects of your child technically being an adult, I've found. You might lose the cuteness of baby teeth and cuddles and bed-time stories, but you gain a slave who can legally purchase booze on your behalf.

"The fact that Henry Cavill isn't here!"

"Ah. Right. Well, yes, I can see why you're upset about that. Do you want me to call him and see if he fancies a pint?"

My eyes pop wide, and for a moment I dare to dream.

"Really? Do you know him?"

Zack grins and shakes his head.

"Nah," he replies, "sorry. I probably know someone who does, but we're definitely not on night-in-the-pub terms."

There is a communal sigh of disappointment around our table as Cally, Sam and myself give up on the idea. At least for the time being – I'm sure there's a way!

I introduce Zack to Sam, and start counting in my head. It takes less than twelve seconds for the words 'I have a great concept for a show' to come out of his mouth. I meet Cally's eyes and she laughs – she was obviously doing the same.

To give Zack credit, he doesn't even flinch. I'm guessing that he must get pitched to by random strangers everywhere he goes. As soon as people find out who he is and what he's involved with, he probably stops being a human being and starts becoming An Opportunity.

"Go for it," replies Zack. "But I need it in less than two minutes, or it's too complicated."

"Really?" I say. "Too complicated if it takes more than two minutes?"

"Absolutely. We're not talking Oscar-winning documentaries here, are we?"

"That's fine!" says Sam. "Mum, time me!"

She nods and gets her phone out, waits until it hits a minute on the stopwatch screen, and signals for him to go.

"It's called *Charity Shop Challenge*," Sam announces confidently. "You assemble a panel of expert judges drawn from a variety of fashion backgrounds – haute couture, street style, urban, a cross-section. What they all have in common is that they're looking for originality, and a fresh eye. Then you bring in your contestants – either individuals or in teams – who are given a budget, a geographical location, and a theme, and they have to create a runway show from their findings. Example: two best friends with an eye for style are given £200 to spend in the charity shops of Liverpool, with the theme of 'Somewhere Under the Sea' – models are provided, but they have to source the clothes, accessories, anything extra for stage design."

He pauses, even though he obviously has more to say, glancing at the stopwatch on the phone. Under a minute – not bad.

"The charities get loads of free publicity, plus maybe video segments on what they are and who they are helping. The experts get to find new talent, and get their faces and brands on telly. The contestants get... well, that could be flexible. It could be cash. It could be glory. Or, if it played out right, it could be even better – it could be the chance to get a job or an internship with one of the experts. A life-changing opportunity, plus fantastic entertainment! It's *Bargain Hunt* meets *Project Runway* meets *The Apprentice*. What do you think?"

Zack sips his orange juice, now delivered by Marcy, and seems to be weighing up his words. Personally I think it sounds great, but what do I know?

"I think," he says eventually, "that it has some potential. It draws together a lot of formulaic elements, but in a different way. It could even expand – you could have the same concept for interior design, for example. Let me give it some thought, Sam. I'll make sure I get your contact details before I leave."

Sam stands up, does an ornate little bow, and moves further along to join the rest of the Young People. Cally is staring after him, shaking her head.

"That was actually pretty good, wasn't it? Probably because Sam's been living *Charity Shop Challenge* for years. It's one of the reasons he started his TikTok and Insta."

"Does he have a lot of followers?" Zack asks, looking even more interested. I guess this whole influencer generation has changed the way everyone looks at stuff, certainly in the media.

"He does," Cally tells him. "Nearly twenty thousand on

TikTok now. Mainly people who are interested in sustainable fashion, plus watching Sam tart around in a new hat or whatever. He curates his own little collections – when we moved here, he raided George's wardrobe and did a whole run of stuff called 'country classics made fresh'. He's genuinely very passionate about it all."

"That's a good thing," Zack replies. "You can fake a lot of stuff these days, but viewers tend to be able to spot it when people are authentic. I'll have a think about it all, anyway."

Cally looks a little befuddled by the idea, and decides on the only sensible route – getting stuck in to that bottle of Prosecco. She pours herself one, then says: "I'm getting another glass from the bar. I feel like a proper alkie."

"Will you drink less if you have two glasses?" I ask.

"Nope, but it'll look like it, and that's what counts!"

As she heads over to the bar, I notice Zack looking on as Marcy shares a story at the other end of our row of tables. She looks animated, and everyone is laughing.

"It's nice to see them all getting on so well," I say.

"It really is. It's all you want at the end of the day, isn't it? For them to be happy?"

"Exactly. Especially at this age – there's plenty of time for the tough stuff later in life! I know our kids have been put through the wringer more than most, but here they are, looking like they don't have a care in the world. How was your day together?"

Marcy and Sophie have now technically finished their placement, and I have given them both glowing reviews in their online logbooks. I've listed the skills they've gained, the tasks they've done, and highlighted a few areas for improvement. It made me feel all grown up, and I kind of wished I'd been able to just draw smiley faces instead of making constructive comments.

"It was good," he says firmly. "We went to Corfe Castle, and walked along Studland beach, and generally mooched around having a nice time. Has Sophie told you they're planning on heading to Crete?"

"She has. I felt guilty about using them both as free labour for the past fortnight anyway, so I've given them a little leaving gift – I suspect it will be translated immediately into either cheap flights, or a lot of alcohol. She said there's a villa there they can stay at?"

"Yes. It's not mine, it's her godfather's – one of my work colleagues. It's in a nice, quiet part of the island. More of a cocktails-by-the-pool vibe than getting off your head and dancing till six a.m."

"I'm sure one could lead to the other if they were determined."

"True. We'll just have to hope not, or we'll be in for a lot of sleepless nights. Anyway. How do you feel about it?"

"I'm okay," I reply, knowing exactly what he means. "Dan and James are here for a bit, though I suspect both of them have their own plans too. I'll be busy with the café once the school holidays start. I'm... well, I'll be all right. What about you?"

He shrugs, and can't quite hide the sadness in his eyes. I see him try, though, and recognise the gesture. Us parents get very good at hiding our sad moments.

"I'd be lying if I said the last few weeks haven't been a bit of a let-down on the whole 'spending quality time with daughters' front – they've basically both been too busy. But this is what life looks like now, isn't it? And that's good, I want them to be busy. I want them to have friends and jobs and plans, and not to feel obliged to set aside time for their ancient dad. Besides, it's been a lot of fun in other ways. I got to hang out with this cool chick I used to know back in the day."

"Really? I bet she was awesome."

"She was. In fact I'll miss her when I go back to London."

"Well, a wise woman would probably point out that London isn't exactly Timbuktu—"

"Which is in Mali, did you know that?"

"Funnily enough I did, yes. Anyway. You can visit – we won't ban you from the village or anything. And I'll probably be in London more seeing Sophie anyways, so we can always meet up again. When are you heading back?"

"Well I can be flexible. Technically I have five days left, so I'll play it by ear. If it works out I can give the girls a lift to the airport."

"Ah. So you have time for your date with Susan, then?"

Susan is the woman he contacted from the dating app. The one with the perfect hair and the slim figure and the annoyingly warm smile. I'd quite like to hate her, but she looks too nice.

"Yeah, maybe. We've been chatting and she knows I'm not down here permanently. She still seems quite keen on meeting up though."

Of course she does, I think, schooling my face into a neutral expression. She must think she's hit the jackpot – Zack is, as Archie said, a silver fox. He's hugely attractive, clearly successful, and as far as I know has all his own teeth. He's quite the catch.

I do hate her, I decide – I don't care how nice she looks. This is not the most mature of responses, I know. In fact it's a very silly reaction for any number of reasons. I have no claim whatsoever on Zack, and it should be irrelevant to me who he dates. We are just friends – although I must be an especially bad friend. He has done his best to encourage me to go on dates and look for happiness, whereas I am secretly hoping that when he meets Susan, she will have crippling halitosis.

What kind of monster am I? I don't have the courage to tell him how I feel, but I still don't want him to see anyone else, at least while he's here. It's hypocritical and cowardly, which are two words I don't especially like to associate myself with.

"Anyway," Zack says, finishing off his drink and then stifling a yawn. "I'm going to head up to my room for a bit. Bear needs a nap."

"Are you sure it's Bear who needs a nap?"

I have noticed that Zack is a real fan of naps, and often disappears for a quick midday slumber.

"Yep, for sure. I'm a human dynamo. It couldn't possibly be that I'm exhausted after a day of keeping up with my super-fit, annoyingly energetic daughter... um, are you doing anything later?"

"As you've spectacularly failed to get Henry Cavill here, no."

"Marcy said the younger lot are heading out for the night – something about a music festival on a farm?"

"Ah. Well, 'music festival' is a slight exaggeration, but it does make it sound a lot more exciting. Ged – he of the Funky Farmhands – has organised it. His parents run a dairy farm nearby, and he's always keen to diversify. I think he has in mind that he's creating the next Glastonbury, and this year is a soft launch – lots of local bands, two stages, kegs of ale and free camping."

"Right. Sounds fun. Are you going to it?"

"Nope. My camping days are over, and believe me, I've seen these particular bands and singers about a million times each. They'll have fun, but I'd just wake up with creaking joints and a sore back."

"I could drive us, if you want to go?"

He stands in front of me, all tanned skin and stylish hair and gorgeous smells, and I realise that it's this kind of thing I will miss when he leaves. The easy way we have paired off, spent time together, enjoyed each other's company. Even if you take away the 'fancying him rotten' aspect, there is a lot left to like.

"I don't think I do," I say eventually, after giving it some thought. "It's actually walking distance anyway, though admittedly quite dangerous walking distance up a big hill if you were drunk... but no. I think I'll leave them to it. All I can offer you is a very dull night in front of the telly, possibly with some pizza and popcorn."

"Is there a dress code?"

"Strictly scruffy casual. Anyone too smartly dressed will be turned away at the door."

He nods and says: "Great. I'll see you about eight? After Bear has had his nap..."

Cally returned for the tail-end of this conversation, waving goodbye as he disappears towards the back of the building and the stairs that lead up to the hotel rooms. She raises one eyebrow at me as she sips her Prosecco. I can never do that – it's both or nothing – and I'm jealous of her skills.

"You like him," she says after a few silent moments.

"Yes, he's nice – don't you like him?"

"No, I mean you *like* like him."

"What are we, twelve?"

"No, about fifteen I'd say – at least from the way you're reacting. Look, why don't you do something about it?"

"Like what – get one of my mates to tell him I fancy him?"

"Maybe!" she replies, laughing. "I'd do it for you! Or you could scratch 'CL Loves ZH' on one of the benches at the edge of the green. Or send him a note asking him if he wants to walk you home from the school disco..."

I throw a beer mat at her head to shut her up, and she spills her booze as she dodges it. Serves her right, I think.

"I'm too old for any of that nonsense," I say firmly. "I know I've been on a couple of failed dates, but that doesn't mean I'm ready for anything more than a coffee."

"I'm calling bullshit on that one, Connie. The way you look at him? The way you are together? It's obvious there's something there."

"It's called friendship."

"No, it's more than that – why are you even bothering to deny it? That's a genuine question – it's not like it would do any harm if you two had a fling."

I take a deep breath and lean back against the wall. I know she's not even asking to wind me up – she's really curious. I bite my lip, and try to rally some words that make sense when they're strung together. I also glance further down to my side, checking that none of the younger crowd are listening in. Of course they aren't – we're not that interesting.

"It's hard to explain," I say eventually. "I'm not quite sure how to express it."

"You fancy him, but you're worried in case he doesn't fancy you and then you make a tit of yourself?"

"Okay, so maybe that bit isn't so hard to explain – yes, there is an element of that. But even more scary would be if he actually did fancy me. What would happen then?"

I see Cally bite back laughter before she replies: "Oh, I don't know – really hot sex? Would that be so awful? You're never too old for really hot sex!"

"I totally agree... but I'm not sure how good I'd be at that."

"At sex? I mean, I know it's been a while for you, Connie, but it's not like you'll have forgotten what to do..."

"I don't mean that – of course I remember what to do, and of course it would be excellent! No, what I mean is, I'm not sure how good I'd be at really hot sex that was casual. The last person I felt this kind of attraction to was Simon, and I married him."

Cally, of course, knows my history, linked intimately as it is with Archie's. She considers what I've said, and all mockery drains from her face.

"Right," she says quietly. "I get that. It was terrifying for Archie as well, when we got together. So terrifying that he almost blew it."

"I know. I'm glad he didn't. I'm glad you gave him a second chance. But this isn't the same."

"Why not?"

"Because you and Archie were just so right for each other. You and Archie were just so right for Lilly and Meg as well. It was the perfect fit, for all of you, and it was worth fighting for. Me and Zack? I'm not sure either of us wants anything serious. I'm not sure either of us is ready for that, and maybe we never will be. Maybe we're better off staying as friends."

Cally leans across the table and takes one of my hands in hers.

"I understand what you're saying," she says seriously. "And they are valid points. But come on, woman – what about the really hot sex?"

TWELVE

By the time Zack arrives, the house is in a state of extremely pleasant chaos. It's full of teenagers and noise and clutter, which is exactly the way I like it.

Marcy, Sophie, Dan, Rose and Sam are all here, preparing for their night at the alleged music festival. James left earlier, planning to drive there for an hour or so later, along with Miranda and baby Evan. I offered to look after Evan for the night to give them some time off together, but he said they were happy just 'dipping in'. I'm a bit disappointed – Evan is hard work but adorable, and a huge amount of fun to sit for.

I've made a feast of pizza and garlic bread, arranging it all on the kitchen table with a big bowl of salad and a range of sauces. I've been experimenting with 'nduja recently, because I'm wild and crazy like that, and am especially pleased with the spicy dip they are plunging the pizza crusts into.

Some of them are sitting at the table like civilised humans; others are lurking around holding slices in their hands, too hyped to be still. Dan is standing on his skateboard as he eats, which is not an unusual scenario. Someone has put music on their phone, and everyone is shouting over it. Like I said, chaos.

It's so loud I don't even hear Zack come in, only noticing when Bear barrels into the kitchen, tail wagging and nose twitching. I quickly push everything into the centre of the table to avoid a Labrador raid, and he looks up at me in disappointment.

His human follows him in, gazing around at the carnage and smiling. He's wearing what looks suspiciously like pyjama trousers paired with a black T-shirt. I stare at him and he says: "What? You said casual. I was worried my jeans might be too posh! Have I violated the dress code?"

"Nah," I say, "you'll do. I'm surprised you're not wearing your elf slippers."

"So am I. I should have brought them with me really."

Marcy springs over to give her dad a kiss on the cheek, leaving a trail of glitter on his skin from the butterfly face paint she's wearing. She's gone full festival girl and I hope she's not disappointed when she realises she'll mainly be sitting on a hay bale while middle-aged men sing about cider.

Their overnight gear is scattered around the room in random heaps of sleeping bags, backpacks and tents, and the whole place has the feel of a base camp for an especially badly planned expedition. Luckily they're only going to a dairy farm a mile away, not scaling Everest.

I make Zack a plate of food, going heavy on the salad because I've noticed he eats disgustingly healthily – in fact he doesn't eat much at all, and I always want to feed him up. I add a dollop of the 'nduja dip and a slice of margherita with fresh parmesan shavings.

"Try that," I say, pointing at the dip.

He does as he is told, swirling a slice of red pepper into it, and the look on his face when he takes a bite is eminently gratifying.

"Oh, Lord," he says, once he's finished chewing. "That tastes so good it should probably be illegal."

"We aim to please," I reply, smiling. I love cooking for people, which is really lucky given the fact that I run a café. But I especially love it when a new recipe goes down well – it's just very, very satisfying seeing people's reactions. Unless that reaction is 'yuck, that's disgusting'.

There is a temporary increase in the hubbub as the youngsters prepare to leave – a last-minute flurry of 'I just need my power bank' and 'is it going to rain?' and 'has someone got the marshmallows for the campfire?'

Sophie and Marcy are driving there with the heavy gear, and the rest walking with rucksacks. It seems highly unlikely that this operation will go smoothly, which is proved right as soon as they try to actually go. There are two false starts where someone runs back inside because they've forgotten the loo roll and then Marcy's neck cushion, and one more when Sam realises he's left behind his gin. Just when I think they're finally done, Sophie dashes back through the door.

"What did you forget?" I ask.

"This," she says, coming over to give me a hug. "Thanks for the pizza. Have a nice night!"

This, of course, is very sweet, and leaves me with even more of a smile on my face than Zack liking my 'nduja dip.

Once she's skittered out again, Zack and I both stand still in the kitchen, listening out.

"Do you think they've finally gone?" he asks, head cocked to one side.

"I think they have... we can finally drop some ecstasy and have a middle-aged rave to the sounds of *Now That's What I Call Music 15*..."

"Why specifically 15?"

"Because it's got *Baby I Don't Care* on it by Transvision Vamp – that's brilliant to dance to!"

"You know exactly which songs are on each *Now That's What I Call Music* album?"

"Don't be daft – only from the first one through to about the thirtieth... I gave up after that."

He shakes his head and laughs, then helps me clear the table. I throw Bear a small slice of carrot, which he snatches from the air with way too much enthusiasm. I think he looks disappointed when he realises what it is, and I give his ears a rub to compensate.

I wrap up the leftover pizza and pop it in the fridge, and Zack stacks the dishwasher while I prepare more snacks. Heaven forbid we run out of snacks – the sky would probably fall in.

It feels strangely quiet in here now that the kids have all left, and I tell myself off when I feel a twinge of nervousness. I have nothing to feel nervous about – I am in my own home, with a man who I enjoy spending time with. I might have the occasional less-than-pure thought about him, but that doesn't mean anything should be awkward between us.

It's a good pep talk, and it almost works – except when we make our way into the living room, and he sits next to me on the sofa, I almost squeal out loud when his thigh brushes against me. It's not a weird place to sit – the sofa is right across from the TV and the best place to view it from. It's just that I maybe expected him to take one of the armchairs instead.

I shuffle up a bit, and put a bowl of popcorn in between us as a chaperone. I press the button on the side of the sofa that makes the recliner bit come up, and he looks delighted as he does the same. Simple pleasures.

"What do you want to watch?" he asks, as I pass him a blanket. It's not cold at all, but there's just something cosy about having a blanket while you watch the telly isn't there? It's more about snuggle value than warmth.

"Something really scary."

"Why? Are you hoping I scream like a girl?"

"Well, that would be an amusing extra bonus – but mainly

because I really love horror movies, but I'm too much of a scaredy cat to watch them when I'm on my own."

"Surely these guys would protect you?" he says, gesturing behind to my cardboard cut-outs of Chris, Henry and Daniel.

"You'd think so, but they're incredibly passive for action heroes."

"Lazy swines. So, what was your favourite scary film from when we were kids? I remember being absolutely petrified by *The Shining*."

"Oh God, yes," I reply, grimacing. "I didn't even see that until I was about sixteen and it was horrifying. I was very partial to *Poltergeist* – still am, actually. Plus *The Lost Boys* – I loved that one! And *The Fly* – the effects look dated now, but back in the day it was so frightening..."

"Yeah – especially that bit where all his flesh is disintegrating and his fly face emerges, and poor Geena Davis is screaming her head off! Still gives me the shivers now!"

"We could watch one of those, I suppose, for old times' sake. Or there's the sequel to *The Shining* – I haven't seen that, have you?"

He agrees, and within minutes we are settled and ready. The lights are low for extra scariness, and we're both comfy beneath our blankets, ready to be terrified. We are not disappointed – it is a tense watch. There are lots of creepy bits and a few jump scares, and we keep shocking Bear by letting out our own yelps.

Once it's over, Zack says: "Wow. That was... intense. Can we watch something else now? Something mellow and nice to help my heart rate steady?"

"Like what?"

"I don't know... something that doesn't feature evil immortals driving around in camper vans sucking out people's life essence, maybe?"

"Um, how do you feel about *Paddington*? I mean, Nicole Kidman is pretty scary in it, but mainly it's nice?"

"Perfect. Just what Doctor Sleep ordered."

We both take what is politely called a 'comfort break' – in my case about my millionth, because, you know, three kids and middle-age. I let Bear out to do the same, and laugh as he mooches around the garden, pushing an old football around with his nose for a while before deciding to just pee on it instead. It's been a pleasant day, weather-wise, but I notice that it's started to rain and a strong breeze is stirring the branches of the cherry trees. I'm extremely glad not to be spending the night in a tent.

I look up at the clock, and see that it is still only half past nine. It was a long movie, but we started early. I let Bear back in and stifle a yawn, realising that I am indeed pretty tired. I'm usually in bed by ten, because most mornings I am up bright and early opening the café.

"I'll just stay for another half hour or so," Zack announces when I walk back into the living room. "Get myself calm enough for the long walk back to the inn. Don't know about you but I'm whacked."

"I know, me too! I feel like if I do an especially slow blink it might turn into an eight-hour nap... not that I ever get those anymore."

"You don't sleep well?" he asks, as I sit down beside him.

"No. I'm told it's hormones. They seem to be responsible for everything from a bad night's kip to world hunger. You?"

"Same. Though not sure if it's the hormones. Mainly I think it's my brain – I have a lot of trouble switching it off. I've been better since I've been here, though. Last night I managed a whole six uninterrupted hours, which is pretty much unheard of."

"Isn't this the most old-person conversation ever?" I say, frowning. "Young people never ask each other how they slept, do they? Now I feel like I start most chats with 'did you sleep well?' It's like the holy grail when you're older, a good night's sleep!"

"I know," he replies, smiling. "And it's only going to get worse... before long we'll be comparing blood pressure pills and discussing the waiting lists for hip replacements."

I have been feeling a few twinges in my hip recently – I suppose a combination of being a teensy bit (okay, almost a stone) overweight and having a job that involves being on my feet all day. I shudder slightly, and say: "Enough! This is even scarier than *Doctor Sleep*. I need to fill my mind with cute bears from darkest Peru!"

"You're right. And this has been nice, Connie."

"Talking about our declining health?"

He shrugs. "Maybe that's part of it – I tend to spend a lot of time with younger people in my professional life. They're bloody exhausting, all fresh and energetic and ambitious."

"Sounds disgusting."

"It can be. So, anyway – it's been nice being here with you. Enjoying your company. Even just chilling out and watching the TV together, you know?"

I nod, because I do know. I've enjoyed it too, and I am starting to feel a tug of sadness at the thought of him leaving. Not just because of the crush thing, but because it has felt alarmingly good to have his companionship. When you lose your life partner, there are many things you miss about the life you had before, and some of them are so simple. Sitting together and watching the TV is right up there, boring as it might sound – just the plain act of sharing a mundane experience, and talking about it afterwards.

"Yes. I know – and the feeling is mutual. Maybe we can watch TV together over Zoom when you're in London? Like, our own personal *Gogglebox*?"

He laughs out loud and says: "Brilliant idea – I'm in!"

I press play on *Paddington*, and let my mind wander as everyone's favourite bear begins his adventures. It's an odd thought, Zack being back in London in that big family home, all on his own – and me here, in a similar state once the kids have gone back to college. Maybe we can help each other through it. Or maybe he's just being polite, who knows? Maybe once he's back in the city he'll forget I even exist. I have no control over that so it's probably best to ignore it.

The movie helps, and is the perfect distraction. I find myself imagining how people here in Starshine Cove would react to a stray bear looking for a family, and decide that Paddington would be inundated with offers of free board, lodging and marmalade sandwiches. We would embrace him into all aspects of our community, and he would be the most loved bear ever.

This is the last conscious thought I have – picturing a fictional talking animal playing cricket on the village green – before I slide into sleep. I don't notice it happening, of course, it sneaks up on me – I must get ambushed by one of those slow blinks. I'm not sure exactly when it happens, but it definitely does, because the next time I glance at the TV screen Paddington has found his happy ending and the film has finished. Yikes.

Even more of a yikes is the fact that somehow, during my snooze, I have scooted all the way across the sofa to Zack. Or, as we've met in the middle, maybe it was a mutual scooting. Either way, I am now snuggled up against him, my thigh across his lap and my face resting against his chest. His arm is slung around my shoulders, and one of mine is wound around his torso. We are completely entwined with each other, and for a blissful moment I simply let myself enjoy it.

I am a tactile person. I like hugs and cuddles and physical affection. My poor children are used to it, and I have plenty of friends in the village who are always happy to have a hug as well. But this is different – this is very different. I have not been in this kind of position since Simon, and part of me is thrilled, even if it did happen by accident.

There is just something so lovely about being in someone's arms, feeling safe and protected and small, allowing yourself to let your guard down for a while. I've been Mum and Dad to my children for a long time now, which means I've always been on high alert. Always vigilant, looking around corners for everyone else. This feeling – this sense of warmth, of comfort, of security – is not one I've experienced for years. It is sublime, but in its own way it is also much scarier than any horror film.

I don't want to move, but I know I have to. I can't let myself stay here, in this lush cocoon, imagining that any of it is real. That any of it might last. He is leaving, and even if he wasn't, I think it's pretty much been established that I'm not his type. Maybe, I tell myself, I will find this again – maybe one of my dates will amount to more than coffee and awkward conversation. Maybe there will be a time in my life when I find a man I can enjoy moments like this with again – but that time is not now, and that man is not Zack.

I let out a little sigh at the thought of having to disturb him, and am shocked when he speaks. And when his arm tugs me even closer to him.

"Don't move," he says quietly, his voice a deep whisper. "I've been awake for a few minutes, wondering how we ended up like this – then deciding I didn't care how. I was just glad we did."

I'm grateful he can't see my face, because I must look ridiculous, like a cartoon version of surprised. My eyes have popped open wide, I feel a flush sweeping across my cheeks and I'm suddenly very hot. I don't think it's menopausal – but it might be hormones. Just different ones. Even the air around us seems to sizzle, like there is electricity floating through it.

He nuzzles into my hair, and I feel the warmth of his breath against me. My hand burrows beneath his T-shirt, making contact with the bare skin of his chest, and I suck in a quick breath. God, it feels so good – to touch and be touched like this.

I feel his fingers stroking my curls away from my cheeks, and then his thumb is beneath my chin, gently tilting my face up to look at his. His green eyes are intense, his slight smile full of promise. He pauses, and I know he is giving me the chance to object. To pull away. To decide that this is a stupid idea and to put a stop to it before anything has even happened.

That is the last thing I want to do, though, and instead I reach up, lay my hand on the back of his neck, and pull him in for a kiss.

It starts softly, both of us taking our time and feeling our way through it. The touch of his lips against mine is everything I thought it would be, and the restrained beginning soon builds into something so much more. It's as if both of us suddenly go on turbo-charge, and the kiss races from quiet and curious to hot and hungry in just a few seconds.

I barely notice myself moving, but somehow I do – and I find myself sitting astride him, his arms tugging me close, our mouths never parting. I hold his face between my palms, and he groans as his hold on me tightens.

I find myself writhing in a decidedly un-ladylike way against him, moaning out loud as his lips move from mine to trail kisses along my cheekbone, my jaw, down to my neck. Every spot he touches seems to be ablaze, and I can't get enough of him. It's as though every minute we've spent together until this moment was extended foreplay, and I am now on fire with need for him. I'd almost forgotten what this felt like – this unstoppable physical pleasure that chases all other thoughts from your mind. The way the body can take on this life of its own, detached from common sense and thought.

He kisses his way up to my ear, and whispers: "Are you sure?"

"Do I seem sure?"

"Yes, you do…"

"So stop asking me that, and take me to bed."

I can't quite believe that I have been so brazen – so demanding. But this feels too good to be wrong, and even if it is wrong, I just don't care. I deserve this. We both do. I'm not going to spoil this fragile magic by over-thinking it, I decide. I don't want to think at all – I just want to feel.

I clamber off his lap, and hold out my hands. He takes them, and soon he is there, looming above me, eyes shining and lips quirked up in a grin. He looks flushed too, and that makes me want him even more – seeing how much this is affecting him is a massive turn-on. It doesn't matter that I'm not his type. It doesn't matter that his previous girlfriends were all young and skinny and gorgeous. None of it matters, because he is here, and he so very clearly wants me, and boy, is the feeling mutual.

We stand a few inches apart, holding hands, both catching our breath and gazing into each other's eyes.

"You are so bloody sexy," he says, a rough edge to his voice. "I've tried so hard not to notice, but you kind of make that impossible."

I raise an eyebrow, and know that I am smiling the smile of a woman who also *feels* sexy. I pull him closer, and say: "You're not so bad yourself."

"Thank you. Should we go upstairs and discuss this in more depth?"

"We can go upstairs, for sure, but I'll be extremely disappointed if all we do is have a discussion."

"Don't worry. I can think of plenty of ways to avoid that. This is one of those situations where actions speak much louder than words."

I nod, and keep hold of his hand as I lead him towards the stairs. Bear looks confused, but thumps his tail a couple of times and goes back to sleep. I'm glad he approves.

I'm halfway up the stairs when I feel him suddenly freeze.

He stops, without any warning, a couple of steps below me. He's still holding my hand, so I'm forced to stop too. I am fizzing with anticipation here, and can't quite believe that he's delaying things any further. Haven't we waited long enough, for goodness' sake?

A few random and unwelcome thoughts slalom through my mind, taking advantage of the unexpected pause to ambush me: has he gone off the idea? Has he had a change of heart now he's seen how big my bum is from behind? Was he just carried away, and now he's having the grown-up version of that moment when the lights go on at the end of a disco and everyone suddenly looks sweaty and crap?

"I think... I think I heard a car," he says, frowning. His hair is furrowed into messy rows where I've run my fingers through it, his T-shirt is creased, and he looks deliciously dishevelled. I want to go up these stairs and make him look even more messy, but I do exactly the same as he is doing – freeze on the spot, go silent, and strain my ears. Every parent is familiar with this routine, the stop-and-start rhythm that your love life takes on once you have children. They're usually just a lot smaller than ours when this happens.

I think I can hear something in the distance, but I'm not quite sure – until Bear lets out a huge booming woof, and skitters across the hardwood floor heading towards the hallway. I look at Zack, and see that he is as frustrated as I am as we hear the now unmistakable sound of a car door slamming. I am the only person who lives in this little cul-de-sac other than George, and I know he will be firmly asleep by now. Plus he doesn't have a car anymore. It's got to be one of our darling offspring, because this isn't the kind of place that people drive to at random.

"One day," I say, dropping his hand and dashing back down the stairs, "we will look back at this and laugh."

"You're probably right," he says, as I reach up to straighten his hair and then do the same for myself. "But that day is not this day, and I feel more like punching a hole in the wall than laughing. Okay. Game faces on!"

I laugh, and we both wander through to the kitchen. Marcy and Sophie are standing there, shivering and soaking wet. The two of them look thoroughly bedraggled, and I instinctively go and warm up some milk for hot chocolate.

"What happened?" I ask as I work. "I didn't expect to see you until the morning!"

I notice Marcy's gaze flicking from her dad to me, and spot the slight raising of an eyebrow.

"I feel asleep on the couch," Zack says quickly, obviously picking up on the same vibe. "We were watching *Paddington*."

As far as it goes, he is telling the truth – but my increased heart rate is still evidence of the fact that there was a lot more to our cosy night in than the innocent watching of a movie. I turn back to the milk pan to hide my grin, feeling like a naughty schoolgirl caught out by her parents and loving every minute of it. Being naughty is fun – I'd almost forgotten that.

"Something went wrong with the tent," Sophie says, peeling off her socks and grimacing at her cold feet. "Or maybe something was wrong with us, I'm not sure. The gig was fine. Usual sort of stuff, but a couple of new acoustic acts as well. Loads of booze. Bit of line dancing. I don't think Glastonbury's got anything to worry about yet, but it was fun."

"Until it started raining," Marcy continues, gratefully accepting her hot chocolate from me and using the mug to warm her hands. "I mean, rain is fine – but it just kept getting worse and worse. We'd had a few drinks so we just danced our way through it, as you do. But then when we tried to get to sleep, the tent just kind of... blew off us!"

"Did you peg it down properly?" I ask, sounding as though I know what I'm talking about. Truth be told I've never been a huge fan of sleeping under canvas, and when we did do it when the kids were younger, I left most of the logistics to Simon. I do, however, remember that you have to knock in the little ropes with a big hammer. I kind of liked that bit; it was cathartic.

"Well," Sophie replies, sipping her drink, "I'd like to be annoyed with you at this point and say 'of course we did, Mum, we're not idiots!' But evidence suggests that possibly that's exactly what we are."

"Right. And did you put the tent up before or after you started drinking?"

They both giggle, and it seems I have my answer. Drunk in charge of camping equipment. They're probably not the first young people that's happened to, and I'm certainly not one to judge.

"What about the others?" I ask. "Are they okay?"

"Yeah," Sophie replies. "They ended up sleeping in the barn. It was only us who decided to make a run for it, because we were so wet, and because we're giant wusses I suppose. We just wanted to be in the warm with mattresses and blankets."

"Can't say that I blame you, love."

"I'm amazed you're still awake though," she continues, glancing at the kitchen clock on the wall behind me. "I assumed you'd have been in bed for hours by now. Don't you have work in the morning?"

I realise that I have absolutely no idea what time it is, and turn around to check for myself. I do a little double take when I see that it's almost two in the morning. Wow. Time flies when you're having fun. And sleeping through movies.

"Umm, yeah, I do. Might open up an hour later than usual. Like Zack said, we just fell asleep. By accident. Because we're, you know, ancient."

Sophie gives me a slightly suspicious look, and I stop talking – I think I might be straying into the-lady-doth-protest-too-much territory. I force myself to meet her gaze head on. I have nothing to hide. Well, I do, but I am determined to hide it.

"You two should go and get into some dry clothes," I say, using my best mother-knows-best voice. I add: "You'll catch your death," just for fun.

Zack has been taking in this whole exchange, perched on the edge of the dining table. He straightens up, and announces: "I'm exhausted. I'm going to head back to the Starshine Inn. Marcy, Sophie, do as Connie says. You'll be off to Crete soon and you don't want to be doing it with a cold, do you?"

I nod in grown-up agreement. Gosh, we are absolutely nailing this responsible parenting thing.

Both of our daughters, miraculously, do as they are told. I think they're too fatigued to resist. They head off upstairs, leaving behind a soaking wet, half-unpacked tent that is now sitting in a pool of rain on my kitchen floor tiles.

"I suppose I really had better be going," Zack says, swiping his eyes with his hands. "I am actually tired."

"You didn't seem tired a few minutes ago."

"I know. Strange that, isn't it? It's like I found a reserve of extra energy from somewhere."

I laugh, and walk with him and Bear to the door. He pauses just before he opens it, and leans down to kiss me. It's on the lips, and it is lovely, but it is a pale imitation of the kisses we shared earlier. The moment has been well and truly shattered.

"See you tomorrow?" he asks, looking at me a little uncertainly. Maybe he thinks the moment isn't just shattered, it's gone forever. Maybe this gorgeous man, despite his surface style and sleek confidence, is capable of feeling insecure as well.

I stand up on my tippy-toes and give him another kiss – one with a bit more oomph to it.

"You most definitely will," I reply. "To be continued."

He smiles and disappears off into the wild and windy night. It's still raining heavily, and the wind is howling up from the bay. I watch until he is gone from sight, and close the door. I lean against it, and let out a loud sigh.

I am tired, of course I am – but I also feel more alive than I have for years. Every part of me is tingling. Every part of me feels hopeful. Every cell in my body feels electrified.

I head up the stairs, and feel like I am floating all the way to my bed.

THIRTEEN

I wake up the next day feeling both incredibly good, and incredibly terrified. But even the terrified is enjoyable in its own way. It's exciting – a fun kind of terrifying, the kind that makes your nerves sizzle and your heart beat faster. The kind that reminds you that anything worth having comes with its own set of risks.

I only managed a few hours' sleep, which I don't suppose was surprising. I had an extended nap during most of *Paddington* and beyond, plus I was just too wired to fall into anything resembling a deep slumber. I felt like I'd injected caffeine directly into my veins, I was so hyped up.

The rest that I did manage to get was fitful and full of vivid dreams. Some were strange and psychedelic, almost like some kind of acid trip involving Labradors that could talk and tents that flew through the sky like flocks of geese relocating to warmer climates. My other dreams were... well, my other dreams were quite clearly related to my intimacy with Zack. Which is of course a polite way of saying I was having sex dreams – absolutely gorgeous sex dreams as well! So gorgeous that every time I drifted anywhere close to consciousness, I'd try to go back to sleep and pick up where I left off.

Needless to say, when I finally wake up properly at just after seven a.m., I have a very big, very stupid smile on my face.

I lie in bed for a few minutes, letting my mind roam free, letting my imagination go crazy. It might only have been a bit of a snog and a bit of a fumble last night, but it had a spectacular effect on me. It's like a button has been switched, and I am suddenly sensationally aware of what I have been missing for so long. My whole body is craving more, to the point where I'm starting to think this whole menopause thing is a myth – because right now I feel like a teenaged girl who has just realised what all the fuss is about when it comes to sex.

I had genuinely forgotten how fantastic it can feel to spend time with the right man, to be swept away by the right chemistry – or maybe I hadn't forgotten exactly, I'd just suppressed the memory because it made me too sad to remember it and then live without it.

I climb out of bed, opening the curtains to see that it is still raining lightly. The sun is bright and clear though, the sky a vibrant pastel blue despite the downpour, seagulls streaking white stripes across the heavens. It's perfect rainbow weather, I reckon, with all that sunshine and the ongoing shower. I love rainbows, so that is a very good omen.

I have a quick shower, do what I can with my hair, and get dressed. As I add a pair of pretty earrings with tiny dangling seashells, I realise that I am not at all worried about my clothes, or whether I should wear make-up, or how I should look when I see Zack again later today. That comes as a bit of a relief, because I'd found it super-stressful when I was getting ready for my dates. I'd maybe expected that I would feel the same today, and it is a joy to find out that I don't. In fact, I feel extremely groovy, baby.

Last night, I was dressed in my scruffs and had been at work all day – and Zack still wanted me. It would be the very height of stupidity to wake up today and become obsessed with my appearance, when he clearly likes what he sees already.

It all still feels strange and surreal to me, but the lips don't lie – and he wasn't playing around last night. He wanted me just as much as I wanted him. I look at myself in the mirror, and see the slightly flushed complexion of a woman who has well and truly rediscovered her mojo. I give myself a wink, because why not?

Again, I could over-think this. I could pick at the scab, remind myself that he is London glamour, that our lives run on very different tracks, that this can't possibly work in the real world. I could remind myself of how much I have to lose – of how it would feel to be rejected, or how sad and lonely I am going to be when he goes home. I could focus on the fact that this isn't a long-term thing, that this isn't even remotely feasible as a lasting relationship.

I could focus on any of those things, and maybe I should. Maybe that would be sensible. But this morning does not feel like the right time to be sensible. This morning feels sweet and sexy and hopeful and full of potential. It feels like rainbows all over. I can't remember the last time I woke up feeling any of those things, and I am not going to burst this bubble before I really need to. I shall ride this wave of optimism for as long as I can.

I emerge onto the landing to be confronted by Sophie coming out of the bathroom. She looks pale and exhausted, her hair in tangles and dark circles beneath her eyes. There was definitely a bit too much alcohol consumed last night.

"Mum, why are you *singing*?" she says, sounding repulsed.

"Was I?"

"Yes! You were singing *Walking On Sunshine* really loudly! That's just not a reasonable thing to do this early!"

"Oh. Sorry. Well, I do love that song... how are you?"

"Tired. See you later."

She walks back into her room and slams the door behind her. Ah, what a sweetie she is! I don't care. Nothing's going to bring me down today. Besides, she has a point. It is unsociably early to be singing out loud.

I hum it quietly to myself instead, and head downstairs. Coffee, a slice of toast and home-made rhubarb jam, and I'm ready to go. I'll have the doors to the Cove Café open by eight, which is right on time – yet another reason to be joyful. I am so winning at life.

I let myself in and pause for a moment, enjoying the familiar scents of the place – the lingering remnants of the blackberry and apple crumble from yesterday, the lavender and sea salt from the wax melts, the hint of floral fragrance from the vase of tulips and hyacinths on the counter.

I walk straight through the building to the back, where the vast French doors lead out onto the terrace. I gaze down at the beach, and smile at what I see. A huge arcing rainbow is anchored on one side by the red-gold cliffs that line the cove, then stretches in a gloriously bright semi-circle right out over the waves. It looks like it's magically hovering over the sea, its brilliant colours reflecting up from the shimmering water.

It doesn't happen often, seeing a rainbow out on the bay, but I had a feeling that today it just might. I allow myself a few seconds of peace and quiet, simply watching what I know is a scientific phenomenon but feels like so much more.

I tear myself away from the view, and get busy. I chop lettuce and cucumber and tomatoes, plate up slices of carrot cake, prep the coffee machine, and bring in supplies from the bigger fridges in the back. Little Betty calls in with a selection of freshly baked croissants and apple custard pastries, along with a spectacular Black Forest gateau that I'm almost tempted to sample there and then. It's a good cake day, for sure.

My first actual customer is Lucy, Rose's mum, who is on her

way to work. She's only lived here permanently since September, and works with Dr Wong, the local vet. I immediately get her coffee to go – black, no sugar, pretty easy to remember – and she orders two almond croissants to take away. Dr Wong has a very sweet tooth, to the point that it seems like a miracle she has any teeth at all. I chat as I put everything together for her, telling her she really should go out back in case the rainbow is still there. Then I tell her how much I love rainbows, possibly in too much detail.

"Are you all right?" Lucy asks, staring at me suspiciously. Her lovely red hair is swept up into a bun, and the white lab coat she's wearing over her clothes makes her look like she's a sexy super-villain in a Bond movie.

"I'm great! Has anyone ever told you that in your work outfit, you look like a sexy super-villain in a Bond movie, by the way?"

"Funnily enough, no. Especially when I'm trying not to get bitten by an angry Alsatian when I stick a thermometer up its bum."

"Mmmm, yes, I can see that isn't the sexiest of scenarios... but still. I bet you look stylish doing it."

She narrows her eyes and replies: "Are you sure you're okay? You seem a bit... odd this morning. Even more odd than normal. You look tired but you sound like a toddler after a full bag of Haribo."

"I told you, I'm great! All is well in the world! Have a good day, Lucy!"

She doesn't look convinced, and I wonder if she'll be calling in to see Ella on the way to the vet surgery. I can just imagine the conversation, as the two of them discuss whether me seeming especially perky first thing in the morning might be a cause for concern. These science types are always looking for logical explanations for things – I bet they don't enjoy rainbows half as much as I do!

I serve a few other regulars, mainly people who are calling in before their commute or want to begin their working-from-home day with a treat. It's always pretty quiet at this time of the morning, and I mainly serve up coffees and simple snacks like the pastries and toast to take away. Sometimes I get parents in early doors as well – the ones with little kids who think the most fun thing in the whole wide world is to wake up and demand cheerful activity at the crack of dawn. I remember those days myself, and always make sure their coffee stays topped up while their brain tries to catch up with their body.

I don't get any bedraggled mums and dads this morning, though, and the first rush-hour is over by nine. It has consisted of five customers, all of whom arrived at different times. Not exactly stressful, or indeed much of a rush. I know I'll get a fresh wave in at about ten, so I do what I normally do and use the quiet time to get a head start on lunch prep.

I do exactly the same thing pretty much every day. It is a tried and tested routine that I could probably perform in my sleep. Today, though, as I make sandwiches and pasta salad and put the jacket spuds in the machine for later, I find that everything feels a little bit more fun. Even the things that go wrong can't bring me down.

I laugh in the face of the exploding mayonnaise bottle. I pour scorn over the smoked salmon that slithers out of my hands. I mock the macarons that crumble as I try to arrange them in colourful pairs. None of it has a chance of affecting my mood today, because I am walking on sunshine. In fact I'm walking on sunshine with a rainbow over my head.

I even maintain my good cheer when Sam turns up for work half an hour late. I had kind of expected it, given the previous night's events, and luckily we're not too swamped by the time he staggers in looking slightly the worse for wear by his usual standards. His usual standards are very high, though, so that's okay.

"I'm so sorry, Connie!" he says when he arrives, whipping on his Cove Café apron and immediately starting to stack the dishwasher. "I'd try and come up with an elaborate excuse, but I don't think there's much point as you know exactly where I was last night. I can only apologise and blame the callousness of youth. Plus some exceptionally strong scrumpy. Did the girls make it home okay?"

"They did, and don't worry, Sam – I'll let you off. Can you clear some tables if I finish this?"

He nods and heads out into the main room of the café. I smile as I watch him wander off, gathering plates and trays and chatting to customers as he goes. He's a natural with people, is Sam – even if he has no interest whatsoever in hospitality, he'd be brilliant at it. I wonder if he'll end up with a glittering show-business career instead if his *Charity Shop Challenge* idea takes off.

Thinking about that, of course, makes me start thinking about Zack. I've been quite careful all morning not to allow myself to think about him – I have enjoyed the sensation of feeling floaty and excited, and have most definitely had a smile on my face. But I haven't as yet gone down the route of considering when I will see him next, and what will happen then, and how absolutely mindblowing it might be if last night's taster menu was anything to go by. I am at work, and it would just be plain rude. Nobody should look that excited over a tuna mayo sub.

Now, though, as I serve the last lunch order and see that Sam has everything under control, I nip into the kitchens for a quick break. I get out my phone and feel a silly little flutter of disappointment when there are no messages from him. It's silly for a couple of reasons – first of all, because I'm not a sixteen-year-old girl. Secondly, because the wifi and phone reception in Starshine Cove are notoriously poor, and he could have sent fifty messages without any of them even landing.

I consider sending one of my own, but both of the above reasons still hold firm, and I don't bother. I'll be done here at about four, and I'm sure I'll see him then – Starshine isn't big enough for anybody to hide in, that's for sure.

We get a busy spell after that, which is probably a good thing. We sell out of my pea and mint soup, and the smoked salmon and asparagus quiche flies from the shelves. The Black Forest gateau is mere rubble by the end, along with the carrot cake and half the raspberry pavlova. The coffee machine works overtime, and the drinks fridge is looking pretty sad by the time we wave goodbye to our last customer of the day.

As Sam turns the door sign to closed, we both breathe a sigh of relief before we begin the tidy-up routine. This is the least fun part of my working life, but I know it has to be done or I'll regret it tomorrow. I clear and wipe and wash, and do the food safety checklist I was teaching Marcy and Sophie not so long ago.

I help Sam restock the fridge, and get some toffee fudge cheesecake out of the freezer ready for tomorrow. I chat to Sam as I work, but my mind isn't really on our conversation, or on the jobs that I am doing. My mind is very much elsewhere, and mid-way through passing Sam some cloudy lemonade bottles, I decide that enough is enough.

"Stick these in and we're done," I announce, standing up and stretching my back. I might be feeling a little giddy today, but my back is still fifty-five years old.

"Are you sure? What about the Cokes?"

"I'll do it first thing tomorrow. Nobody asks for a chilled Coke in the morning, it'll be fine. I've had enough for one day. Jog on, sunshine – go and have fun!"

"Aye aye, captain," he says, giving me a little salute. "Lilly and Meg will be out of school by now. Might go and see if they fancy a trip to McDonald's with me."

"Is there even a remote chance that they won't?"

"Based on previous evidence, it seems highly unlikely. Their collection of Happy Meal toys has got much bigger since I moved in. What are you up to tonight?"

"That'd be telling," I reply, raising my eyebrows in an attempt to be mysterious.

"Ooh-la-la," he says, fanning his face with his hands. "Sounds interesting! See you same time tomorrow?"

"No, actually, Sam – see you at the right time tomorrow!"

"Absolutely. Scout's honour."

Once he leaves, I head off to the ladies', where I keep a little emergency spruce-up kit in a cupboard, glamorously located next to the spare loo roll. I spray on a bit of deodorant, then run a brush through my hair before I hoist it up with combs at the sides. I still have a sparkle in my eyes when I look in the mirror, and give my curls a little *zhuzh* as well.

"Okay," I say out loud to myself. "What now, gorgeous?"

It's a good question, and not one I have an immediate answer for. Things were a little chaotic last night, and neither Zack nor I actually made any definite arrangements for when and where we would see each other again. It was left loose, and now I'm a bit at a loss as to where to head next. After a normal working day, I usually pick one of three options – I go straight home, I go to see George or Ella, or I go to the pub.

Today, I should really go home. If I go home, I'll be able to check in on Marcy and Sophie, and make sure Dan survived his night of barn-surfing. I could also call at Miranda's on the way, and see if James is there. Yes, that would most definitely be the most sensible option.

Obviously, having considered all the angles, I grab my bag, switch off the lights, and head straight for the Starshine Inn. Being sensible has never exactly been my strong suit.

It's a beautiful day now, the air crisp and fresh in that way it can be after a storm, as though the wind and the rain have blown everything clean. The sky is still a vibrant blue, and the sun is casting a golden glow over the cottages that line the green. I wave to Trevor as I walk past his Emporium, and smile as I pass the Bettys' home next to their bakery. They're addicted to uber-violent movies about Navy SEALs or the SAS, and I hear the merry sound of a sub-machine gun blasting out from their TV as I walk by. Everyone's happy place looks different, I guess.

I take a deep breath as I pause outside the door to the inn, realising that I am feeling a delicious blend of nerves and excitement. I am jittery, like my insides are skittering around. Classic butterflies in my tummy, I suppose. I have no idea why – I am simply about to do a completely normal thing and pop into my local. There is usually someone in here who I know, and if not, I can always sit at the bar and chat to Jake if he's working, or his bartender Matt if he's not.

This is not a big deal, I tell myself, as I push open the door. This is all totally one hundred per cent normal. I just wish my body was listening.

The place is busy but not full, and I spy a few familiar faces as well as a group of walkers tucking into pints of ale and plates of sandwiches. Starshine is on a popular coastal walking path, and more people seem to find us through hiking than driving. The jukebox is playing *It's Raining Men* by The Weather Girls, which of course is a bit like *Walking on Sunshine* – impossible to not sing along to.

I see Jake behind the bar and he gives me a wave as he serves a young couple with an adorable Springer Spaniel. I wave back, and glance around the place with a bit more scrutiny. I let my eyes roam over the little alcove seats, and the tiny side rooms with only one table in each. Not that I'm searching for anyone in particular, of course.

Once Jake has finished, I wander to the bar and perch myself on one of the high stools. I'm so short that my feet dangle and swing, which always makes me feel like I'm at school.

"What can I get you?" asks Jake, smiling as he joins me.

"Oh, I don't know... what do you think?"

"Well, what kind of a day have you had?"

"Busy but fizzy."

"Ah. Right. Well in that case, maybe a nice sparkling rosé? How does that sound?"

"Like heaven. How's Kitty?"

His already handsome face breaks out into a doting smile that makes him even more attractive. Wowzers.

"She's fabulous! Not only did she sleep through last night, but this morning she rolled over all by herself!"

He couldn't look prouder if his daughter had won a Nobel Peace Prize, and his happiness is so infectious it makes me grin.

"Amazing. She'll be up and about before you know it, and then you'll be in trouble."

He pauses midway through pouring my drink and frowns. He's obviously turning that idea over in his mind, and shakes his head as he says: "I know. We really need to sort our living arrangements out... I'm not sure a pub is the right place for a baby."

"I shouldn't worry too much. A pub is a fine place for a baby. Just make sure she's not living in a pub when she's fifteen."

Jake nods, passes me my drink, and predictably enough refuses to take any money from me. We all kind of operate on a barter system here, and I can't remember the last time I charged Ella for her coffee either.

I sip my drink, revelling in the slightly decadent sensation of doing a tiny bit of boozing in the afternoon, and find myself staring in the direction of the stairs that lead up to the guest rooms. Maybe he's up there, I think. Maybe I should just take my drink back through with me, and go and knock on his door. That could be a lot of fun, and I'm very much in the mood for fun.

Jake notices me looking, and I have a brief moment where I

panic in case he's read my mind. Not that it would matter – we're both single. We're both adults. We're both very much consenting. There's nothing to be ashamed of, I know, but I'd still like to keep things as discreet as possible for the time being. Apart from anything else, our children might die of embarrassment if they found out.

He nods towards the stairs and says: "It's a shame he had to leave early, isn't it?"

I stare at him, wondering if I've been so distracted that I missed a conversational shift. Have we moved on from Kitty to something completely different?

"Sorry?" I reply. "What?"

"Zack," he explains, frowning slightly as he looks at me. "He left a couple of hours ago. Checked out early, saying there was something he had to deal with at work."

I blink several times in a row, and feel the world freeze around me. The sound from the jukebox fades into the background, almost as though someone has turned the sound down, and the noise of people chatting becomes a dull buzzing drone. I stare at Jake some more, and put my glass down on the counter.

"Oh," I say, aiming for nonchalant but not at all sure I'm hitting the mark. "Right. He's gone, has he?"

"Yep. Some kind of emergency he had to deal with at the office, he said. Connie, are you okay?"

The concern in his voice helps to snap me out of my reverie, at least long enough to pull myself together for a few seconds.

"All good, Jake, thanks. Just tired. Like I said, a busy day."

He nods, but I can tell he's not convinced. He'll probably be yet another person reporting in on my emotional state to Ella. Luckily, one of the walkers arrives at the bar to order another round, which distracts him and gives me some much-needed space.

I take some deep breaths, and try to blink the confusion out of my eyes. Everything feels unreal and hyper-vivid, but at the same time blurred and out of focus.

Zack has gone. He has left Starshine. He has presumably driven back to London with Bear, without any explanation and any attempt at saying goodbye. I know that messages aren't reliable here, but I've been in the café all day long – not exactly hard to find. If there was really a work emergency – and it's hard to imagine that there was anything that couldn't be sorted out on the phone – then there was no reason at all that he couldn't simply call in and tell me.

I sip my rosé, my hands so shaky the liquid sloshes over the side of the glass, and revisit the way we'd left it the night before. We'd kissed on the doorstep after the girls had gone to bed. He'd asked if we'd see each other tomorrow, and I'd said yes, definitely – that it was 'to be continued'. He seemed happy, eager, as pleased with the situation as I was. At least that's how I interpreted it – could I be misremembering? Did I just hear what I wanted to hear? Have I rewritten the whole thing in my mind? I feel so uncertain that I think possibly I did. Because if I didn't, then that makes his sudden disappearing act a callous and cruel way to behave, doesn't it?

I feel tears stinging the back of my eyes and swipe them away. I am half angry and half sad, which is always a lethal combination for me when it comes to crying. I'm sad that I misjudged him – that I took him as a decent guy – and I'm angry that he's been so disrespectful. Even if he'd changed his mind, even if in the cold light of day he decided it wasn't such a good idea, then I thought our friendship was strong enough that he would discuss it with me face to face, not just run away, leaving me feeling like this. Like an idiot.

I put my glass down again. It's probably not a great idea to start drinking right now. Because added into the sad and the angry there is also a sprinkling of self-loathing – a little voice inside my own head saying: "I told you so." Telling me I've been foolish to assume a man like him would be interested in a 'to be continued' with a woman like me. Telling me I'm a terrible judge of character. Telling me I was a fool to let myself get so carried away by something that he clearly saw as a mistake. I've been walking on sunshine all day after what happened between us, whereas he obviously woke up with so many regrets he left the county. Way to go, Connie – still got the magic touch.

I wave goodbye to Jake, and head outside. As I stroll around the green and back towards home, I can't quite believe the change in mood – how different I feel walking in this direction to how I felt walking towards the inn only minutes earlier. I know I'm being stupid – I know I'm a grown-up and I'm tough enough to handle a little rejection – but I can't help it. I feel deflated and down and a teensy bit humiliated. Nobody knows anything about it all other than me and him, so there's no call for the humiliation – it's still there, though, niggling away at me. I decide I will delete the dating app as soon as I have time. I suspect I was right all along – this dating business is not for me. I will go back to my nice, quiet, boring life, because at least it was safe.

I open the door, and pause in the kitchen for a moment. I can hear a racket coming from upstairs, which tells me that Dan is playing one of his shoot 'em up video games, and the sound of the television in the living room, which tells me the girls are probably here too. I put my game face on, and remind myself to smile before I walk in to greet them.

"Greetings, earthlings!" I announce as I enter.

They both look up from their spots on the sofa, and Sophie replies: "Mum! We're watching *Bridgerton* – want to join us?"

"Maybe later. Do you want dinner?"

I really, really hope they want dinner. I might have been doing it all day, but I feel like cooking. It will distract me, and comfort me, and it is something I know I am actually good at – unlike interacting with members of the opposite sex, it seems.

"Nah, thanks, Mum – we've already eaten. Zack left a note for you, it's on the kitchen table."

Sophie says this with complete indifference, and why wouldn't she? She doesn't know that just last night, Zack and I were on that sofa snogging each other's faces off. She doesn't know that I've spent the whole day looking forward to doing it again. She doesn't know that my heart has sunk so low it's somewhere around my ankles right now.

"Oh, right. He's left, I believe?" I say, oh-so-casually. Part of me hopes I'm wrong. That Jake was wrong. That it's all been some kind of misunderstanding.

"He has," Marcy replies, tearing her eyes away from yet another stunning Regency ball, "he said he had to go in to work. He's always doing that."

"I thought he was supposed to drive you two to the airport the day after tomorrow?"

"He was, but he didn't think he'd be able to get back here so soon, so he transferred me some cash so we could get an Uber."

An Uber, I think, almost laughing. She'll be lucky. Maybe Ged will give them a ride on his tractor.

Both girls turn back to the screen, and I suppose I am grateful that they seem so unconcerned. They definitely don't have a clue that anything has gone awry.

I head back into the kitchen, taking solace from its familiar sights and smells. The pots and pans hanging from the ceiling. The crammed surface of the island. The little notepad I always keep at hand to jot down recipe ideas in. This is my turf, my terrain, and I am safe here. I almost convince myself that I am completely fine, that I am simply over-reacting and that I will be perfectly okay as soon as I've had a chance to recalibrate. I'll probably even laugh at it some time very soon, this minor disappointment.

I pick up the envelope from the table, and see that my hands are still shaking. I'm not sure I even want to read what's inside.

I'd quite like to simply throw it in the bin, or maybe even set it on fire. I remind myself again that I am a grown-up, and that this note might explain all. It might be a full and wonderfully acceptable reason for him running away without even bothering to say goodbye.

Inside the envelope I find a postcard that shows a picture of the beach, the words *Hello from Starshine Cove!* emblazoned above the shining blue sea. He must have bought it from Trevor's Emporium; he has racks of them outside the shop every day. So, I think, frowning and feeling the angry part of me rise up again, he had time amidst his alleged emergency to go to the store, buy a postcard, write me a message and come to my house to deliver it – but not to call in at the café and actually talk to me in person? Am I that repulsive? Was seeing me again such a horrendous prospect?

I flip the postcard over, and see his loopy handwriting scrawled across the back of it.

Connie, I'm so sorry, it says, *but I have to leave. This isn't the right time for any of this. You're fantastic, and I promise it's not you, it's me. Corny but also true. Forgive me – Zack.*

I sit down at the dining table and lay the postcard flat before me. I have no clue what to make of it, other than he's right. It is corny. And I am fantastic.

I sigh, feeling about a hundred years old. I glance at the fridge, and see that picture of Simon. The one where he's wearing the Mickey Mouse ears. It almost feels like his brilliant blue eyes are staring out at me for real. Like he could step out of the picture and into my arms any second.

I smile at him, and allow myself the luxury of letting my tears flow.

FOURTEEN

The next week passes on autopilot. Sophie and Marcy successfully make it to Crete, where they are having a wonderful time lounging on inflatable flamingos in their swimming pool and sipping cocktails beneath the stars. James and Miranda have gone on a little trip to Cornwall with baby Evan, making the most of their time together before James heads back to Jersey. Dan is in Surrey, visiting his film student girlfriend, Julia. Basically, they're all busy and I'm on my own again.

I have made a little deal with myself not to care about that – not to sink into a blue mood, or let it get me down. My children are all healthy, happy and moving on with their lives, which makes me far luckier than some. It is the way it is meant to be, and all is right with the world.

I have been keeping myself as busy as possible, helping Ella organise the annual breast screening van visit, sorting out a programme of activities for the next few months in the community centre, and signing up to help Archie and Rose with their fruit and veg delivery project. I've taken George out for dinner, painted my downstairs loo a nice shade of blush, and made a head start on the menu for the Summer Feast event. I've also opened the café every single day, and kept it open until six instead of three. Sam's been delighted with the extra hours.

All of this frantic activity has gone some way towards keeping me out of trouble, and has certainly been very effective at making me tired. The days have passed relatively easily in a blur of busy-ness. The nights, though, as ever, have been a different matter. I try to ban Zack from my mind, to pull up the mental drawbridge as soon as I think about him – to hold up a giant "Stop!" sign whenever he starts to creep in there. I try, but I don't always manage. Sitting on the sofa watching TV in particular makes me sad, which is utterly pathetic. He was here for less than a fortnight, and I have no right to miss him, especially when he behaved like he did.

Despite the surface reassurance of the words on the postcard, I still feel hurt and disappointed that he didn't say goodbye in person. Sexy fun times aside, I genuinely thought we had become friends. I have considered calling him, but my final shred of self respect always stops me as my fingers hover above his name in my contacts. He is obviously fine, or Marcy would have mentioned something. He is back in his real life, and I am here in mine, and never the twain shall meet. I suppose I'll get used to it again.

Tonight, I decide to do a spot of spring cleaning in the kitchen. This seems to involve taking every single item I own out of a cupboard, and piling it somewhere on the floor, the counter or the table. It starts well enough, and I rediscover a really nice marble pestle and mortar I'd forgotten existed. I also find out that I own four colanders, way too many saucepans, and approximately seventeen thousand slotted spoons.

I try to sort the piles out ready to get rid of some. We have an event here every year called the Spring Greening, where we all set up trestle tables and arrange our unwanted stuff on them. Essentially it's like a giant swap shop. The idea is to declutter, but I usually end up coming home with more crap than I got rid of. Sometimes, as was the case with my lovely singing fish, I get rid of things one year, miss them, and get them back the next. I am never going to be a minimalist.

By the time a knock comes at the door, I am sitting on the parquet surrounded by pots, pans, mismatched lids, serving plates, cheese graters, Kilner jars, casserole dishes and baking trays.

"Come in!" I yell. "I can't let you in, I'm trapped!"

It's just after eight in the evening, which is a little late for house callers in Starshine Cove, but I assume it's someone I know and not an axe murderer. They only hang out on dating apps after all.

The door opens, and Ella makes her way through the hall and towards me. She's carrying a bottle of wine, and stops dead in her tracks when she sees me. Her little dog Larry trails behind her, and jumps over a forlorn toastie maker to come and lick my face.

"Oh," she says, stepping carefully over a teetering pile of tea towels. "What happened? Was there an explosion?"

"No. My kitchen is trying to eat me. It started as a spring clean but it's all taken a very dark turn. I see you come bearing gifts."

"I do indeed. I realised I haven't seen you on your own for ages. Plus Kitty is teething and I really wanted to get out for an hour."

I push some of the pans away, and she holds out her hands to help me up. I pick a careful path through the detritus, knowing that I need to sort it all out at some point but also knowing that I won't be doing it tonight.

Instead, I grab two glasses, and Ella and I decamp to the living room, where she pours us both a generous glug of something red and fruity that most definitely isn't Ribena. I bring a tin of home-made macadamia nut and white chocolate cookies with me, just in case either of us is at risk of starvation.

"So," she says, kicking off her trainers and curling her legs up beneath her on the sofa, "how are you?"

"I'm great. Apart from the messy kitchen."

"You're lying."

"No I'm not. The kitchen really is messy."

She sighs, and shakes her head. I suspect she is a little bit exasperated with me.

"Connie, you know how when I first arrived here, you grilled me at every possible opportunity? And eventually you broke me down and turned me into a blubbering wreck who discusses her *feelings* all the time?"

"You're welcome," I say, raising my glass.

"Well, how come you expect everyone else to do that, but you won't talk about your own feelings at all?"

I take my time swallowing the wine, and try to come up with an acceptable answer. I completely fail, and end up just shrugging. "Not sure. Maybe I've just got huge double standards? Or maybe I don't have any feelings worth discussing at the moment?"

"That's not true. I know you're unhappy. And I know you've been like that since Zack left. Why won't you admit it?"

"Because, my darling friend, I don't want to. If I admit it, I make it real. Whereas if I ignore it all for long enough, I'm pretty sure it'll go away."

She picks a cookie up out of the tin, and throws it at me. It bounces off my head and lands in a crumby mass on the sofa cushions.

"That's not healthy, Connie – and I'm a doctor. I know about these things."

"Right. So what do you prescribe then, Dr Farrell?"

"Drinking this wine, and telling me what's going on. You've been working all hours, running yourself ragged, and I've never seen you so down."

"Oh. That's disappointing. I thought I'd fooled everyone."

"You might have fooled people who don't know you that well, but not me. Or Archie, or George – we're all a bit worried."

I hate the idea that the people closest to me – the people I love – are fretting about my emotional state. I hate being a worry to anyone, or imagining that I'm upsetting them.

"I'm sorry," I say quietly, for once all out of jokey comments.

"Don't be sorry, Connie – just be honest. Talk to me."

I pause for a few moments, pretending to be chewing a cookie. No, actually, I am chewing a cookie – but I don't even taste it. It's just a way to stall for time. I am scared of opening up to Ella. I am scared of being honest with her, and honest with myself. I am scared that if I open those floodgates, I will be washed away in a river of tears. Larry jumps up onto my lap and curls up in a ball, which definitely helps.

"I miss him," I say simply. Best to start with the easy stuff I suppose.

"I can imagine. You spent a lot of time together. You were friends."

I nod, and force myself to meet her eyes. She takes in my expression, and adds: "Ah. I see. You were more than friends?"

I nod miserably. This whole talking about your feelings business is so much harder from the other side.

"So why did he leave? You seemed to get on so well!"

"I know. I thought so too. But it's not just that he left, Ella, it's that he didn't even say goodbye. We'd arranged to see each other the next day so we could continue being... more than friends... and I never saw him again. He just left, without a word. Left me a lame note saying he was sorry but he had to go."

She takes this in, and I see her turning over the words in her mind. Ella is a logical and fair person. She will try and see it all from both sides before she responds.

"Well. That makes him a complete prick in my opinion."

Oh. Maybe not. I laugh out loud, because that pronouncement is very much not what I expected.

"Yes! It does, doesn't it? I mean, he could have popped into the café, couldn't he? It wouldn't have killed him! It's just that I was so looking forward to seeing him again, and then I felt like such a fool when I realised he'd run away. It's not nice, getting all hot and heavy with a guy one night, and him doing a runner the next morning. Not good for the ego, that's for sure."

"Well, he's not only a prick, he's rude. And an idiot. And I'm sorry. I'm sorry that happened – you don't deserve it. Did he give you the impression that he was, you know, into you?"

I suppress a smile at her rom-com turn of phrase, and answer: "Ella, I don't mean to be crude…"

"Why spoil the habit of a lifetime?"

"Fair enough. Okay, to be crude – yes, he was into me. It's been a long time since I've been intimate with a man, but I still recognise the signs. Some of them are really pretty hard to ignore – especially when you're sitting on them."

It's her turn to laugh now, and I realise that I am feeling a little better. A problem laughed at is a problem halved.

"And now I miss him. But I'm also upset with him. I'm going from angry to hurt to sad, all in the space of five minutes. Is this menopause again?"

"Maybe. But I think it's also a symptom of being a woman who is suffering from a bad case of the Three Ls. You remember those, don't you? I seem to remember you diagnosed me with them almost two years ago…"

I stare at her and pull an 'as if' face. The Three Ls are sacred. The Three Ls that Ella was very much suffering from were Love, Lust and Like, all for the man who is now her husband and the father of her child. The Three Ls are often found singly or in pairs, but rarely found together.

"I don't think so, Ella. I mean, I barely know him really… I know I first met him decades ago, but it's only really been weeks in the real world."

"Except you do know him. Except time has nothing to do with these things, does it? The Three Ls have a mind of their own. They don't care how long you've known someone, or what you *should* be feeling, or why it could all be a terrible mistake to feel anything at all... they just exist. And they aren't often wrong."

I examine what she's saying a bit more closely, determined to decide that there is no possible way it could be true. Yes, I like Zack. Yes, I lust after Zack – I was doing that even before our night of curtailed passion. But love? Isn't that a bit too dramatic? Isn't that a bit too big for what this is? I'm still half convinced that if I ignore it, it will all go away.

"Look," Ella continues, "I didn't know you when Simon was around. But the way you seemed when you were with Zack... well, you were happy, Connie. And not just in your normal way. You seemed happy in a way I've never seen you. I know you're probably struggling acknowledging that final L exists, but at least consider it."

"I'm fifty-five, Ella – not fifteen! I'm way too old to fall in love – I was lucky to have that once, and I've never expected to have it again!"

"Fifty-five is young these days. You'll be here till you're at least a hundred. You're barely halfway through, Connie – are you sure you want to give up on that last L for the rest of your life? Isn't that why you went on your dates?"

I nod, because I can't deny it. Against my better judgement, almost, I have allowed that part of myself to open up again – I'd allowed myself to hope, I'd allowed myself to move on, even though I felt guilty for doing so.

"But look how it all turned out, Ella! Two failed dates, and then a spectacular rejection from Zack – the only man who I've really been interested in for years. The only man who triggered even two of the Ls, never mind the third... he walked out, without even explaining why."

"That must hurt, and I know you said you're angry. Would you feel better if you had a proper explanation?"

"Yes, I would – because anything's better than 'it's not you it's me', isn't it?"

She cringes and nods.

"It really is. So, then, Connie – I suppose the next thing to figure out is, what are you going to do about it?"

"What do you mean?"

"I mean, ask yourself your usual question – what would Dolly do?"

I'm not at all sure what Dolly would do. It's pretty hard to imagine a man dumping Dolly in the first place, never mind how she'd react to it. I drink some more wine, and think it over.

I might not know what Dolly would do, I decide – but I do know she wouldn't sit around feeling sorry for herself. And neither will I.

FIFTEEN

I call Zack as soon as Ella leaves. I have had wine, and I have had a pep talk, and I have definitely had enough of my pity party. If I'm so keen to point out that I'm a grown woman, why aren't I acting like one? Zack has hurt me. He has behaved badly. I am still suffering because of it, and that's not fair. Ella is right, I would feel better if I had an explanation – and it's up to me to get one. I deserve that much at least.

This is all rather fabulous motivation, but doesn't help at all when there is no answer. I'm so geared up to talk to him that when I hear his voicemail message instead, I immediately crumble and hang up. Then I fret about the fact that I've hung up, and call straight back and simply say: "It's Connie. Please call me."

He doesn't call me, and I can live with that – it's late, and he might already be asleep. Or, of course, he might be out living it up at a glittering showbusiness party, or on a date with a retired supermodel who now runs her own successful eco-friendly pet portrait business. This is the kind of woman I fully expect Zack to be with, and the fact that he seemed interested in me at all could very well have been a glitch that he now regrets. But if it is, why not just be honest? Why run like that? Why leave me hanging?

It's all very difficult to figure out, and when he still hasn't returned my call by lunchtime the next day, I feel exhausted by it. I make loads of mistakes at the café, to the extent that Sam is giving me some seriously concerned side-eye, and as soon as it's quiet I close up.

"Are you all right, boss-lady?" he asks as we finish cleaning. He's a baby, but I seem to have reverted to being a teenager, so maybe I should get his view on it all.

"I'm not sure, Sam. How would you react if you met someone, really liked him, he seemed to really like you, things got steamy, and then he just left without speaking to you? And then never called you, and didn't return your calls either?"

"Ouch," he says, hands on hips and eyes narrowed. "You've been ghosted?"

"Not necessarily. I could be asking for a friend."

"Of course you could. Well, I suppose the obvious answer is to say, 'Screw him, his loss' and draw a line under it. Give the whole situation the emotional finger. But personally I think it depends on a few things, things they should consider before they just throw it all away. Like how much your friend likes this person – because if he, she or they really like him, then it's worth the extra effort isn't it? It's worth a bit of angst to get to the bottom of it? Could there be a good reason he's ghosting you? Has he previously seemed like the kind of person who would treat you like that?"

"You mean my friend? And no. He hadn't seemed like that kind of person. And I suppose there could be a good reason, but the silence is overwhelming, and doesn't help to explain anything. Maybe he's just not that into my friend."

Sam, who is very tall, leans all the way down to give me a little kiss on the cheek.

"I'd say he's an idiot then, because your friend is *hot*. And also super cool. Don't let it get you down, okay? Don't let somebody else's bad behaviour affect the way you see yourself."

"Wow. That's excellent advice. I shall pass that on."

He winks at me and saunters out onto the green. I make myself a hot chocolate with all the extras, and take it out onto the terrace at the back of the café. The spectacular view down to the bay works its magic, and the squirty cream and marshmallows help too.

I gaze at the infinity of beauty before me, and let the sound of the waves rolling onto the sand soothe my soul. Maybe Sam's right, and this whole thing is worth some angst. I am questioning my own judgement now, going over and over events and replaying the things that were said, the things that were done. The things that were felt. It's like I have a rewind button in my brain and can't stop using it.

I veer between feeling sure that what we had was real, and feeling like I'm the world's biggest idiot for even considering that option. It's like I'm hitching a ride on a giant emotional yo-yo, and I absolutely hate it.

I pick up my phone, and shockingly see that there are no calls. The little bars that show how much signal you have are pretty non-existent out here, so I go back inside and use the good old-fashioned landline. His number rings out, and then my heart leaps as it's actually answered – just as I have my message ready for voicemail. Damn. I'll never get the hang of this.

"Hello?" he says, in that uncertain tone we all use when answering a call from an unknown number. He obviously doesn't have the landline saved in his contacts, and maybe that's the only reason he picked up – he didn't know it was me.

"Zack, it's Connie – surprise!"

I am greeted with silence apart from background noise – the sound of other people talking, of a TV in the background, a random beeping noise I can't quite identify. All kinds of sounds, none of them the sound of Zack's voice. He finally speaks.

"Connie. Um... I can't really talk right now. Could I call you back?"

"No. Because you won't, will you? Look, Zack, I don't want to be some kind of bunny-boiler here, but I think I deserve a bit more than your note, don't you? I get that you changed your mind. I get that you didn't want to take things any further between us. All of that is fine, but the way you left it? That's not fine."

I hear someone shouting a name in the background, and realise he's in some kind of waiting room. Maybe he's getting his nails done. I also realise that I am crying as I talk. They're those tears that come when you're not just sad, but angry as well. The kind that seem to curse women of all ages, turning us from articulate and intelligent creatures into soggy disaster zones that nobody can take seriously.

"I'm sorry," he says simply, sounding deeply uncomfortable. "And it's not that I didn't want to take things any further... I just didn't think it was a good idea, for you."

"For me? What do you mean? And since when did you turn into my dad and get to make my decisions for me?"

"Look, it's complicated, okay, and you'll have to take my word for it – you don't want anything to do with me. I've got to go now."

And just like that, he hangs up. I stare at the phone for a few moments, listening to the humming noise that tells me the line is dead, and swipe at my face. I'm annoyed that I'm crying. I'm annoyed at myself, I'm annoyed at him, I'm annoyed at the universe.

I close up the café and stride over the green towards Archie and Cally's cottage. I knock and go in as soon as Cally shouts a greeting. Meg and Lilly run over to me, ginger plaits bouncing, and I scoop them in for a hug. Lilly is almost as tall as me now, and she's only nine. She's going to be an amazon in a few years' time.

"Is Archie around?" I ask, once the girls have lost interest in me. "I need to blow off some steam."

"I'm around," he says, walking in from the kitchen bearing a packet of biscuits. "What kind of steam do you need to blow off? Long walk on the beach, six pints and a whinge, or something more aggressive?"

I can see that both Archie and Cally are looking at me with concern, and remember what Ella said about them all being worried about me. Zack hasn't just upset me, he's upset the people I love as well, damn him.

"More aggressive, definitely. I feel like punching something but I know I'd probably just hurt my own hands."

He ponders for a minute, then replies: "Okay. Log chopping it is. Follow me."

I do as I'm told, and half an hour later I'm exhausted, panting, and sweating. Archie had taken me out to the huge garden at the back of the cottage, given me an axe, and let me go at it. I discovered that I'm not very good at chopping logs – it's a lot trickier than it looks – but it serves its purpose. It was indeed very cathartic to swing an axe at innocent chunks of wood, plus Archie now has a full load of admittedly randomly shaped logs to use on the burner.

He pops his head around the kitchen door and makes the universal gesture for 'would you like a cuppa?' When it comes, I soon discover that it's not just a cuppa, it's a cuppa with a glug of brandy in it.

"You looked like you needed it," he says, sitting beside me on the bench and surveying my log kingdom. "Didn't want to offer until you'd finished chopping though. Never good to be drunk in charge of an axe. Feel better?"

"Yes. Thank you, for both. It really helped to use up some energy, you know?"

"I do. I'm a fan myself. Anything I can help with? Anything you want to talk about? If it's any use to you, Cally says she'll happily use the axe on a real person if they've hurt you."

I laugh and pat his hand. "I have no doubt she would! I'm okay. Just working some stuff out. I'm going to go home and bake now. That always helps."

"Excellent. I look forward to the end result."

I head back to my place, and before I can sit down and start feeling sad or angry again, I immediately get out my supplies and start to whip up an apple and rhubarb crumble. I love making a crumble. There's something very relaxing about using your fingers to rub together the butter and flour and in this case chopped almonds. I know it's quicker in the whizzer, but this is very much a hands-on exercise for me.

As I work, I turn over the conversation I had with Zack earlier. The way he spoke. The way he hung up on me before we'd even really been able to communicate. The way he shut me down, closed me out, disregarded me. That cryptic comment about how I don't want anything to do with him, which was arrogant as well as confusing. The distance in his voice, as though we'd never even been friends.

I don't deserve that. I really don't. And more to the point, I'm not going to accept it.

SIXTEEN

The very next day, I find myself back in London. Specifically, in fact, I find myself in Wimbledon. This time I came on the train, because I had the sneaking suspicion that whatever happens next, I might not be in a fit state to drive. I could be too emotional, or too distracted, or possibly so drunk I forget my own name. The journey to London took just over two and a half hours, and then onwards via the Tube.

I arrived here a little while ago, but called in to a coffee shop on the high street first. I needed a few moments to get my head together, and to give myself a final chance to chicken out. Part of me really, really wants to chicken out – to go running back home with my tail between my legs, and forget all about Zack Harris and the chaos he has brought into my formerly calm life.

I know, though, that if I do I won't like myself very much. I waited for a call back last night, but it never came. I consoled myself with a rather fine crumble, but it didn't take the pain away. I'm deeply unhappy with how things have gone, and I need to make those feelings understood. Face to face. Even if it's just a totally cringeworthy encounter where Zack looks horrified to see me and threatens to take out a restraining order, I need to do it. If I don't, then I'll struggle to move on.

I'm also aware that Marcy and Sophie are now BFFs, as the kids say, and there will probably be occasions in the future where Zack and I are in the same room. I really don't want to ruin my daughter's graduation ceremony by yelling at her pal's dad. We are adults, and we need to clear the air.

I've found out sneakily from Marcy that he's working from home, and plan to simply knock on his door and say 'hi'. I'll take it from there and see where we end up – my usual carefully crafted and perfectly sensible plan.

I pay the bill, leave a generous tip, and head purposefully down the road to Zack's place before I change my mind.

I don't see his car in the driveway, but there is a garage to the side so I don't read too much into it. I stride up the steps to the handsome front door, and ring the bell. There is no answer other than Bear's barking, and I gaze around in case it's one of those video bells with a little camera attached – maybe he's in there looking at the security feed, hiding from me under the kitchen table.

I give a sharp bang with the brass knocker, but there is still nothing but Bear woofing away.

"Sorry, boy!" I shout, and his bark at least subsides into a whine. Poor Bear – so near to a human he knows might have treats, and yet so far.

I'm not quite sure what to do now, and feel a bit deflated. I arrived here after a righteous march, pumped up on my own determination. I'd imagined many scenarios – him being furious, him sweeping me into his arms and kissing me, him telling me pityingly that it had all been a mistake and he'd quite like to never see me again. Somehow, though, I'd never quite imagined this far more mundane scenario – that he simply wouldn't be at home.

I take a sneaky glance through the front windows, still half suspecting that he might be in there somewhere, and then make an annoyed *hmmmph* noise and plonk my backside down on the front steps.

It's a pleasant afternoon, with a pale blue sky and enough sunshine to build up a bit of warmth on your skin when you face the right direction. The birds are singing in the trees that surround the house, and I spot an early bee buzzing around a pot of beautiful blue hyacinths. I will sit here a while, I think, and see what happens. I've sat in far worse places, and I have come a very long way after all.

I get out my phone, and make the most of the fantastic signal to browse random websites and send silly messages to all three of the kids. I'm content enough plugging my brain into the matrix for a while, and sit quite happily. Every now and then Bear gives me a little woof just to remind me that he's still there.

I've probably been waiting for almost thirty minutes when Zack's fancy grey Audi rolls slowly into the driveway, its wheels crunching on the gravel. I put my phone away and sit upright, suddenly feeling swamped with nerves now that he is actually here. It all seemed like a good idea until it was really happening, and I wonder if it's too late to sneak away without him noticing.

For a minute it looks like that might be a feasible option, because he is incredibly distracted. He stays seated behind the wheel for a few moments, staring into the distance with eyes that don't seem to be seeing anything, certainly not me. His hair is ruffled in the way it gets when he's been running his hands through it, and his usually golden skin tone is a shade more pallid. I know I've been angry with Zack, but my very first thought when I see him is: what's wrong?

I stand up, and as he climbs out of the car he freezes dead on the spot and stares at me. His green eyes go wide in surprise, and he does a double take, as though he can't believe what he's seeing. I don't suppose I can blame him for that.

"Connie?" he says quietly, shaking his head in confusion.

"In the flesh!" I reply, walking towards him. When I get closer I see that he looks tired, with dark circles beneath his eyes. I reach up, and stroke his face, keeping my hand on his cheekbone. He leans into my palm and sighs out loud, as though he's exhausted and ready for bed.

"Are you okay?" I ask gently. "Because you don't seem okay."

"I'm... getting there. This hallucination is certainly helping."

"Well, this hallucination is desperate for a pee – any chance of popping in to use the facilities?"

"I know the feeling – you take the upstairs, I'll take the downstairs! God, this is terrible, isn't it? This never happens in romantic movies, two geriatrics racing to the loo!"

He manages a smile as he opens the front door, and Bear comes hurtling to greet us. Zack gives him a quick pet and heads down the hallway, and I gallop up the stairs.

A few minutes later, we reconvene in the kitchen, where I find Zack putting the kettle on. He leans against the counter, and swipes his fingers across his eyes as though he's wiping sleep from them.

"I'm sorry," he says simply, meeting my gaze.

"Elaborate on that, please."

"I'm sorry I ran away like that. I'm sorry I didn't say goodbye. I'm sorry I didn't explain. I acted like a coward, and I've hated myself for it ever since. I've been on the verge of calling you ever since, but I've been too much of a wimp. You deserve better, on every level. In my defence I did try and call you back last night, on your landline number, but nobody answered."

I'm surprised at that, and wish I'd known – maybe I wouldn't have had such an awful night. But maybe I wouldn't have turned up like this either, and I think that needed to be done. It is also, as we both know, a bit of a cop-out.

"It was the café number, that's why. You could have tried

my mobile, couldn't you? Or emailed me, or sent a text? There are so many ways to get in touch with someone these days, and you didn't desperately try any of them..."

He shrugs and looks sad. "This is true. I suppose I was being a coward again, and I know you deserve an explanation."

"You're absolutely right, I do, that's why I'm here. I intended to give you a piece of my mind about the way you behaved, and now you've gone and taken the wind out of my sails by bloody apologising straight away!"

"Well, I apologise for that as well, then. Look... it's complicated. It's messy." He sighs and runs his hands through his hair in that way I'm now so familiar with. "I'm giving you the opportunity right now to walk out of the door, go back home, and never think about me again. You have your apology, and if that's enough, you'd probably be better off leaving."

I take two mugs from a stand, and start to make us both a coffee. He seems too exhausted to do it himself.

"Well, thank you for the offer, Zack, but now I've had my apology, I find that I want more. Like an explanation."

He nods, and gestures towards the garden.

"Shall we sit out? It's warm enough."

We head back to the table and chairs outside, and Bear gallivants behind us. He runs straight to a stone planter and cocks his leg against it. Looks like we weren't the only ones who needed the loo.

Once we're settled, Zack goes quiet again. The sun is glinting against the silver in his hair, and despite the fact that he's obviously not firing on all cylinders, I can't help but notice the way he fills out his navy blue sweater. He really is appallingly handsome – how am I supposed to stay annoyed with someone who makes me tingle like this?

When he shows no sign of speaking, I put my mug down and say: "You're clearly not feeling good, Zack – is there anything I can do to help? Can I get you anything? Do you want to talk about whatever it is that's affecting you?"

He shakes his head, and gives me a sweet smile that melts my heart. It's full on eye-contact, no shying away, intense and deeply personal. The kind of smile that somehow makes me feel like we are the only two people left in the entire world.

"I don't want to talk about it, no – but I know I should, and you're pretty much the only person I want to talk to anyway. A few months ago, I was diagnosed with something called chronic kidney disease, which pretty much does what it says on the tin. They grade it in stages, from one to five. One is minor, five is... well, let's just say there isn't a six. By the time I found out, I was a three."

The words immediately bury themselves in my brain and start to burrow around in there. Chronic kidney disease. I'm not precisely aware of what it is, but that combination cannot possibly be good. I feel my nostrils flare a little, but I hope that is the only sign of stress that I show. This is not the time to over-react. This is the time to listen.

"Okay. So, what does it mean, then? Longer term?"

"Well, that's an interesting question. I was at the clinic when you called yesterday, and in fact I've just come back from seeing my nephrologist at the hospital. The night we first met, in the restaurant, you remember I was glued to my phone?"

"I do. I assumed you were bidding on a rare porcelain tea pot on eBay."

"Ha! No, I was reading some emails I'd had about test results. Results that suggested my kidney function was declining. And then the day you were doing your practice run for the Spring Feast, and I turned up late?"

I nod, and he continues: "I'd been on the phone with the consultant to discuss it, and to make arrangements to see him again. Today, I found out that the news isn't great. I'm now officially stage four, which means I need to start really considering the future. Four isn't exactly a barrel-load of laughs. My back aches, I pee all the time, and I often feel sick. But if I'm lucky, things might stay like this for years – but they might not, and I was told I need to have a think about what comes next. About my options."

"And what are they?"

"Fun stuff, like dialysis or a kidney transplant. I'm also now at increased risk of stroke, heart attack and bone disorders. For most people with this condition, it won't get that serious. Only about one in fifty do go on to the nasty bit, apparently. I guess I'm just lucky."

I reach out and gently push his hair back from his face. He looks unbearably sad, and I can't stand it. I lean across the table and kiss him quickly but decisively on the lips. It seems like an effective way of reassuring him.

"And you haven't told anybody about this?" I ask, already knowing the answer. Suddenly, so many things fall into place – his constant naps, his lack of appetite. His plan to concentrate on the work he loved rather than the work he usually did. The comments he made about his fear of leaving the girls alone. I can only imagine how much that thought has tortured him since he was diagnosed, especially after losing his wife when his daughters were so young.

"No. I've been stupidly macho. I have been cutting down on work, because I've been told to reduce stress, but other than that I've just carried on as normal. I didn't want to worry the girls, and I'm just not close enough to anyone to tell them. Until I met you. I wanted to tell you, I really did – I'd just got too good at hiding it. At telling myself I'd be fine, no matter how tired I was. And then... then, Connie, I started to fall for you, and everything changed. I tried so hard not to – I even drove you to dates with other men, all the time secretly hoping that you'd hate them! I didn't expect any of that to happen... it really wasn't part of the plan."

I take his hand in mine, and squeeze his fingers. Despite the terrible circumstances, my heart is thumping a little faster at hearing that he was falling for me – because, of course, Ella was right all along. Being here with him, hearing this news, I can't deny it anymore. This is most definitely a triple L situation – for both of us, it seems. I should be rejoicing, and part of me is, but I know this is not anywhere near simple for either of us.

"I felt the same, Zack," I say. "And I had no clue at all what was going on in your mind, so congrats on being an Oscar-level actor. It wasn't part of my plan either, but I can't tell you how much I've missed you since you left. I felt terrible, mainly because I'd opened up to you and then it seemed like you'd rejected me."

"It wasn't that at all, Connie – I desperately wanted to stay. To be with you. To enjoy your company. To confide in you. Also, to be honest, to pick up where we left off on the canoodling front..."

"Canoodling? That's a fantastic way of putting it!"

"It is, isn't it?"

We both smile, and it feels good to share that moment of light-heartedness with him.

"So, why did you leave? If you didn't want to?"

"Well, I guess there were a couple of reasons. I have to admit I was scared. I've dated quite a few women in recent years, but none of them scared me before. Except maybe for Simone the yoga instructor, she was terrifying. But you... you were real. We were real. I could see myself staying with you, building a life with you. That was overwhelming, because I'm not entirely sure what my life is going to look like in the future. And I didn't want to do that to you."

"Do what to me?"

"I felt like there was a real connection between us, Connie. I could imagine us together in the same way I was together with

Rowena – heart and body and soul. Did you feel any of that, or am I imagining it?"

I shake my head. Of course he wasn't imagining it. I'd felt every one of those things, much as I'd tried to fight it. I'd fallen for Zack in exactly the same way, and can completely understand how scary it felt for him because it was the same for me. When he left in the sudden way he did, I was convinced that everything had been one-sided – that it was only me who was feeling like that. Hearing him say otherwise is making me feel giddy and excited and thrilled, but all of that is tempered by the fact that he still looks so very sad. This should feel like a happy exchange, and yet it doesn't.

"You weren't imagining it, Zack. I felt the same. I do feel the same. What I'm not quite sure about is why you didn't tell me. Why you left the way you did."

He nods and strokes my palms with his fingers, a delicate and intimate touch that almost undoes me.

"Fear. Not just fear about finally meeting a woman I could love after years of keeping my heart locked away – but fear about the future, and what effect it could have on you. I know what you went through when you lost Simon. I know because I went through the same. I couldn't bear the thought of us being together when the future is so uncertain. I couldn't bear the thought of you finally loving someone again, only to lose them again. It didn't feel fair. I hated the idea of us moving forward, only for you to end up with a man stuck in a sick bed – a burden. A man who might not even be around for long. It was too much to ask of you. I know I should have handled it differently, but I wasn't thinking straight. I'm so sorry."

He looks devastated, on the verge of tears, and I drag my chair round so we are next to each other. I pull him into my arms and stroke his hair, soothing him and consoling him. There is a lot to unpack here, a lot to think about. I'd be lying if I said he didn't have a good point – the way I feel about Zack has already shown me how hard I find being vulnerable. The thought of loving him, of being fully committed to him, and then losing him to sickness? I'm not going to assume that I can cope with that. I am not superhuman, and I know how much that loss hurts.

But for now, none of that matters – for now, the only thing I need to do is make him feel better. Give him the comfort he needs. Provide him with some respite, even if it's only for a night. Tomorrow, as they say, is another day.

I pull back from our hug, and look him in the eyes.

"It's okay, I forgive you. Forget about that now. I'm here, and I'm not going anywhere. You've been spending too much time alone, dealing with all of this. Human brains don't cope well with that kind of pressure. You need a break. So, here's the plan – you're going to go up to bed and have one of your famous world-class naps. I'm going to make us some dinner in your disgustingly tidy kitchen. Then we are going to talk about all of this, and you are going to be honest and open and share all the gory details."

He pulls a face and says: "Do I have to?"

"Yes. It's absolutely essential. But then, after our dinner, we will stop talking about it. If you have the energy, we will take Bear for a little walk, and then we will come back here. We will settle down on the sofa, and we will put blankets over our knees like the old people we almost are, and we will watch the telly. Because in our world, that is an exciting night."

He laughs, and I see some of the sparkle coming back into his eyes.

"Okay, boss. Sounds like a plan. But what will we watch?"

"Doh! We'll watch *Paddington 2*, obviously – have you not been paying attention?"

He nods, stands up and stretches his arms above his head. He seems to be feeling a bit better. Maybe it's me, or maybe it's the simple relief of finally telling someone, I don't know.

I stand up to join him, and he throws his arm around my shoulders. He drops a gentle kiss on top of my curls, and says: "And after the film? Will you be going home?"

I can tell that he is trying to keep his voice neutral. I suspect he doesn't want to put any pressure on me to stay. He must have spent countless nights alone in this house, trying to think his way through his situation. Zack is the kind of man who is used to being able to control things, to find solutions and fixes, and this must have been torture for him. A health problem like this would be a nightmare for any of us, but dealing with it all alone? So much worse.

"I won't be going home, no, Zack. I'm so sorry, but you're stuck with me for the night."

"What about the café?"

"What about it? The world isn't going to explode if I don't fire up the coffee machine in the morning. There won't be a day of national mourning if I'm not around to provide pain au chocolat to the citizens of Starshine Cove."

"I'm not so sure about that... but thank you. I can't tell you how much I appreciate it. The thought of another night staring at these walls and worrying was driving me mad."

"Well, no need for that now. I can drive you mad instead."

SEVENTEEN

I wake up the next morning in Zack's arms, my head on his chest and my hair spilling over his shoulders. I glance up and see that he is still asleep. He looks peaceful, slumbering deeply, and it makes me smile.

We had, as per the plan, eaten some dinner – a very simple prawn and garlic linguine as I was working with a limited range of ingredients – and he had told me everything. Apparently his dad had suffered from 'kidney problems', but nobody had ever discussed what it was in detail – which is pretty par for the course for men of his dad's generation, who would go to work in a coal mine with one arm missing and call it 'just a scratch'.

After that, we'd drawn a line under it, but I could see how much of a relief it was to get it off his chest. I suspect bottling everything up had made him feel so much worse. Perhaps because of that relief, sitting together and watching yet another silly-but-uplifting movie seemed to put him in an exceptionally good mood.

When it reached bedtime, he had offered me the spare room like a gentleman, and I had refused it like a complete hussy. I'm fed up with messing around – we've both said how we feel, so why should we pretend any longer? It hadn't been the sexiest of evenings, discussing things like blood tests and biopsies, but I for one need that physical closeness, and I suspect he does too.

Even though we slept in the same bed, we didn't actually do the deed. He was still physically worn out, and I was a little more anxious than I was allowing him to see. We cuddled, and enjoyed some rather delicious slow kisses, and basically confirmed what I've always suspected – that I absolutely fancy the arse off this man. He clearly feels the same, and our chemistry is off the scale. There will be plenty of time for us to explore that aspect of things, but right now everything feels fragile and delicate. Including me. Waking up in bed with a man isn't something I expected to do ever again.

I manage to slip out of his embrace without disturbing him, and gaze down at his sleeping form. His hair is splayed on the pillow, and the golden skin of his chest is stark against the white sheets. He is absolutely gorgeous, and part of me wants to jump straight back into bed and wake him up in the most saucy way imaginable.

But that wouldn't be right for all kinds of reasons, and instead I grab my things and go to get dressed. I hadn't brought an overnight bag with me, and slept in one of Zack's T-shirts. I keep it on, with the addition of a bra, because I am not of the age or physique where it's advisable to go without one unless I want to do myself an injury.

I like wearing his T-shirt, though. It smells of him, and makes me feel like I'm still in his arms. I realise that I am smiling as I make my way downstairs and get coffee on the go. He has a fancy pod machine and I treat myself to something sinfully chocolatey, sipping it while I root in the cupboards for food. All I find is some disgustingly healthy granola, its cardboard box screaming that it's sugar free. I might as well eat the box, I decide, putting it away.

Bear is now awake and following me around the kitchen. I

have no idea what his usual routine is, but I let him outside into the garden, and find some tins of food for him in the utility room. I give him a tin and a handful of mixer, and he wolfs it down in about twenty seconds. He stares up at me pleadingly, begging for more, but I am not fooled – I know he's on a diet.

"Sorry, boy," I say, patting his head. "I know how you feel. Shall we go out for walkies?"

Zack hadn't felt up to it the night before, so Bear looks insanely excited when I find his lead and hook him up. I get the house keys out of the little bowl on the table, and we are off out into the outside world. It's almost nine in the morning, which is very late for me, and I am childishly excited by what I see of morning life in the pretty London suburb. There are people everywhere, rows of shops and cafés, boutiques, galleries and restaurants. I know it's just a suburb, but compared to Starshine Cove it is a bustling metropolis.

Bear is obviously used to the route, and takes it all in his stride. A few people stop to stroke him and know him by name, giving me curious looks as they do. Even though it is London, there does seem to be a sense of community here that is warming. I grab some amazing-smelling pastries from a cute little bakery, and let Bear take me towards a big green space.

I let him off the lead for a gambol around, then find a wooden bench to sit on while I nibble on an apricot crown. He immediately zooms back to me and goes on alert at my feet, just in case I drop a crumb.

I gaze around, taking in the pretty surroundings, having no clue where I am. Maybe, I realise, I'm on Wimbledon Common – the place where the Wombles used to hang out in the old children's TV show. Seeing Great Uncle Bulgaria would be exciting.

I look behind me at the bushes, but see no signs of a Womble. I know I'm just letting my mind have a few silly moments before it gets down to business. I have a lot to think about. I have decisions to make. I have consequences to balance. I have so many thoughts running around in my mind that I can't quite grab hold of any of them. It's like herding cats on acid.

I take some deep breaths, and get out my phone. I need to talk to someone who knows more about this stuff. And someone who knows me.

I catch Ella at home at the inn, which has pretty much the best phone reception of any building in the village. This is one of her mornings off, though the sound of a wailing baby in the background when she answers implies it's possibly not that restful a morning off at all.

"Everything okay?" I ask straight away.

"Yes. No. Bah. Hold on a second..."

I hear the phone laid down, and some mooching movements in the background. After a few moments, she picks it up again and says: "Feeding time at the zoo. Bloody hell, this teething business isn't for the faint-hearted, is it... it's been very humbling, being an actual mother. All these years I've seen women for pregnancy problems, and helped with nappy rash and childhood ailments, and now I finally realise why they all seemed so strung out! Anyway. We are guaranteed a few minutes' peace and quiet now. How did it go? Where are you?"

"I think I'm on Wimbledon Common, but don't hold me to it."

"Oh. You spent the night, did you? I assume it went well then, you dirty stop-out!"

"Umm. Kind of. Ella, what do you know about chronic kidney disease?"

"Quite a lot. Why? Are you all right? What are your symptoms?"

I hear the change in her voice immediately, the switch from pal to professional.

"I don't have any – it's not me, it's Zack. He's sick, and that's why he left. He said he didn't want to burden me. He said he might decline, and he said he's not sure how long he's going to be around for."

My voice cracks slightly as I say this, and I think it is really hitting me for the first time. Yesterday, I kept it all tucked away inside me for his sake – it was very much all about him, because that's what he needed. Now, I am feeling the emotions sweeping over me – wondering how life could be so cruel as to show me that love is possible again, but then threaten to take it away again straight away. Tears spill from my eyes, and Bear whines a little at the sight of me being so upset.

"Oh. I see. Do you want me to be a friend right now, or a doctor?"

"Can't you be both?"

"Not at the same time. Let's do doctor first. Do you know what stage he's at?"

"He's just gone into stage four."

"Right. Well, that's not wonderful, but it's also not terrible. People can stay in stage four for years. Some never go any further. But you have to be realistic – sometimes they do. It can cause other serious health problems, and it can progress to stage five. That might mean dialysis, or a transplant. Neither of which is easy."

I nod, then realise she can't see me. I wipe the tears from my eyes and tell myself to hold my shit together.

"Yeah. That's what he said. He's scared, Ella, which you can understand, can't you? But I'm scared too... and I have no idea what to do here. He's told me he feels the same about me as I do about him."

"Full list of Ls on both sides?"

"Yes. And in normal circumstances, I'd be so happy this morning. But if I'm brutally honest, I have my concerns. I don't know if I can do it. I don't know if I can let myself fall in love with a man I might lose. I don't know if I'm strong enough to survive that again. Does that make me a terrible human being? Because it makes me feel like one!"

I hear baby Kitty squawking, and Ella comforting her. It feels like they are a million miles away.

"Connie, no – of course it doesn't make you a terrible human being! This has all come as a shock to you. You've only just found out, whereas he's had time to adjust. Don't be so hard on yourself. You're one of the kindest, most generous people I've ever met. Your heart is as big as the moon, and you always put others first. But that doesn't mean you get to ignore yourself, and your own feelings. If you have doubts, you need to consider them, because it wouldn't be fair to him or to you if you didn't. Look, if you took the CKD out of the equation, how would you see this working out?"

"I'm not sure," I say, scratching Bear behind the ears as I talk. "I mean, it's new. All new things come with complications, don't they? Like the fact that he lives in London and I live in Dorset. Like telling our kids. All of that stuff. But to be honest, I don't think I'd care about any of it... I love him, Ella, even though I kind of think that's ridiculous at my age. I love him so much it actually hurts to think of being away from him."

"Oh gosh," she replies, and I hear the emotional catch in her voice. This is rare for Ella. "That's... beautiful. It's exactly how I felt about Jake. And stop going on about your age, will you? So – he feels the same?"

"Yes, I think so. No, I know so. He does. I can see it in his eyes, hear it in his voice. Feel it in every touch. This is real."

"Real wins every time. Would he consider moving to Starshine, do you think, because I really can't see you in London... at least I hope not. I'd miss you."

I turn the concept over in my mind, wondering if I would be capable of another big life change. I mean, there's no real reason not to. My kids are grown enough to handle it. I could sell the café, or get someone to manage it. My finances are sound. I like this area of the city, could just about imagine a life here. Except... I'm not sure it's one I'd want. There would be no George, and no Archie, and no Ella. All of my friends would be so far away, and I'd miss the sea and the sand and the stunning countryside views. Starshine is a special place, and it has been my home for so long that it's hard to separate myself from it. We kind of come as a team.

"I don't know. But I think he'd like to stay in Starshine. He said as much last night – that he could imagine building a life with me there. Now, though, it all feels so big. What about his condition? What about his hospital and his doctor and his treatments? He has no idea what's going to happen next – how his health will hold up, how long he has left, any of it! We have no clue what the future might look like!"

More tears spring up, just as I'd got rid of the last ones. Damn them.

"Oh, Connie, I know... It is complicated. It is big. But I have to say this – there are hospitals where we live. There are doctors where we live. If he especially wanted to stay with his current team, he could. I could do all his tests and monitor him, and liaise with them. It's not the other side of the world. That stuff can be managed. As for the rest... well, who *does* know what the future looks like, Connie? None of us do. Even without illness, none of us have a clue. We don't know how long we've got, or how long our loved ones have got, or what is around the corner. That's the way life is. It's scary, but it doesn't mean you can stop living it."

On those words, I hear Kitty start crying in earnest, and my friend's helpless attempts to calm her down.

"Ella, it's fine. Thank you. You've given me a lot to think about. Go see to the baby, and I'll call you later, okay?"

"You promise?"

"I do."

I switch off my phone, and let her words sink in. I know, of course, that she is right. I should, of all people, understand that life is a gamble. The last day Simon was alive was totally normal. I'd reminded him to put the bins out, and I'd gone to work as normal, and I'd planned to cook us a nice lasagne to eat for tea while we binged on *Line of Duty*. It was a mundane day full of what I now see as absolutely blessed boring domestic detail. He wasn't sick. He wasn't a thrill seeker. He wasn't an extreme sports addict. He was a normal man who simply gave his pregnant sister a lift to the hospital.

The accident came from nowhere, and our entire family's life was never the same again. There was no warning. No time to prepare or say goodbye – there was just the before, and the after. Would it have changed how I felt about Simon, if I'd known that when I met him? If I'd known that our time together would be so limited, would it have stopped me from falling in love with him? From marrying him?

I don't think it would. We might not have had the forever that we wanted, but we had enough time together for me to know that it was special. That not many people are so lucky as to meet their soulmate. And now I might have met another – the question is, am I brave enough to take the chance?

EIGHTEEN

By the time I get back to the house, I've been out for well over an hour. I needed that time and space to try and bend my mind around things, as well as to give Bear a good run around.

I let myself in, and find that Zack is up, showered and dressed. He looks ten times better than he did yesterday, with some of his old energy back. Bear ambles over to him and thumps his tail.

"Has he been fed?" he asks.

"He has. He's trying to con you."

"Not for the first time. And you... have you been fed?"

"Yes. I ate an apricot pastry that I got myself from the bakery. Then I ate an apricot pastry that I got for you from the bakery as well. Soz."

He laughs, and walks over to me. He reaches out and puts his hands on my waist, pulling me so close to him our bodies collide. He keeps me there, and I can't say it's an unpleasant feeling.

"You look good in my T-shirt," he says, running a hand up my back so slowly it makes me shiver. His fingers twine themselves into my hair, and he gently turns my face upwards to look at him. My heart starts to go crazy at the contact, and at the look in his eyes. When he finally leans down to kiss me, I'm already desperate to feel his lips on mine. I fling my arms up and around his neck, pulling him closer and letting the moment claim me. He edges me backwards until my back is against the wall, and I am deliciously trapped against him. Wow. This man can really kiss, and in my experience, men who can really kiss can usually do everything else really well, too.

When we come up for air, I feel almost lightheaded, and cling on to him for balance. He grins down at me, his eyes twinkling and his smile almost smug when he sees my reaction. He knows he's just unravelled me, and he's enjoying it.

"You seem to be feeling better," I say, letting my hands settle on his shoulders.

"I do, don't I? And a lot of the time I'm fine. Yesterday was especially tough, right up until the moment I found a mad former celebrity chef sitting on my front doorstep."

"Yeah. Well, that would cheer most people up, to be fair. Can we talk, do you think? Without you touching me?"

"I thought you liked me touching you!"

"I do. A bit too much. I can't think clearly when you're touching me."

He nods, and we both take chairs around the dining table. Bear realises it's a no-go on the second breakfast front, and slumps at his master's feet.

"So," he says, sipping a glass of orange juice, "how are you feeling about everything this morning? I know that was a lot to take in. I know this isn't ideal. And I wouldn't blame you at all if you left – I'd completely understand it."

"I do plan on leaving, Zack. Maybe not immediately, but sometime very soon."

He nods, and I see the effort it is taking for him to keep his face in neutral, the way his hand trembles slightly as he puts his glass down. He presses his lips together as though he's trying to stop himself from talking, and he closes his eyes for a second as he digests what I've said. He's hurt and disappointed and trying to hide it.

"I understand. Thank you for everything."

"Hang on, pal – I haven't finished!"

"Oh. To use one of your words, soz."

"As you should be. Look, Zack, we're both too old to play games, aren't we? So let's not. How do you feel about me? Straight-up honest answer please!"

He looks taken aback for a moment, but then replies, with heart-warming conviction: "The way I feel about you is the only simple thing about all of this. I love you, Connie."

I feel a little spike in my pulse, and give myself a second to enjoy the absolute thrill of hearing those words. Words that I haven't heard for so long, other than from the lips of my children and my extended family. Words that certainly haven't been accompanied by one of those spectacular kisses.

"Well, that's handy, because I feel exactly the same. I love you, even though I'm still surprised by that. And I want to be with you."

He opens his mouth to speak, and I know that he is about to object. About to point out all the complications, all the drawbacks, all the potential problems.

"No, Zack, don't do that. I already know the issues. But a wise woman – okay, Ella – just made me really think about all of this, and I've decided she's right. None of us can predict the future. None of us know how much time we get to spend with each other. I don't know, and neither do you. All I do know is that I want to be with you. I feel alive when I'm with you, and I'm not ready to turn my back on that. So, as we're old and don't play games anymore, how would you feel about coming back to Starshine Cove with me when I leave?"

"It would be complicated," he says, gazing past my shoulder and seeming to think about it.

"Pah to complicated."

"It would be an adjustment for both of us, after all this time alone."

"Pah to adjustment."

"It would be a surprise for the girls."

"Pah to the girls, they're old enough to understand."

"It would be... wonderful."

"Pah to— Oh. Okay. Wonderful. I like that. Wonderful doesn't deserve a pah."

We look at each other across the table, and we both smile like teenagers. He holds out his hands, and I take them in mine. I hold him tight, and vow that I won't let him go.

"That was a big decision," he says. "And neither of us seems to be regretting it yet."

"No. I'm glad. And I know there will be stuff to sort out, but we'll manage it. Together. We'll figure it out as we go."

"Together," he replies, that big dumb grin going nowhere fast. "That sounds good."

He nods decisively, and suddenly stands up. He keeps hold of my hands, and does that thing where he whooshes me up and catches me in his arms.

He turns around and walks into the hallway, leading me by the hand.

"Where are we going now?" I ask, looking at the stairs and hoping we're going where I think we're going.

"To bed. I'm sick of 'to be continued', aren't you?"

NINETEEN

Six months later

It is just about autumn in Starshine Cove, but the weather is magnificent. The sky has been blue all day, the air fresh and crisp and clean. Night is falling much earlier now, and the fairy lights that are strung along the buildings around the green kick into life and make the place look like a birthday cake. It's one of my favourite times of year, when the leaves turn golden and the woods become a wonderland of whirling leaves.

It always starts to feel a little Christmassy round about now, I think, and Christmas is one of my favourite times of the year too. In fact, they all are – there's something to love in all the seasons, especially here in my gorgeous little corner of the world.

Tonight, though, the fairy lights have some competition. Tonight, the entire place is lit up. There are roving floodlights roaming over the cottages and the inn, projectors are casting bright coloured sparkles over the treetops, and a red carpet has been laid out from the inn all the way to the community centre.

Archie and Jake have rigged up a 'photo op' area, and the village teenagers are currently pouting away in front of it, taking selfies.

Cally has been working overtime doing hair and make-up, and everyone looks fantastic. Cally herself is wearing her traditional wrap dress, Archie is in a vintage seventies tux from George's extensive wardrobe, and Lucy and Josh look like an actual Hollywood power couple. Everyone is here, from baby Kitty all the way through to villagers who are on the verge of getting their telegram from the King.

I've gone for a red dress that is way more revealing than normal, and my curls are in an elaborate up-do. I feel a bit overdone, but if you can't gussy up for a film premiere, when can you? Besides, my two handsome escorts for the evening are looking so good in their penguin suits that I'm glad I made the effort.

Everyone has been taking it in turns to do their strut down the red carpet, and it's almost our go. George offers me his arm to link on one side, and Zack on the other.

"I'm a very happy old man tonight," says George, leaning down to speak to me. "Seeing Archie with his Cally, and now you with Zack... well, I couldn't be more pleased, my love. You deserve it."

I pat his hand, and give him a big smile. I've not given up hope on George finding love again, even though he insists he's well and truly 'past it'.

I turn to Zack, and raise my eyebrows.

"Are you ready, Mr Director?" I say, squeezing his arm.

"Of course. I hope you all like it."

"How could we not?" I ask. True to his word, Zack finished his editing of his Starshine Cove movie, as well as continuing to work on his idea for a show about refugees. He's now officially semi-retired from his company, taking on an executive role rather than day-to-day. He's moved in with me, and none of our children were anywhere near as surprised as I expected – in fact they all seem delighted for us.

His health is stable, and as she promised, Ella is working with his nephrologist in London to monitor him and carry out all the routine tests. He has regular chats with the London team on video call, and so far so good – there have been no big changes. His medication is working, and he is doing well. It might not stay like this forever, and there might be tough choices to make further down the line – but for now, he is fit, healthy, and absolutely yummy.

As for me, well, my life has totally changed. I have opened up in a way I never believed was possible. I have accepted love into my life, and delight in this new version of me – this new chapter that I am still turning the pages on. I am happy again, it is that simple.

We enter the community hall, and everybody stands up to give Zack a round of applause. He turns around, bows in all directions, then kisses me before we take our seats.

As the music kicks in and the film starts to play across the giant screen, the initial shots are ones that Zack did with his new toy, a drone camera. It captures the glorious green fields, the red and gold cliffs, and the dramatic sun-kissed shimmer of the sea stretching out from the bay. There is a communal gasp as everyone recognises our tiny speck of a village, nestled at the heart of all that natural splendour.

The gasps are followed by laughter as the setting changes to my café, and a shot I never even knew he was taking – me, singing along to the Girls Aloud classic *Sound of the Underground* as I wipe down tables. I'm going great guns, really feeling the chorus, and the entire room is in hysterics as they watch me hop and shimmy my way around the room.

I turn to him and smile, punching his arm playfully. He puts his arm around my shoulder, and tugs me close.

"See?" he says, as we both tuck into our popcorn, "it might have taken me twenty-five years to finally get you on screen, but I always knew you'd be a star..."

A LETTER FROM THE AUTHOR

Dear reader,

Huge thanks for reading *Starting Over In Starshine Cove*; I hope you enjoyed Connie's story. You can sign up to find out all about Storm books, and the great releases they have in store (including mine!) by signing up here:

www.stormpublishing.co/debbie-johnson

You can also sign up to a newsletter that I send out myself – you'll be the first to hear all my news, book gossip, and more – there will be giveaways, free samples, and short stories. It's totally free, I won't send so many your inbox hates me, and I promise it will be fun!

debbie-johnson.ck.page/32bc38fdb7

If you enjoyed this book and could spare a few moments to leave a review that would be hugely appreciated. Even a short review can make all the difference in encouraging a reader to discover my books for the first time. Thank you so much!

Thanks again for being part of this amazing journey with me and I hope you'll stay in touch – I have so many more stories and ideas to entertain you with!

Debbie Johnson

KEEP IN TOUCH WITH THE AUTHOR

 facebook.com/debbiejohnsonauthor
 x.com/debbiemjohnson

ACKNOWLEDGEMENTS

Those of you who follow me on social media know that this hasn't been the easiest of years. I badly broke my ankle after an accident (yes, I was sober!), ended up in hospital for a month and had two surgeries to repair the damage. It was a grim time, but also in its own way strangely positive – I made new friends, received so much kindness, and learned a lot about resilience and inner strength. I thought I was pretty sorted on that front, but it turns out you're never too old to learn. I've had times where I've been incredibly low and convinced my life would never look 'normal' again, but having to accept that recovery is something you quite literally do one step at a time has probably been good for me. Unlike my fictional world, I can't control everything in real life!

I owe a big debt of gratitude to the NHS, in particular Longmoor House in Liverpool, and Prof Lyndon Mason, the ortho guru who carried out my second surgery and helped me get back on my feet again. Mainly, though, it has been friends and family who have kept me going – my pals who never stopped messaging, or who turned up even when I said I was too fed up to have visitors. The ones who basically sat with me while I cried, either in the flesh or virtually – I thank you all, in particular: Sandra Shennan, Karen Murphy, Pamela Hoey, Paula Woosey, Jane Wolstenholme, Milly Johnson, Andrew Campbell, John Mitchell, Terri McQueen, Rob Page and Suzanne Di Mascio. Special thanks also to my lovely Auntie Christine, my surrogate mum. On the home front, I've been humbled by the sheer magnificence of my family – looking after someone isn't easy, either physically or emotionally, and they've been amazing. So, to Dom and my brilliant children – Keir, Daniel and Louisa – THANK YOU! I'll never, ever forget how kind you've all been.

Thank you as ever also to my fab agent, Hayley Steed, and her team at Janklow & Nesbit, and to the Storm squad – in particular my editors, Kathryn Taussig and Vicky Blunden.

Mainly, thank you to you – the reader who got to the end of the book. I can't tell you how much I appreciate your support.

Printed in Great Britain
by Amazon